THEODOSIA

—and the—

STAFF of OSIRIS

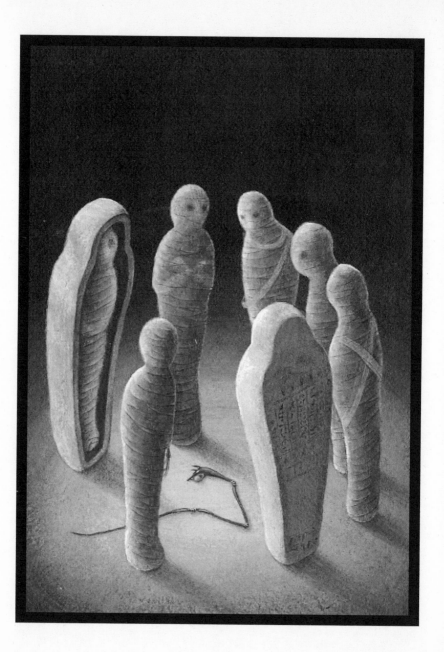

THEODOSIA

— and the —

STAFF of OSIRIS

R. L. LaFevers

illustrated by Yoko Tanaka

sandpiper

HOUGHTON MIFFLIN HARCOURT
BOSTON NEW YORK

The text of this book is set in Minister Book.
The illustrations are acrylic on board.
Map of 1905 London used courtesy of the Harvard Map Collection.

Library of Congress Cataloging-in-Publication Data is on file.

ISBN-13: 978-0-547-24819-6

Manufactured in the United States of America
EB 10 9 8 7 6 5 4 3
4500328346

For odd ducks everywhere.
Remember, "odd duck" is just another name
for a swan.

And since this book had so very much to do with mummies,
it seems only right that I dedicate it to my mummy,
Dixie Young,
who ran with the wolves (or maybe it was the jackals!)
long before there was a book written about it,
and had to find her own way through the wild woods.
And even with all that, she managed to hold the path open for others.
I only wish I'd understood earlier how hard it must have been.

CHAPTER ONE
A GRAND FETE

THE LACE ON MY PARTY FROCK itched horribly. I don't understand how they can make things as complex as motorcars or machines that fly but can't invent itchless lace. Although Mother didn't seem to be plagued with this problem, I would have to pay close attention to the other ladies at the reception this evening to see if they exhibited any symptoms.

"You're surprisingly quiet, Theodosia," Father said, interrupting my thoughts.

"Surprisingly"? Whatever did he mean by that, I wonder?

"I would have thought you'd be chattering a mile a minute about Lord Chudleigh's reception."

Tonight was to be my big introduction to professional life. And I planned to savor every second of it. I would be the first eleven-year-old girl ever to walk in their midst. What if they should ask me to make a speech? Wouldn't that be grand? I would stand there, with all eyes on me—keepers and lords and sirs and all sorts of fancy folk—and then I would . . . have to say something. Maybe having to speak wouldn't be such a great idea after all.

Mother put her gloved hand on Father's arm. "She's most likely nervous, Alistair. The only young girl among so many important dignitaries and officials? I would have been tongue-tied at her age."

Well. *That* wasn't very comforting. Maybe I should have been more nervous than I was. The carriage turned a corner and my stomach dipped uneasily.

We reached Lord Chudleigh's residence in Mayfair, a large red brick mansion with white columns and windowpanes. At the door, a butler bowed and greeted Father by name. Then we were motioned inside, where we joined an absolutely mad throng of people, all dressed in fine frocks and evening coats. There were marble floors, and the hallway sported Greek columns. Actually, the whole place had the touch of a museum about it: Grecian urns, a bust of Julius Caesar, and even a full coat of armor standing at attention. Suddenly I was glad of all that itchy lace—otherwise I would have felt dreadfully underdressed.

I slipped my hand into Mother's. "Lord Chudleigh's house is even grander than Grandmother Throckmorton's," I whispered.

"Don't let her hear you say that," Father said.

"How could she possibly hear me?" I scoffed. "She's miles away in her own grand house."

The look on Father's face gave me pause. "Isn't she?" I asked hesitantly.

"I'm afraid not." His tone was clipped, as if he wasn't very happy about it, either. "She moves in the same social circles as Lord Chudleigh."

That was the sort of news that could ruin an entire evening. One might think it was a bit of an overstatement, if one didn't know my grandmother.

I stared out at the crowd of people, desperate to spot Grandmother. If I saw her first, it would make avoiding her all that much easier.

Although really, I oughtn't worry, I told myself as we moved into the enormous ballroom. I was on my best behavior and had no intention of drawing any unpleasant attention to myself. Not even Grandmother would be able to find fault with me tonight. Except she believes children in general, and me in particular, should be seen as little as possible and heard even less. Just my being here would be an enormous affront to her sense of propriety.

Music played in the background, but people weren't dancing—they just stood about talking and drinking champagne. We weaved our way among the guests until a tall man who looked vaguely familiar waved us over. Father immediately altered his course and began herding Mother and me in that direction.

When we reached the gentleman, he leaned forward and thumped Father on the back. "It's about time you showed up, Throckmorton. At least you had the good sense to bring your lovely wife."

Mum put her hand out, but instead of shaking it, the man lifted it to his lips and kissed it! *He'd better not try that with me*, was all I could think. Luckily, he didn't. In fact, he ignored me until Father cleared his throat and put his hand on my shoulder. "And this is my daughter, Theodosia, Lord Chudleigh. The one we spoke about."

"Ah yes!" Lord Chudleigh bent over and peered down at me. "Our newest little archaeologist, eh? Following in your mother's footsteps, are you, girl? Well done." He reached out and patted me on the head. Like a pet. I'm sorry, but you simply don't go around patting people on the head like dogs!

Father tightened his hand on my shoulder in silent warning. "So. What's all this I keep hearing about an artifact of your own?"

Chudleigh looked smug. "After you came rushing home in such a hurry, I had to make a quick run down to Thebes to secure the site."

Father winced slightly. "So you've mentioned." Under his breath he added, "Three times." Then, louder, "I'm terribly sorry about that. If my son hadn't been so ill . . ."

"Eh, it felt good to get out into the field and get a taste of what you do." Chudleigh nudged Father with his elbow. "I got a chance to find a little something of my own down there, too. Standing in plain sight, it was. Don't know why you and your wife didn't send it straight along with the first batch. In fact, I have a treat for everyone tonight." He puffed up his chest and rocked back on his heels. "In honor of my most recent find, we're going to have a mummy unwrapping!"

A mummy unwrapping! My stomach recoiled at the very idea. Didn't he understand that mummification was a sacred death rite of the ancient Egyptians? That unwrapping a mummy would be the same as undressing his grandfather's dead body? "Sir," I began, but Father's hand pressed down on my shoulder again. Surely I was going to be bruised black and blue from all this hand clamping.

"Fascinating, sir," was all he said. "We'll look forward to it."

"Good, good. Thought you might." Chudleigh nodded. Father excused us, took Mother's elbow and mine, and began to steer us away.

Mum muttered under her breath, "I thought unwrappings went out with Queen Victoria."

I whirled around to Father when we were out of earshot. "Why didn't you say something? That's desecration, isn't it?"

"Yes, I suppose it is, Theodosia. But I'm not personally responsible for every mummy that comes out of Egypt, you know. Besides, the man's on the museum's board. I can't risk getting on his bad side, and telling him that unwrapping his new mummy is bad form would certainly do that."

I turned to Mother.

"Oh, no," she said. "Don't look at me. I've already got a hard enough row to hoe being a woman in this field. I can't afford any appearance of sentimentality or emotion."

Well, it had been worth a try. "Where do you think Chudleigh found the mummy?" I asked. "I never saw one in the tomb or annex. Did you, Father?"

"Well, no. But then again, I was preoccupied with getting you out of there safely. Now, let's get this wretched evening over with. *Oomph!*"

Mother removed her elbow from Father's ribs. "Tonight's supposed to be a treat," she reminded him.

Indeed, I had hoped for a lovely evening out with my parents. I had also hoped that my dressing up in fancy clothes and attending one of their social events might have allowed them to see me a little differently.

Or simply *see* me, rather than spend the entire evening looking over my head at other adults.

Pretending I hadn't heard them, I raised up on my tiptoes, trying to spot the mummy. I couldn't believe I would have overlooked a mummy lying about in plain sight, even if I had been being chased by the Serpents of Chaos.

It was hopeless. There were too many people, all of whom were taller than I was. When I pulled my gaze back down, I found an elderly man examining me through his monocle as if I were a bug at the end of a pin. A very round woman dressed in mustard-colored ruffles lifted her lorgnette to the bridge of her nose, then tut-tutted. Honestly! You'd think they'd never seen an eleven-year-old girl before.

"I suppose we'd best go pay our respects to Mother." Father made the suggestion with the same enthusiasm he might have shown for leaping off the London Bridge straight into the foul, icy water of the river Thames.

Which was precisely how I felt about seeing Grandmother, frankly. Luckily, the crowd shifted just then and I spied someone I recognized. "Oh look, Father! There's Lord

Snowthorpe." And although he wasn't one of my favorite people, he *was* standing next to one of my favorite people, Lord Wigmere. Only, I wasn't supposed to know Wigmere even existed, as he was the head of the Brotherhood of the Chosen Keepers, a secret organization whose sworn duty was to keep watch over all the sacred objects and artifacts in the country. Because the British Empire had amassed quite a few relics and ensorcelled items, it was quite a job. It was the Brotherhood that stood between our country and any of that ancient magic getting loose and wreaking horror upon us. Well, them and me, that is. I waved at the two men.

"No, Theo!" Father hissed. "I don't wish to speak to—"

"Throckmorton!" Lord Snowthorpe called out.

"Oh, blast it all. Now look what you've done."

Didn't Father realize that Snowthorpe was a hundred times better than Grandmother? Besides, I was hoping one of these gentlemen might be as repulsed by the mummy unwrapping as we were. Since they didn't work for Lord Chudleigh, perhaps they could put a stop to it.

When we reached Snowthorpe, Lord Wigmere winked at me, then ever so slightly shook his head, letting me know I wasn't to let on I knew him. I winked back.

There were a lot of false hearty hellos and good-to-see-yous exchanged, then Snowthorpe got down to his real reason for wanting to say hello: snooping. "I say, did that Heart of Egypt of yours ever turn up?" he asked.

Father stiffened, and Mother raised her nose into the air. "I'm afraid not," she said. "The burglar got clean away."

That was a subject I wouldn't mind avoiding for a while longer. Say, a lifetime. My parents had no idea that I had been the one to return the Heart of Egypt to its proper resting place in the Valley of the Kings. It had been the only way to nullify the dreadful curse the artifact had been infected with. Of course, I'd had a bit of help from Wigmere and his Brotherhood of the Chosen Keepers. But my parents didn't know that, either.

"What was all that rot you fed me about having it cleaned, then?" Snowthorpe demanded.

"We . . ." Father turned to Mother with a desperate look on his face. She stared back, fumbling for something to say.

They couldn't have looked more guilty if they tried, so I spoke up. "The authorities had asked us to keep quiet until they made a few inquiries. They didn't want the perpetrators to catch wind of how much they knew or who they suspected."

Four pairs of eyes looked down at me in surprise.

"Isn't that what they said, Father?" I prompted.

"Yes," he said, recovering nicely. "Exactly what they said."

Wigmere's mustache twitched. "Do introduce me to this charming young lady, Throckmorton."

As if we needed any introduction! We'd only worked closely together on averting one of the worst crises ever to reach British soil.

"Forgive me. Lord Wigmere, this is my daughter, Theodosia Throckmorton. Theodosia, this is Lord Wigmere, head of the Antiquarian Society."

I gave a proper curtsy. "I'm very pleased to meet you, sir."

"And I you."

Before Snowthorpe could begin jawing on again about the Heart of Egypt, I decided to raise my concerns. "Have you heard what Lord Chudleigh's planning for this evening?"

I felt Father scowl at me, but I did my best to ignore him, which was rather difficult when his heated gaze threatened to burn a hole through my skull.

Snowthorpe brightened. "You mean the mummy unwrapping?"

"Yes, but don't you think it's wrong to do it as . . . entertainment?"

Snowthorpe dismissed my words with a wave of his hand. "Gad no! It's good for business, that. People love mummies, and whenever their interest goes up, so do museum ticket sales."

"But isn't it desecration?"

The pleasant expression left Snowthorpe's face and he looked down at me, almost as if seeing me for the first time. "You sound just like Wigmere here. He'd have us ship all our artifacts back to Egypt if he had his way."

Well, certainly the cursed ones, anyway. I sent a beseeching look in Wigmere's direction, but he shook his head sympathetically. "I already tried and got nowhere. Chudleigh's too intent on having his fun."

Disappointment spiked through me. I looked over my shoulder. The crowd had broken up a bit. I caught a glimpse of a table with guests clustered around it, but I still couldn't see the mummy itself.

Really, this fete of theirs was no fun at all. Not what I thought of as a proper party. I caught yet another old codger staring at me and realized that such scrutiny had made me beastly thirsty. I suddenly craved a glass of lemon smash or cold ginger beer. As I searched the crowd for the man with the refreshment tray, yet another old lady examined me through her opera glasses. I wrinkled my nose. Didn't these people realize how rude that was?

The woman dropped her glasses, and I was dismayed to find myself staring into the shocked face of Grandmother Throckmorton! I quickly turned away, pretending I hadn't seen her.

Seconds later, a very stiff-looking footman appeared at

Father's side. "Madam wishes me to request you attend her immediately."

"What?" he asked, then caught sight of his mother. "Oh yes, of course!" He bid goodbye to Wigmere and Snowthorpe, then herded us over to where Grandmother was conversing with a rather short, barrel-shaped man.

When we reached her, she offered up her cheek to Father for a kiss. He did so (grudgingly, I'm sure), and then she turned to Mother and inclined her head slightly. "Henrietta."

"Madam." Mother nodded back.

Grandmother ignored me completely. She still wasn't speaking to me for having run away while under her care. Even so, I wanted to prove I could be polite even if she couldn't and gave my very best curtsy. "How do you do, Grandmother? It's very good to see you again."

Grandmother sniffed in disapproval, then asked Father, "What is she doing here?"

"Now, Mother. She did make a rather remarkable find, locating that secondary annex to Amenemhab's tomb. Lord Chudleigh suggested we bring her along to celebrate her first find for the museum."

"This is no place for children and her schedule is already far too irregular. If you cannot see to her proper upbringing, then perhaps I shall take her to hand." Grandmother studied me for a long moment before continuing. "Have you had any luck in locating a new governess for her?"

Mother and Father exchanged guilty glances. I could tell they'd forgotten all about it. "Not yet. But we'll keep looking." Mother missed the look of scorn Grandmother sent her way, but I didn't. I narrowed my eyes and glared at the old bat.

Except she was so busy ignoring me, she missed it and turned to the man standing beside her. I was left to stew on the idea of Grandmother overseeing my upbringing. I was torn between horror at the thought and fury at her treatment of Mother.

"Alistair, I'd like you to meet Admiral Sopcoate."

Admiral Sopcoate had a jolly face. He was quick to catch my eye, then smiled. I liked him immediately.

Admiral Sopcoate shook Father's hand. "What is it you do, again, Throckmorton?"

Father opened his mouth to respond, but Grandmother talked over him. "He's the Head Curator of the Museum of Legends and Antiquities."

When Grandmother said nothing more, Father quickly stepped in. "And this is my wife, Henrietta. She's the museum's archaeologist and brings us a number of our most spectacular finds."

Grandmother sniffed.

"And this is my daughter, Theodosia," Father continued.

Admiral Sopcoate reached out and took my hand. (No head patting or hand kissing here! I knew I liked him for a good reason.) "Pleased to meet you, my dear."

"And I you, sir." Still determined to be on my best behavior, I added, "Perhaps you'd like to come by and see our museum someday? We'd be happy to give you a tour."

Grandmother's eyes flared in irritation. She fixed me with a gaze that clearly said, *Do not dare speak again in my presence,* then turned back to the admiral. "We were just discussing Admiral Sopcoate's newest addition to the home fleet, the *Dreadnought.*"

"Yes! Have you seen her yet, Throckmorton?" Sopcoate asked.

"I can't say as I have," Father said. "Although I've read a bit about it in the paper."

"The *Dreadnought* is the newest crown jewel in Her Majesty's fleet," Sopcoate explained. "Makes every other battleship in the world obsolete."

"If you ask me," Grandmother butted in, "we can't have enough battleships. Not with Germany's determination to become the world's greatest naval power."

"Now, now, Lavinia," Admiral Sopcoate reassured her.

"The British Navy is twice as strong as the next two navies combined."

Lavinia! He'd called her by her Christian name! I'd forgotten she even had one.

"Not if Germany has its way," she answered darkly. "They are determined to challenge our naval supremacy."

"Don't worry." Sopcoate gave a jolly wink. "Once those Germans see the *Dreadnought*, they'll put aside their misguided ideas of naval equality with England."

"But isn't that rather like baiting a bear?" Father asked. "How do you know they won't come out swinging, determined to build even more battleships of their own?"

Couldn't grownups talk of anything besides politics and war? I knew that the Germans and the British were on the outs with each other, but if you asked me—although no one did—that was mostly the fault of the Serpents of Chaos. They were a secret organization dedicated to bringing about disorder and strife in their quest to dominate the world. Specifically, they wanted Germany and Britain at each other's throat. They wanted instability and utter chaos so they could move in and seize power. However, now that Wigmere and I had foiled their plans, this whole war-cry nonsense would surely die down.

Luckily, before the adults could go on too long, we were

interrupted by a faint clinking sound. Lord Chudleigh was striking his champagne glass with a tiny fork. "Time has come, everyone. Gather round. Here's your chance to see a mummy unwrapped, the unveiling of the secrets of the Egyptians."

An excited murmur ran through the crowd, and everyone shuffled over to the table on which the mummy lay. I tugged on Father's hand. "Do I have to watch, Father? Can't I wait over there?"

He patted my shoulder. "There's nothing to be afraid of, you know."

Of course I knew that! *That* wasn't the issue. It just seemed wrong to be unwrapping the poor mummy in front of all these gawking visitors who didn't give a fig about ancient Egypt or the scholarly pursuit of Egyptian burial practices.

As we drew closer, I made a point of hanging back behind Mother and Father, but then Admiral Sopcoate stepped aside. "Here, young lady. Come stand in front of me so you can see better. You don't want to miss this!"

Of course, he was just being kind. I opened my mouth to say, "No thank you," but caught Grandmother's eye. The warning glint told me that refusing wasn't an option. Biting back a sigh, I stepped forward and found myself in the front row, merely three feet away from the mummy on the table.

"This unidentified mummy was found inside the newly discovered tomb of Amenemhab," Chudleigh went on. "We're hoping that by unwrapping him tonight, we will learn more about who he was, as well as insights into the mystery of mummification. Are you ready?"

A wave of assent rose up from the gathering.

"Throckmorton, Snowthorpe, would you do the honors, please?"

Father blinked in surprise. He quickly hid the look of distaste that spread across his face and stepped dutifully forward.

"Let's start from the feet, shall we?" Snowthorpe suggested.

I thought about closing my eyes, then wondered if Grandmother Throckmorton would be able to tell. Testing the theory, I screwed my eyes shut—just for the merest of seconds. Immediately there was a sharp poke in my shoulder blade and a disapproving sniff.

I opened my eyes and thought briefly of handing her a handkerchief. Honestly! I didn't see how it was rude to close one's eyes but perfectly all right to sniff constantly, like one of those pigs that can root out truffles.

I turned my attention back to the front, but looked steadfastly at Father instead of the mummy.

It takes a surprisingly long time to unwrap a mummy. To entertain his guests, Lord Chudleigh jawed on about mummy legends and curses—the most sensational rubbish he could find, and most of it not even close to the truth. When he got to the part about how they used to grind up mummies to be ingested for their magical properties—that part true, unfortunately—I was so utterly revolted that I blurted out, "You're not going to grind this one up, are you?"

There was a long moment of silence in which everyone chose to stare at me, and I suddenly remembered my promise to do nothing to call attention to myself.

Chudleigh gave a false laugh. "No, no. Of course not. This one will become a part of my own personal collection."

"Oh. I beg your pardon," I said, vowing to keep my mouth shut from now on.

At last Father and Snowthorpe came to the mummy's head. I studiously kept my eyes glued to Father's face. When the last bandage was lifted away, the crowd gasped in delighted horror.

I will not look, I will not look, I told myself. But sometimes the more you concentrate on *not* doing something, the more drawn you are to doing it. In the end, my curiosity got the better of me and I looked.

"Behold—the unknown priest of Amenemhab!" Lord Chudleigh called out.

A smattering of applause ran through the crowd. Unable to help myself, I stepped forward, my eyes fixed on the mummy's face.

It was a face I had seen only a few short months ago, when I'd been forced to confront three of the Serpents of Chaos in Thutmose III's tomb. Their leader's words rang in my ears. *That is twice he's failed me. There shall not be a third time.*

"Oh no, Lord Chudleigh." The words bubbled out before I could stop them. "That isn't an unknown priest of the Middle Dynasty. That's Mr. Tetley. From the British Museum."

CHAPTER TWO

CHAOS RETURNS

THE CROWD ERUPTED INTO SHOCKED EXCLAMATIONS. Father looked at me strangely. "You know Tetley?"

"What on earth are you talking about?" Chudleigh asked.

Behind me, I heard Grandmother declare, "She's gone too far this time." Just as her clawlike hand reached for me, I took three giant steps forward, answering the least dicey question first.

"I'm trying to explain that this isn't a mummy from ancient Egypt, but a very recent fake."

A look of indignation passed over Chudleigh's face, which he tried unsuccessfully to cover up with a jolly bluster.

"Now, now. What could a young girl possibly know about mummies, eh? Not much, I'd wager."

"Well, you'd be wrong, sir." Grandmother's gasp of shock made me realize that I had sounded rude, although I was just trying to point out that I most certainly did know things about mummies. "See how there aren't any amulets among the bandages? Most unusual. And look here. He's not wearing a linen tunic or skirt or even a loincloth. He's wearing . . . a combination suit." I felt myself blush and heard a commotion behind me. A voice called out, "Get me some smelling salts!"

I glanced over my shoulder to find Admiral Sopcoate dragging Grandmother Throckmorton over to a settee. I gulped and turned back to face Father and Lord Chudleigh.

Chudleigh's face was quite red. "Now, see here . . ."

Father tugged at his collar. "I'm afraid she does point out some very legitimate irregularities, sir."

Chudleigh did not look happy to have my opinion confirmed. Afraid he would think that Father was only sticking up for me, I addressed Lord Snowthorpe. If anyone could recognize Tetley, it would be he. "What do you think, sir?"

With great reluctance, as if he had no wish to be near the center of this brewing controversy, Snowthorpe looked from me to Chudleigh, who was growing redder by the minute. I was afraid the poor man was going to have apoplexy.

"Do you recognize the mummy, sir?" I asked.

Snowthorpe gave me a patronizing look. "Now, now, my dear girl. I appreciate your faith in me, but I can't possibly recognize every mummy in Egypt."

Honestly, the man had a brain the size of a pea. Fighting down a growing frustration, I tried again. "Yes, but doesn't he look familiar? Haven't you seen that face before?"

Snowthorpe seemed horrified. "Where would I have seen this face before?"

I winced. "Just have a quick look, sir. If it really is Mr. Tetley from the British Museum, you'd know better than I."

Chudleigh said, "Yes, yes. Come have a look and prove this poor child is gravely mistaken."

Snowthorpe stepped up to the mummy's head and lifted his monocle. "Well, Tetley *has* been missing for the past few weeks. Left the office one morning and never returned."

"So it *is* possible," I said.

Chudleigh glared at me. "But that doesn't prove he'd go all the way to Egypt and get himself turned into a mummy!"

"I'm sure he didn't do it on purpose," I pointed out.

Father grabbed my elbow and walked me a few paces away from Chudleigh. "How on earth did you know Tetley?" he asked in a heated whisper.

Oh dear. I was so hoping he'd forget that particular question. "Um, he was very helpful to me once. On my last visit to the British Museum."

"What in the blazes were you doing there?" he asked.

I lowered my voice. "Just checking out the competition, Father. I didn't enjoy it a bit."

His face relaxed. "I should hope not," he said. Then he called out to Snowthorpe, "Well? What do you think? Is it this Tetley fellow?"

Snowthorpe lifted his gaze, his face deathly pale. "Yes," he said in a low voice. "I'm afraid it is."

The crowd erupted again and shocked whispers echoed throughout the room. Chudleigh speared me with a glare that clearly said he thought this was all my fault, as if I'd gone and masterminded the deception myself.

Someone moved forward to stand next to me, and I was relieved to find Wigmere at my side. Now we'd get somewhere.

Wigmere motioned the others to come closer, then lowered his voice. "If this really is Tetley, then we need to consider foul play and summon the authorities."

Chudleigh recoiled in horror. "Are you mad? Think of the scandal!"

I wasn't so sure what Chudleigh thought the scandal was—foul play or his being exposed as an ignorant boob.

"It can't be helped," Wigmere said.

"Well, let me at least get these people on their way, then," Chudleigh said. He glanced down at me as if I were an old rotten headcheese that had just appeared on his floor. "Clever girl," he said, but it was no compliment. More like a curse.

"I'm terribly sorry, sir," I heard Father say. "My daughter has been around Egyptian artifacts ever since she could walk. She was bound to pick up some of this knowledge along the way."

"Most unnatural way to bring up a child, if you ask me," Snowthorpe muttered.

"But we didn't ask you," Father said, bristling.

Chudleigh began walking away, stiff as a board. "Unnaturally clever," he grumbled.

With one last glance at me, Father hurried after him to try to smooth things over. I was left standing alone next to Wigmere. "It is Tetley," I whispered. "I'm sure of it."

"You know what this means, then?" He pulled his eyes away from the mummy, and the full weight of his heavy gaze hit me. "The Serpents of Chaos wanted us to find this. They wanted to send a message."

At the mention of the secret organization, my mouth grew dry. I was almost afraid to ask, "And what message is that, sir?"

"That we haven't seen the last of them. They'll be making another move. And soon."

I turned and looked out into the crowd, half expecting to see von Braggenschnott or Bollingsworth lurking there. But no, only Lord Chudleigh, bidding his guests a hasty farewell. "Do you think *he's* involved, sir?"

Wigmere followed my gaze. "I doubt it. I'm not sure the man's smart enough, for one thing. Chaos doesn't usually employ dimwits."

Wigmere appeared convinced, but I wasn't. It seemed to me it would be easy to hide a sharp mind under all that bluster and joviality.

I caught a movement out of the corner of my eye. Grandmother Throckmorton was waving Admiral Sopcoate away. She looked up just then, and our gazes met. Her wrath toward me seemed to give her strength and she surged to her feet. I glanced about desperately, looking for Mother or Father, but they were still hovering over by Lord Chudleigh, hoping to appease him.

When Grandmother reached me, she stared down at me with pinched nostrils. "You have finally gone too far. Someone needs to bring you to heel. If your parents won't see to it, then I will."

It wasn't as if *I* had done anything to the poor fellow. I just happened to notice the mummy wasn't an ancient

Egyptian! And didn't anyone realize this meant someone had been murdered? And that the murdered body was propped up against the watered silk wallpaper right under our noses?

If you ask me, some people have no perspective.

CHAPTER THREE

ANUBIS RISING

FATHER SPENT ALL OF BREAKFAST glowering at me over his newspaper. It's surprising how being scowled at chases one's appetite clean away. I mostly picked at my toast.

Finally, he finished his eggs and kippers and put his paper down on the table with an angry rattle of the pages. "I've half a mind to leave you home today, Theodosia," he announced.

His words stopped me cold. He didn't really mean it, did he? He hadn't left me at home for years. "B-but Father . . . if I'd known it was going to cause this much trouble, I would have kept quiet. It was just so clearly a fake. And," I said in a very small voice, "I just wanted to make you proud of me."

I should have known by now that trying to impress Father never went as planned. Usually my efforts ended up being ignored, but now it appeared I'd graduated to inciting a near riot. I risked a glance at him just in time to see him exchange a look with Mother. With relief, I saw his expression soften.

"I do admire your ability to detect a fake, Theodosia. No emperor's new clothes for you, no matter how many others who should have known better were duped." He broke into a broad grin. "A true chip off the old block."

Mother cleared her throat.

"Yes, well, you need to learn there is a time and place to announce your findings," Father continued. "And in a way that doesn't shoot other people's conclusions down like a clay pigeon."

What rot! He never took others' feelings into consideration when pointing out the flaws in their theories. However, I knew when not to argue. "I'm sorry, Father. I'll have to pay more attention and see how you do it next time."

He looked surprised. "Very well. Still, I do think it's good that your grandmother is finding a new governess for you. I didn't realize how long the other one had been gone. You need more structure and direction in your studies."

Well, of course I'd love some guidance in my studies! The only problem was, I'd had to help my last governess keep up with *me*, which wasn't exactly the sort of help I needed.

I looked down at the napkin in my lap and began plucking at one of the corners. "I had hoped, now that Mum was home again, you and she would have time to direct my studies." I looked up in time to see them exchange another glance across the table.

"It wouldn't take much time at all," I rushed to add. "I'm a very independent worker and need only a little direction."

There was a long, horrid silence before Mum finally spoke, her voice gentle. "I'm sorry, Theodosia. We couldn't possibly, not with the new items from the dig. There's so very much to do, what with preparing the artifacts and analyzing what they mean. We will be busy round the clock."

I swallowed my disappointment, reminding myself it had been a long shot. "Please don't leave me at home today, Father. I do promise to be good."

"Hm. Better than that, I've come up with a project for you. A way for you to be helpful and not just get in the way."

I perked up at that. Doing something useful at the museum was what I longed to do, after all.

"I've decided to put you in charge of cataloging all the mishmash down in long-term storage. It desperately needs to be done, and it should keep you out of trouble for days."

I tried to keep the horror off my face. "Long-term storage, Father? As in, downstairs in the museum's basement?"

He scowled. "Yes. I clearly said long-term storage, did I

not, Henrietta?" He looked to Mother for confirmation. She nodded, and he turned back to me. "Is there a problem with that?"

"No! I just thought perhaps you needed my help cataloging the things from Amenemhab's tomb. We're not all finished with that yet, are we?"

"No, but I've got that well in hand," Father said. "Besides, I won't be working on that this morning. I've got an interview with a candidate for the First Assistant Curator position. Now, is there a problem with the task you've been given?"

"No, Father," I lied. Perhaps I should have been content staying home after all. Surely it was better than venturing down into the catacombs.

For the first time ever, I found myself wishing my beastly younger brother, Henry, were home from school. If he had been, I would have made him come with me.

Henry claims the basement isn't really a catacomb, and I suppose he's right. Technically. It is, however, a large cavernous room full of old dead bodies (mummies, mostly) and items taken from their graves. Eerily similar to catacombs, if you ask me.

But the worst part is, whenever I open the door that leads

to the crypt, it feels as if there is some malevolent force waiting silently in the darkness below. I'm sure it's just the various curses and black magic that have accumulated over the years, but the air feels thick, almost alive with the power of it all.

Terrifying stuff, that. So I made sure I had on all three of my amulets as well as a pair of sturdy gloves. My cat, Isis, paused at the head of the stairs, sniffed at the cold, dank air, then meowed plaintively.

That wasn't a good sign.

However, there was nothing else to do. Scuffling my feet loudly so I wouldn't startle any entities down there, I descended the steps. I clutched my curse-removal kit with one hand (one can never be too careful!) and the banister with the other, as if it were a lifeline that would keep me anchored to a way out of this pit.

Come to think of it, that was exactly what it was.

The feeble gaslight barely penetrated the thick, rancid gloom. I shivered violently, unsure if it was the dank chill of the murky depths or something more sinister. . . .

That was one of the things that was so unnerving about the catacombs. There were so many ancient artifacts jumbled so closely together. None of them had been near moonlight or sunlight or *ka*—life force—for years. Whatever curses and spells they possessed lay deeply dormant—which meant I had no way of sensing them. It felt like a horrid game of blindman's bluff.

I paused at the bottom of the stairs. Isis lurked near my feet and together we faced the looming, squatting shapes before us.

It was even worse than I had remembered. There was a huge stone sarcophagus that took up most of the right side of the room, its heavy stone lid slightly askew. Seven mummies stood propped up against the wall just behind the sarcophagus. Their painted eyes seemed to follow me. In the far deep corner opposite the mummies lurked an enormous life-size wooden hippopotamus. It was coated with peeling black resin, which gave it a rotted, threatening appearance. As did the leering mouth filled with large square teeth.

It was clearly an Underworld demon of some importance.

I quickly scanned the other side of the room. The faint gaslight glinted dully off three bronze statues—one of Apis the Bull (Late Period, I believe), the falcon-headed Soul of Buto, and a lioness-headed statue of Sekhmet, the goddess of the destructive power of the sun. Funerary masks of long-forgotten pharaohs and ancient priests lined a shelf against the wall, and dozens upon dozens of Canopic jars were crowded together on the shelf below. Clay urns and bronze vessels sat next to stone daggers and knives with flint blades. A large Canopic shrine of gilded wood sat in the middle of the room, on top of which rested a large life-size statue of Anubis in his jackal form. Every available inch of the storeroom was covered with steles and scarabs and amulets and jewelry. It would take months to catalog all this!

I cast one last longing glance up the stairs, then pulled the notebook and pencil Father had given me from the pocket of my pinafore.

I decided it would be best if I started out with the seven mummies covering the far wall. For one, being able to cross an entire wall of artifacts off my list would make me feel as if I was making good progress. And two, if I had to spend days with my back to a bunch of mummies, I'd prefer to know exactly whom I was dealing with.

I took one look at the mummy nestled up against the corner, and my pulse began to race with excitement. It was from the Old Period, Third Dynasty, most likely. One of the oldest mummies I'd ever seen. I peered at the old spidery handwriting on a small tag inserted among the bandages. It was written in English, but it wasn't Father's handwriting. Perhaps this mummy had been acquired long before he'd arrived.

The tag identified the mummy as Rahotep, a powerful priest during Djoser's reign. It was in such excellent condition, I couldn't understand why it was down here in the catacombs instead of on display. I'd have to remember to ask Father about that.

The next mummy stood in a painted wooden case with a lid that had been removed. The mummy itself was still wrapped in its linen shroud (fully intact) and reinforced with linen strips. It was clearly from the Late New Period. I gingerly grasped the small wooden tag around its neck and squinted to read the faded Egyptian. The tag had been placed by the embalmer and claimed this mummy was Herihor, who had been an official of some sort under Osorkon the Elder.

The next two mummies were from the Middle Kingdom: Ankhetitat, a princess; and Kawit, a royal companion of the pharaoh Khendjer. Both were in relatively good condition, but weren't spectacular finds like Rahotep.

The next mummy was a bit of a puzzle. I could narrow him down to the Late Period, but the wooden case had been coated in wax of some sort, which hid most of the markings. Deciding I wasn't expected to identify it, I simply marked it down as Unknown Mummy, possibly Late Period.

The last mummies were also from the Late New Period: Sitkamose, a priestess of Horus; and Isetnofret, a priestess during Nectanebo's reign. Seven total.

After I made the last notation on my paper, I reached up to stretch.

There was a faint rustle behind me. I whipped my head around. "Isis?"

But it wasn't she who had made the noise. She stood frozen in her spot, back arched, staring at the statue of Anubis.

Which yawned.

Or maybe it was more of a stretching of his jaws. Either way, it wasn't something a statue ought to do.

Worried, I stepped forward for a better look, then jumped back as the jackal shook himself, like a dog awakening from a nap.

This was bad. Very bad.

I looked into the statue's eyes and he looked back at me, his hackles rising. He growled.

The growl ran along my skin, leaving a trail of goose bumps in its wake. Isis, who wasn't used to hearing dog noises in her domain, hissed loudly.

The jackal swung his head in her direction, recognized immediately that she was a cat, then leaped off the shrine toward her.

Oh no!

Isis yowled and darted into the small space between the wall and the sarcophagus, and the jackal skidded to a stop. Frustrated, he tried to squeeze in after her, but he was too big.

I had to do something, and quick! But what? Of course, the solution rather depended on what had caused him to spring to life in the first place, and I had no idea. Was it exposure to the light? To my *ka,* or life force? Oh, what to do, what to do?

I glanced around the room, hoping for some rope to tie him up with or even a cloth I could use to try and cover him. If it was light or life force that had activated him, perhaps turning him off would be as simple as putting a barrier between him and the light.

But there was nothing usable nearby. "Hold on, Isis," I called out encouragingly. "I'll be right back!"

I galloped up the stairs, pleased to find a number of thick, heavy coats hanging from the rack on the landing. I grabbed the longest, thickest one and tore back down the stairs, dragging the coat behind me.

The jackal still had Isis cornered between the wall and the sarcophagus. Moving as quietly as I could, I snuck up behind him, then threw the coat over him, trying to cover his entire body without getting too close to his snapping jaws.

He froze.

Was he wondering what had happened to him? Or had I managed to reverse whatever magic had brought him to life?

I searched the shelving in front of me, looking for some kind of weapon or something I could use to keep him at bay. My eyes fell on a long, bent staff on the shelf. Perfect. I reached out and grabbed it. As I grasped the top end, I noticed it had a jackal head fashioned in gold. This could be a good sign. The ancient Egyptians thought it most effective to fight a force with a similar force, rather like fighting fire with fire. So using a jackal head against a jackal just might work.

Reaching out cautiously with the end of the staff, I lifted a corner of the coat, exposing the jackal's left haunch. It was perfectly still. I squinted. It was hard to tell in the murky gloom, but it didn't look as if he'd turned back to stone. Then his haunch twitched and his foot moved. I jerked the staff back, dropping the coat, and he was still again.

Well, no matter what had awakened him, it seemed that covering him up would take care of it. At least long enough for me to think of something more permanent.

"Isis?" I called softly. "You can come out now if you like."

After a long moment she finally poked her whiskers out from behind the sarcophagus. She paused, studying the overcoat for a long while. Deciding it was safe, she began to emerge from her hiding spot. The overcoat twitched, and she disappeared back into her corner.

Bother. The overcoat wasn't going to hold as strongly as I'd hoped. Which gave me about two minutes to come up with a more lasting solution.

I hurried over to my curse-removal kit and rummaged about. My hand bumped into a plump, squashy bag. Of course! The salt I'd kept there ever since last year when a small statue of the frog-headed god Kuk had sported a curse involving a rain of slugs. Although, for the record, I try very hard not to use salt on the artifacts in the museum. Salt is horribly corrosive, and I like to be extremely careful with the museum's treasures.

The overcoat twitched again.

But sometimes during an emergency one had to settle for whatever was at hand. I didn't have time to do any research on this curse to discover the safest way to remove it without damaging the statue. My time was up.

I grabbed a handful of salt in my left hand, then moved back to the overcoat. It was beginning to wriggle now, which meant it wasn't the light that had activated the curse. More likely my life force.

Holding the staff in my right hand, I hooked the end of it under the overcoat, then yanked, exposing the jackal. Momentarily disoriented at being suddenly uncovered, he blinked, which gave me time to toss the handful of salt at him.

It caught him full along the side, and he reared away from the sarcophagus, shaking his head as if stunned. Before I could follow up with a second assault, Isis yowled and shot out from between the gap, racing toward the opposite end of the room. The jackal yipped once, shook off the effects of the salt, then followed. Or tried to. His claws scrabbled against the polished wooden floor, looking for traction, which he finally found and raced after Isis.

The salt had almost worked! It had slowed him down, anyway. Maybe I should have aimed for a more vulnerable part of his body. I grabbed another handful and hurried over to plant myself directly in Isis's path. She darted past me, and when the jackal was in range, I flung the salt into his face.

He yelped and skidded to a stop. After a moment's pause, he shook it off again and headed straight for me. I lunged to the side as he tore past, intent on Isis.

There had to be a way to cover him with salt all at once! But how?

Isis leaped up onto the shrine where the Anubis statue had been sitting before it sprang to life and caromed off the wall behind it, knocking over one of the bronze vessels.

That was it—water! I could dump the salt into the water and then pour it over the jackal, who was now trying to jump up onto the shrine after Isis. Luckily, it was too tall, and my cat was safe. For the moment, anyway.

With the bronze vessel clutched in my hand, I raced up the stairs, then headed down the hall toward the lavatory. I had just reached the door when Father called out. "Theodosia?"

I tried to hide the bronze vessel behind me while looking as innocent as possible. "Yes, Father? Dear?" I added for good effect.

"Is everything all right?"

"Of course! Why wouldn't it be?" Did my voice sound unnaturally high? I couldn't tell.

"Well, you're carrying an artifact into the lavatory."

"Oh. That. I was just going to wash something sticky off it, that's all."

Father frowned. "You *are* being careful with museum property, aren't you?"

"Absolutely! See?" I held up my hands. "I even wear gloves to be sure I leave no smudges on anything."

"I say, good idea."

Of course, that's not why I wore gloves at all. I wore them because sometimes the black magic lingering on the artifacts tried to work its way into *me*, and I'd really rather it didn't.

Satisfied, Father turned to go back down the hall. "Oh!" he said, stopping before he'd taken two steps. "Have you seen Fagenbush about?"

Fagenbush? Hardly. I spent quite a bit of energy trying to avoid our Second Assistant Curator whenever possible. "No, Father. Can't say as I have."

"Well, if you do, let him know I'm looking for him."

Was Fagenbush in trouble? One could always hope. But I

didn't have time for such happy thoughts right then. As Father disappeared down the hall, I stepped into the lavatory, nearly dancing with impatience as I waited for the water to fill the vessel. Once it was full, I raced back to the stairs, praying I wouldn't run into Father or—worse— Fagenbush. As I reached the top step, Isis gave a bloodcurdling yeowl. Certain the jackal had her clamped in his jaws, I tore down the stairs, taking them two at a time.

I found Anubis with his shoulders wedged between the wall and the sarcophagus, scrabbling madly for Isis, who was emitting low, deep warbles of fury.

Keeping one eye on the jackal, I dumped some of the salt into the water, then swirled the vessel around to mix it up.

The jackal yelped as Isis's claws made contact with his nose, but he didn't retreat. He bared his teeth at her and growled low in his throat.

Afraid to wait too much longer, I took three large strides toward the jackal, then dumped the water over his head, thoroughly drenching him.

The jackal snarled, then raised his muzzle to snap at me. But it was too late.

As the water trickled down his body, he began to harden, his live flesh turning back into hard stone piece by piece, until, with one last mournful yip, he was once again a statue.

My shoulders slumped in relief, and Isis stopped her

caterwauling. Cautiously, she crept out from her hiding spot and drew closer to the frozen jackal. She sniffed at it, then gave it a vicious swipe with her paw. *Take that, wretched statue,* I thought as my heart quit trying to pound its way out of my chest.

"Theodosia!" a voice called from the top of the stairs.

"Yes, Mother?"

"Did I hear a dog down there?"

Bother! "Uh, no, Mother. Just me. Playing with Isis."

"By acting like a dog?" She sounded truly puzzled.

"Well, er, I was training her to defend herself. Against a dog."

"But we have no dogs in the museum."

"I know, but in case she should ever encounter one."

There was a long pause. Finally Mother called down again. "Theodosia?"

"Yes, Mother?"

"It would be best if you didn't mention that game to your father, all right, dear?"

"Whatever you say."

"Excellent. Now come along. Your grandmother's arrived with a new governess in tow." Mum's voice was falsely cheerful, as if she could jolly me into believing this was a good thing. "She's waiting in the sitting room, and I'm leaving right now for a meeting with the board of the Royal Archae-ological Society. Your father's in his office. She's asked to see him, too."

"But Mother, do you have to go?" It was much safer to face Grandmother in large numbers.

"Yes, I really must. Duty calls. Goodbye, my darling!" Then there was the rapid click of her heels on the marble as she made her escape, no doubt from the back door where she could be sure to avoid Grandmother.

With a sigh of frustration, I replaced the vessel on the table and made a mental note to be sure to rinse the salt wa-ter out of it when I got back. I would also need to be sure to wash all the salt from the Anubis statue later. But for now, I had a grandmother to confront.

When I reached the top of the landing, I heard voices coming from Father's office. I thought Grandmother was in the sitting room, but perhaps she had gone into Father's of-fice looking for us. I headed in that direction but quickly re-alized that although one of the voices was Father's, the other voice was most definitely not Grandmother's.

"But I have all the same qualifications that Bollingsworth had."

It was Fagenbush. And I must say, I'd never heard him sound so petulant.

"I know you're disappointed, Clive, but I think it's for the best," Father replied. "Bollingsworth had a few more years' experience than you do," he explained.

Bollingsworth. Just hearing that name made me shudder in revulsion. Father didn't know that the former First Assistant Curator had been a traitor. I wondered how much of Bollingsworth's experience had been gained while working for the Serpents of Chaos?

"You are very talented at what you do," Father continued. "But you are quite young still, and I think a few years' more polish and maturity will serve you well. Now, I must go. I have someone waiting." Father stepped out into the hall and spied me. "Oh, there you are! I was just coming to fetch you. Your grandmother is here."

"Yes. I know." Miserably uncomfortable, I stared at the floor and tried not to look at Fagenbush. But I could feel him staring sharp, pointy daggers at me, and almost against my will, I found myself looking up.

Pure hatred flashed in his eyes. There was no question—Fagenbush knew I'd overheard the whole thing. And he would never forgive me for it.

CHAPTER FOUR
MISS SNEATH

FATHER BID HIS MOTHER A QUICK HELLO, then hurried off, claiming he had an applicant waiting for him. Honestly! I couldn't believe that both my parents were abandoning me like this. Didn't they realize facing Grandmother Throck-morton was just as perilous as being stuck in a tomb in the Valley of the Kings? Of course, *then* they'd been willing to step in and save me, but now, when I truly needed them, they ran.

I squared my shoulders and entered the sitting room. Grandmother looked especially fierce in her iron gray gown. Her beakish nose made her look like a bird of prey getting ready to pounce. Next to her sat a severe-looking woman with a large jutting chin and small almond-shaped eyes. Her hair was scraped back so tightly against her head that it pulled her eyes back to a painful-looking slant.

"Well, don't just stand there dawdling," Grandmother scolded. "Come over so I can introduce you. Miss Sneath, this is Theodosia. The child has had a most appalling education, which needs to be corrected immediately." She sniffed.

Then she sniffed again. "Do I smell wet dog?"

"Wet dog?" I repeated. Bother. Wet jackal, yes, but wet dog, no. "Perhaps it's Miss Sneath's coat?" I nodded toward the brown woolen coat that had been laid on the back of a chair.

"Certainly not!" Miss Sneath said, scandalized.

Even so, I gave her my best curtsy and brightest smile. In spite of what grownups think, I do *try* to get off on the right foot. Most of the time. "How do you do, Miss Sneath? What sorts of things shall you be teaching me?"

"First," she said, with a rigid set to her jaw, "I shall teach you to mind your place and manners. Then I shall teach you the sorts of things a young English lady should know, not the frippery your grandmother tells me you've been studying."

Showing admirable restraint, I narrowly kept from pointing out that Mother and Father might take exception to their life's work being referred to as frippery.

Miss Sneath set her small brown satchel on the table, then

pulled out a thick book and a ruler. She placed the ruler on the table in front of her, then shifted in her seat. There was no chair for me, so I remained standing. "One of the first things I do with any new pupil is test her existing knowledge so I can see how much catching up we must do." She opened her book.

"How many continents are there?" she barked, making me jump.

"Six," I barked back. "Seven if you count North America and South America as two separate continents."

She rapped her ruler on the table. "No impertinence will be tolerated!"

"I'm sorry, Miss Sneath. I wasn't trying to be impertinent. Only thorough."

"How many oceans are there?"

"Five."

"What is the capital of Burma?"

"I'm not sure. I do know the capitals of the ancient Babylonian, Assyrian, and Egyptian empires, however."

"Those were not the question. What year did—"

"Wait! Aren't you going to tell me the capital of Burma so I'll know it next time?"

"Of course not! You'll need to look it up yourself. That is how you learn."

This was highly suspicious. "Do *you* know what the capital of Burma is?"

The ruler cracked down on the table again. "Impertinence!"

Grandmother was no doubt pleased with all this ruler slapping, whereas I found it quite tiresome. "Would you like me to share the answer with you once I find it?" I offered.

"I don't need you to tell me the answer." Miss Sneath pressed her lips together so tightly, they almost disappeared.

"Now then," she said after a long moment. "What year did Charles I dissolve Parliament, and how long was it before it met again?"

"Er, I'm not sure . . . but I know that the current Kaiser Wilhelm is Queen Victoria's grandson and King Edward's nephew." Which you'd think would make them just that much friendlier to each other, but apparently not.

The ruler cracked down on the table yet again. "That's not what I asked."

"Well, I know that, but don't you think it's more important to understand today's relationships in politics rather than those of two hundred years ago?"

Miss Sneath turned to Grandmother. "Not only is this girl markedly ignorant, but she's impudent."

Grandmother shifted in her chair. "I did warn you."

"So you did." Miss Sneath looked down at her book. "What is seven times eight?"

Ooh! I love multiplication tables. "Fifty-six."

Miss Sneath scowled. "Nine times nine?"

"Eighty-one!"

Her scowl deepened. "Eleven times eleven!" It felt as if she were pelting me with small, hard pebbles.

"One hundred and twenty-one!"

She began furiously turning the pages in her book. "What are the four principal sources of heat?" she barked out.

"Well, there's the sun, of course. That would be one. The gas in lamps. Oh, and electricity!" But that was only three. "What about steam? Is that the fourth?"

"Wrong," Miss Sneath trilled, sounding triumphant. She looked back down at her book. "The four principles of heat are the sun, electricity, mechanical actions, and chemical actions."

"Almost had it," I said under my breath. Besides, she had to look at the book. It wasn't as if she knew them by heart, either.

"Well, there you have it," she announced, obviously enjoying my wrong answers far too much. "This child is woefully ignorant," she told Grandmother Throckmorton. "You have contacted me none too soon."

My cheeks grew hot. "Don't you think 'woefully ignorant' is overstating it just a bit? I knew much of what—"

"Enough! *I* am a professional, and there is no question your parents have neglected your education horribly."

"Nonsense!" The word burst from me before I could stop it. "You know all that stuff only because you're reading it from the book! And memorizing isn't the same thing as learning at all!"

Miss Sneath stood, her chin jutting forward. She opened her mouth to say something, but I rushed ahead. "I know lots of things. I know some of the classics and a little Latin. I know Greek and hieroglyphic writing. And I know all about Egyptology, the New Kingdom, and the Middle Kingdom, although admittedly I'm not as familiar with the Old Kingdom as I should be. And I'm very good at long division."

"Silence!" Miss Sneath thundered, a bright red spot appearing on either cheek. She turned to Grandmother. "Her lack of a proper environment has ruined her temperament."

The silence grew thick in the room.

"*Do* you know the capital of Burma?"

We all jumped at Mother's voice. She stood in the doorway with her head held high, indignation snapping in her eyes. I wondered how much she'd heard. Enough, that was for certain.

Miss Sneath's eyes slid down to her book, but she'd already turned the page. "One doesn't need to know the answers in order to properly teach," she said stiffly.

While defiantly glaring at Grandmother, Mother said, "I rather think that in this case one does. The one thing I do insist on is a superior education."

The two of them had a staring contest for a few tense seconds before Grandmother looked away. "You're dismissed," she told Miss Sneath.

The governess's mouth opened and closed, but her sense of propriety (or self-preservation) overrode her sense of outrage. She quickly packed her book and her ruler back into her satchel, closed it with a firm snap, then took her leave.

When she was gone, Grandmother spoke. "While this will be much harder than I originally thought, don't think you've had the last word." I wasn't sure if she was talking to me or Mother. "I *will* find you a governess, and she *will* teach you your place."

Just then, Father poked his head back into the room. "What happened? I just saw the governess go storming out the front door. Henrietta! I thought you'd left."

"I had," Mother said. "But I forgot the paper I wanted to present to the Royal Archaeological Society."

And it was a very good thing she had!

She hurried over to retrieve her presentation, then quickly departed again.

When she had left, Grandmother thumped her cane. "You have come very close to creating a monster, Alistair."

"Oh really, Mother . . ."

I tuned out Grandmother's tirade. (It was the only way to handle them—they were just too upsetting otherwise.) As I let my gaze wander away, it landed on a fellow standing next to Father. I hadn't seen him at first, as he'd been mostly in the hallway, but as Grandmother raged on, he'd sidled into the room. My cheeks grew hot as I realized I was being scolded in front of a complete stranger.

Especially this prig. He'd scrubbed his face so hard that it shone, and his dark hair was pasted flat on his head. It was a shame he hadn't thought to use the same paste on his ears, as they stuck out rather dreadfully. His mouth was pressed into a thin line. It was probably why he had a small fuzzy caterpillar of a mustache—so people would be sure to realize he had a mouth. I have observed that people with small, tight mouths are rarely friendly or good tempered.

Needless to say, I disliked him instantly. Not because of his ears or even his mouth, but because he stood listening to Grandmother, nodding his head in agreement the whole time. He clearly had the makings of a toady of the first water.

By the time Grandmother had finished her lecture and left, Father's own mouth was looking a little thin and there was a slight tic in his jaw.

"Ahem." The man next to Father cleared his throat.

"Oh, Weems! I'm sorry. I'd completely forgotten about you. Theodosia, this is our new First Assistant Curator, Vicary Weems. Weems, this is my daughter, Theodosia."

"How do you do?" I said, bobbing a curtsy.

Weems sent a curt little nod in my direction, as if he wasn't about to smile at someone who'd just been so thoroughly scolded. A prig, just like I thought.

There was an awkward silence before Father realized Weems wouldn't be responding. "Yes, well, as you see, we're looking for a governess. Now, let's go meet the other curators, shall we? Theodosia, you have something to do, I believe?"

"Yes, Father." Honestly, I never would have thought the catacombs would look so appealing!

Isis refused to return to long-term storage with me. While she was perfectly willing to brave vile magic, evil curses, and the dangerous, restless dead, she'd clearly drawn the line at dogs and doglike creatures.

Once again I descended the stairs feeling as though I

were venturing into the very pit of the Underworld itself. I couldn't decide if I should have felt safer; surely the worst had happened, with that statue of Anubis? Or perhaps I should have been even more scared, as the statue was just the beginning? That was the rub of Egyptian magic—one never really knew if one was coming or going.

I paused at the foot of the stairs and eyed the statue of Anubis warily. It didn't move so much as a nostril. Deciding it was safe, I went to the small stool near the shelves, picked up my pencil and notebook, and resumed my cataloging.

One set alabaster Canopic jars, lids shaped after the Four Sons of Horus, empty, New Kingdom

One set limestone Canopic jars, human head–shaped lids, empty, New Kingdom

One set quartzite Canopic jars, lids Four Sons of Horus, empty, Middle Kingdom

One set basalt Canopic jars, dome-shaped lids, empty, First Dynasty

One large, lidded ceramic jar, empt—Ew!

Upon lifting the lid I found myself staring at dozens of dried lizards, all standing on end with their noses pointing up toward the mouth of the jar. Gingerly, I closed my gloved fingers around the nose of one of the lizards and gently pulled the lizard out of the jar. I half expected it to disintegrate at my touch, but it didn't. When I had it out of the jar, I gasped. The lizard had two tails! I put that lizard aside and checked the others in the jar. They all had two tails. What a find! The ancient Egyptians believed that two-tailed lizards—any malformed creature, really—were full of extra-powerful *heka*. Many of the instructions for removing curses or making magical potions called for two-tailed lizards. How lovely to have stumbled upon something helpful for a change!

As I started to catalog the next jar, my elbow caught the end of the staff that I'd so hastily thrust back onto the shelf earlier, and it clattered to the floor. I winced at the noise and looked over my shoulder to see if the disturbance had woken anything up from its dormant state.

Everything was still and exactly as I'd left it. I paused, noticing Anubis's eyes on me. Had they always been? I couldn't remember. I'd been more worried about his claws and teeth, frankly. I'd have to keep a close watch on him, though.

I bent over to pick up the staff. What I had originally thought was just crooked turned out to be jointed wooden sections that could be rotated to make the staff straight and long or twisted into unusual shapes, sort of like a puzzle. The jackal head at the end was made of gold and had gaping jaws that looked as if they'd held something at one time.

(Hopefully not a cat!) As I smoothed my gloved hand along the staff, straightening out the sections, it took the shape of a serpent. Of course! It must be a *weret heku*, one of the ancient magician wands!

The middle joint in the wood was stiff and I had to really bear down to get it to straighten. With one final twist, the bottom half snapped into place, knocking over a Canopic jar in the process.

I flinched at the loud thud, relieved the jar hadn't shattered. Except . . . it shouldn't have been that heavy. All the Canopic jars were relatively light because any internal organs in them had dried up and turned to dust ages ago. Even the jar with the dried-up lizards hadn't been heavy.

So what—exactly—was in this jar? What if the internal organs in it hadn't turned to dust?

I stared at the jar for a while, working up my nerve. It could hold something wonderful, like the lizards.

On the other hand, there could be a set of rotting intestines or a putrefied liver lurking inside.

Bracing myself, I squatted down and tapped the lid away from the jar's opening. I expected something nasty to ooze onto the floor, but instead a small golden ball rolled out.

The golden surface was completely covered in ancient symbols, many of them looking older than the hieroglyphs I was used to. But wait! There was a jackal head near the top of the sphere. I picked the ball up and peered closely. Running along the middle was a carving of a long staff, very much like the one I'd just found.

Something niggled at me and I reached for the staff. Could it be? I brought the two together and tried to fit the orb into the head of the staff. It was a tight fit, and I had to work it around some. The jackal's teeth had been designed to keep the ball from falling out, which meant they also made it difficult to get the ball back in.

With a final soft *click*, the orb slipped past Anubis's teeth and settled between his gaping jaws. At the very same moment, the gaslights flickered and a whooshing sensation swept through the room.

A chill ran up my spine, but before I could determine what—if anything—had happened, Father's voice called down the stairway.

"Theodosia! Come along. It's time to go home."

I looked down at the staff in my hand, deciding there would be plenty of time to figure it out the next day. Going home sounded lovely. After spending hours in the dusty old room, I felt horribly grubby and absolutely coated with the whiff of black magic. Perhaps I'd put a handful of salt into my bath tonight—just as a sort of purification ritual.

Besides, I could hear voices arguing at the top of the stairs. Curious, I set the staff down and made my way up the steps until I reached the landing. I paused when I saw Vicary Weems standing with his hands on his hips, glaring at the other two assistant curators.

"What happened to it?" Weems was asking. "Greatcoats don't just get up and wander away on their own."

Uh-oh.

"Of course they don't," Fagenbush said, his voice full of scorn. "But we are responsible for the collections, not other curators' clothing."

Weems stiffened at this. "I don't need to remind you that I'm your superior now, and insubordination of any sort will not be tolerated."

Honestly! Was he by any chance related to Miss Sneath?

I knew I should have stepped in and explained about the missing coat, but how, exactly? Best I should just put it back tomorrow—hopefully that would satisfy him. "Um, are you sure you brought it with you today?" I asked, stepping from the doorway.

"I beg your pardon?" Weems asked, staring down at me as if I were something Isis had sicked up.

"Well, often when I think I've brought my cloak or hat, it turns out I haven't. So perhaps that's what happened to you? You just thought you'd brought it. Besides, it really wasn't that cold out this morning. I'm not sure why you would have needed it."

His cheeks flushed slightly and I realized I'd scored a direct hit. He hadn't worn it for warmth, but rather because he liked the dashing figure he cut while wearing it. I almost snorted but stopped myself in time.

"M-miss Theodosia has a p-point," Edgar Stilton, the Third Assistant Curator, said. "Especially since overcoats have never gone missing before." Stilton was my favorite curator. Not only was he kind, but he acted as a sort of human lightning rod for all the magic afoot in the museum.

"Nonsense. It was probably one of the workmen, and if so, you can be sure I shall report him to the authorities."

"It was not Sweeny or Dolge!" I said hotly. "They've been here for years and nothing's ever gone missing. You probably just left it at home or set it down somewhere you can't remember."

"You think so," Fagenbush drawled, looking at me strangely.

Bother. He was too suspicious for his own good. Or for my own good. "Well, it happens sometimes," I said, trying to lighten my voice. "Now, if you'll excuse me, I believe my parents are waiting for me." And with that, I hurried down the hall.

CHAPTER FIVE
WHERE'S MY MUMMY?

THE NEXT MORNING FOUND ME sitting at the breakfast table trying to hide a yawn. I'd stayed up far too late the night before, making a few extra wedjat eyes to carry with me down to the catacombs. With Chaos returned to London, one could never have too many sources of protection.

I nudged the beige lump in my bowl, wondering who had ever thought porridge was a good idea, when Father squawked.

Usually I am the one doing the squawking, so this was a change.

He stared at the daily paper, his lips moving faintly as he

read and a dull flush spreading up his cheeks, a sure sign he was getting hot under the collar.

"What the devil?" he finally exploded. He looked up from the newspaper at Mother. "Listen to this. 'A series of burglaries have been reported all over London. From private collections to public museums, a large coordinated set of robberies occurred last night. The same item was stolen from each location: mummies. "Someone is playing a deliberate hoax!" Lord Snowthorpe, head keeper at the British Museum, declared when he was reached late last night for comment.'"

Father surged to his feet. "We've got to get to the museum! Those thieves might have hit us as well."

Mother was unperturbed. The truth was, she'd been in a jolly mood ever since her meeting the day before, which had gone swimmingly. "Surely Flimp would have sent a message if there had been anything out of the ordinary last night," she said.

"Unless they coshed him over the head first," I pointed out.

Father speared me with a look.

"I'll just go and get my hat," I said, then hightailed it to the carriage so I wouldn't be left behind.

The authorities were waiting for us when we arrived. Flimp had refused to let them in without Father's consent (good man, our Flimp).

"Sir." The constable in charge stepped forward. "We're here to check and see if there's anything amiss in your museum."

"There better not be," Father mumbled as he waited for Flimp to unlock the door. Remembering their manners, the constables motioned for Mother to go first, then followed her inside. I, of course, brought up the rear. I seem to do that a lot, frankly.

Father led the way through the foyer toward the stairs to the Egyptian exhibit, then stopped, causing all of us to bump into him. "What the blazes . . . ?" he boomed.

Everyone else fell silent. I craned my neck to see around the people in front of me, my jaw dropping when I did.

There, lined up in the hallway, were scads of mummies. Rows and rows of them. I was seized by a violent shiver, and goose bumps rained down my arms.

"What now, Theodosia?" Father said, turning his exasperation onto me.

"Nothing! I just felt a draft, that's all."

"Mebbe the sight o' all those bodies gave her the willies?" the constable suggested, looking a little pale himself.

But of course, it wasn't the willies. Or even a draft. What

the sensation meant was that one of those mummies was either cursed or carrying some beastly sort of magic with it. But which one? There were scores of them, all crowded together against the wall as if they were waiting for a train to arrive. Most of them were still covered in their wrappings, thank goodness! But they were old and dingy, and some of the linen was looking tattered. A few unwrapped heads and limbs poked through, but I tried very hard not to look at those.

The constable cleared his throat. "Is that how you always display your mummies, sir?"

"Of course not! Those aren't even ours."

He was right. They weren't. Which meant . . .

They were probably the missing ones.

I could almost see the gears turning in the constable's head as he drew the same conclusion. "Well, isn't that cozy, guvnor? All the mummies just happen to be here in your museum."

Horrified disbelief spread across Father's face. "Are you accusing me of stealing them?" I could tell by the color his face was turning that he was trying hard not to shout.

The constable shrugged. "They've gone missing from all over the city and now they're here. What am I supposed to think?"

Father glared at the man. "Who asked you to think,

anyway? Our museum has plenty of mummies of its own. We have no need for any of these." He waved his hand at the wall.

With a shock, I realized one of the bodies was staring at me. It took me a moment to recognize it was Lord Chudleigh's mummy. The one formerly known as Tetley.

I forced my attention back to the constable, who was dispatching one of the other constables to go fetch an Inspector Turnbull, who was still questioning employees at the British Museum. As the man hurried away, he nearly collided with Edgar Stilton, who emerged from the hallway just then. When he saw the rows of mummies, the entire left side of his body twitched.

"Sir?" He looked inquiringly at Father.

"Stilton." Father's voice was full of relief. "How long have you been here?"

The constable sent Father a quelling glance. "I'll be the one to ask the questions, if you don't mind."

It was clear that Father did mind, but after a gentle nudge from Mother, he clamped his mouth shut.

The constable turned to Stilton. "What time did you get in this morning, sir?"

"I've been here since half past, sir." Stilton looked from the constable back to Father, not sure whom to address his answer to.

"Were these mummies here when you arrived?"

"I-I don't know. I came in the west entrance, like always."

"I say! What's all this?" a pinched, critical voice demanded. At the sight of Vicary Weems, thoughts of his missing overcoat rushed back into my head. Bother! I had hoped to return his coat to the rack before he got here this morning, but the mummies had driven that thought out of my mind.

"Nothing, Weems." Father waved his arm in dismissal. "Just some mix-up that will be sorted out immediately."

The constable stiffened. "Seems to me I'll be the one to decide when it's sorted out."

"Oh, good gad, man! Take a look around our museum. Does it look like we need any more mummies?"

That was when I realized a curious thing, something no one else seemed to have noticed yet. All of *our* mummies were standing in the foyer, too. As if they'd all decided to come down and have a chat with the newcomers.

"Excuse me, sir," I ventured, in an attempt to smooth things over before they completely fell apart.

Just as the constable nodded at me to continue, a commotion erupted at the door.

"Ah. Now we'll get to the bottom of this," the constable said. "Inspector Turnbull!" he called out, then rushed over to speak to him privately.

Mother inched closer to Father and they began talking in hushed voices. Weems's disdainful gaze fell onto poor Stilton. "What are you doing out here? Shouldn't you be in your office? Working, presumably?"

Stilton slipped a finger into the top of his collar and tugged at it. "Th-They seem to have some questions for me, sir."

"Indeed." Weems looked doubtful. He was clearly the sort of person who always assumed one was lying.

"He's quite correct, you know," I said. "The constable wanted to ask him some questions, so he'd best stay until they dismiss him."

Weems turned his beastly glare on me. I suddenly found myself wanting to tug my frock into place and make sure every button was done up correctly. Instead, I reached up and scratched my armpit, the most vulgar thing I could think of in the heat of the moment.

His lip curled in distaste. "I'd assumed yesterday was some sort of holiday. Surely you don't come here every day?"

Have I mentioned that Vicary Weems has a very nasally penetrating voice?

The inspector left the constable by the door and stalked toward us. He looked like a determined bulldog, which was not promising. "And who might you be?" he asked Weems.

Weems drew himself up to his full height, which was still

considerably less than Inspector Turnbull's. "I am Vicary Weems, First Assistant Curator, in charge of the museum's exhibits, and, I might add, a close personal friend of Lord Chudleigh, who is on the board of directors of this museum."

Turnbull studied him a moment longer. "So you're in charge, then, eh?"

"Yes sir," Weems said, puffing up.

"Well then, you can tell me exactly what's going on and how these stolen mummies got here."

It was as if he'd stuck a straight pin directly into Weems. The First Assistant Curator unpuffed rather quickly. "It's only my second day on the job, sir," he rushed to add, clearly wanting to distance himself from any wrongdoing on the museum's part. "Let me go get the Head Curator." And before Turnbull could say another word, he headed over to Father and Mother.

The inspector followed closely on his heels. As unobtrusively as possible, I trailed after them. When they reached my parents, Turnbull pulled a small notebook from his jacket pocket along with a little pencil stub. He thumbed through the notebook pages and scowled. "Just came from the British Museum. A Lord Snowthorpe gave me a list of the missing mummies. Seems they were out forty-seven of them."

"Showoffs," Father muttered.

Turnbull gave Father a steely look. "How many mummies do you normally display in your foyer?"

"None! The foyer's no place for a display."

"Then it looks to me like those are the missing ones. How d'you explain that, Mr. Throckmorton?"

And of course, Father couldn't. None of us could. However, if they would only give me a chance, I could prove that Father wasn't a thief. I opened my mouth to speak, only to be interrupted by a second commotion at the door. "I say, let me in, you nitwit!" Lord Chudleigh's impatient voice rang through the foyer. "I'm on the museum's board, for gad's sake!"

Properly quelled, the constable let him through.

"I've come to check on our mummies, Throckmorton! How did we fare—I say, what are all these doing *here?*" He peered more closely at the bandaged forms against the wall. "What's *my* mummy doing here?"

"That's what we're trying to find out, sir," Inspector Turnbull said reassuringly.

I studied Chudleigh briefly, trying to determine if his bluster and outrage were an act. If so, it was a very good one. He would bear watching.

Thinking this had gone on long enough, I stepped forward, drawing everyone's attention. "That's what I've been trying to tell you. Some of those are *our* mummies. We don't keep them in the foyer. If you search the museum, I imagine you'll find that all the ones from our exhibits have been moved down here with the others. Clearly, if Father was to steal mummies, he wouldn't steal his own! I think you'll find that someone was going to steal all of them and was just keeping them in one place till he got back with a lorry or something, and then he was going to haul them all off."

A hushed silence fell over the room as everyone turned to count the mummies. "She's right," Father said. (I do wish he wouldn't sound so surprised.) "There's the forty-seven from the British Museum, Lord Chudleigh's, and the eighteen others that have gone missing from private collections. That leaves thirteen more, exactly the number we had on display."

"Biggs!" Inspector Turnbull barked out.

"Yes sir?" The constable in charge hurried over.

"You said there was a night watchman. Fetch him."

"Of course, sir." The constable disappeared down the hallway while the rest of us waited in silence. Or tried to, anyway.

"Hsst!"

I whirled around, wondering what on earth could be making that sound.

"Hsst!" came again, only this time I detected it was coming from behind one of the marble pillars. Glancing over my shoulder to make sure no one was paying any attention to me, I sidled toward the column—cautiously, mind you, as I had no idea who (or what) was hissing at me.

As I drew closer, a hand snaked out and grabbed me. The grimy hand sported an even grimier fingerless glove, but I bit back my surprised scream as I recognized the blue eyes dancing above a dirty button nose.

Sticky Will.

CHAPTER SIX
THAT'S THE WAY THE MUMMY TUMBLES

"WHAT ARE YOU DOING HERE?" I hissed back at him. Instead of answering, Sticky Will pulled me behind the pillar, out of view of the others.

With one last glance toward the foyer, he tugged his cap. "Ol' Wiggy sent me."

"You mean Lord Wigmere?"

"Aye. 'E wonts to talk to you." He grabbed my arm again and began pulling me down the south hallway.

"You don't have to drag me! I would like to see Wigmere as much as he'd like to see me, you know."

Will dropped my arm. "Right, then. This way. 'E's waiting just outside."

When we reached the east entrance, my heart jerked against my ribs. It was unlocked. Was this how the mummies had gotten in?

Will saw me eyeing the lock. "Couldn't come in the front, miss. Not with all them coppers in there," he added apologetically.

"You picked the lock?"

Will shuffled his feet and had the grace to blush a little. "Aye."

I leaned closer to him and lowered my voice. "Could you teach me how to do that?"

Will drew back in surprise. "Ye mean ye aren't mad at me?"

"Goodness, no! As you said, Wigmere and I must talk. And you were on official business." My head reeled with the potential forbidden knowledge I'd have access to if I could pick locks.

"Come on, miss. We shouldn't keep him waiting too long."

"Right. But you will teach me? About the locks, I mean?"

"Sure. Now come on."

The air was cold and brisk, and since it was still early yet, there was little traffic out on the street. A tall, rather greasy-looking man in a tattered undertaker's coat and battered top hat was buying a pie from a pie seller's cart. Farther down, an urchin loitered in a doorway. But other than that, no one was about, which was perfect.

The Brotherhood's carriage lurked on the far side of the street, its hulking form a deep, shiny black unmarked by any crest or insignia. I glanced once more around me, then hurried across to the carriage. When we reached it, Will rapped smartly on the door, then opened it.

The head of the Brotherhood of the Chosen Keepers sat back against the cushion, his hands resting on his cane. The lines on his face seemed deeper this morning, and his eyes were serious. Here was someone who was very good at taking charge and knew just what to do about predicaments. "Good morning, sir."

"Good morning, Theodosia," he said, motioning me inside. As I clambered up into the carriage and settled onto the plush velvet seat, he said to Will, "Keep an eye out. If anyone from the museum or police shows up, give two quick raps, then a hard knock."

Wigmere turned his attention fully to me. "We received some news last night that I thought you ought to know. Plus, with this morning's unpleasantness all over the newspapers, it seemed a visit was in order."

"Oh, thank you, sir! This morning has been a bit dicey. Do you know who piled all those mummies up in our foyer?"

"Well, no. Not exactly. But we do have confirmation that the Serpents of Chaos are back in London, just as we feared. In fact, I'd lay odds that someone from the Serpents of Chaos has had contact with Chudleigh and even planted the idea for a mummy unwrapping in his thick head—in order to ensure Tetley was discovered." He still looked disgusted at the spectacle we'd been forced to witness.

"You mean to let us know we haven't seen the last of them?"

Wigmere's solemn blue eyes met mine. "Yes. To let us know we may have won the first battle, but not the war. As a warning to show us what happens to those who displease them."

I gulped. The truth was, I displeased them very much. "I had *so* hoped that was the end of them." In fact, one of my favorite daydreams was imagining von Braggenschnott still stuck fast to the wall in Thutmose III's tomb, yelling for help for the past three months, even though I knew it wasn't very realistic.

"With Tetley's body showing up so publicly two nights ago, I can't help but feel the Serpents of Chaos must have something to do with this morning's mummy situation. It's too great a coincidence, although I can't quite figure out what their game is. Not yet."

"But it doesn't make any sense! Why would they bring all of London's mummies to our museum?" A thought occurred to me—a horrid, vile thought. "You don't think all the mummies are cursed, like the Heart of Egypt was, and now those curses will fall on our heads?"

Wigmere scowled. "Did they feel cursed?"

"At least one is. Or if it's not cursed, its *akhu* is hovering nearby and most unhappy at being disturbed."

"I suppose that's unavoidable with so many mummies being moved. Can you handle it?" he asked.

I sat up straighter. "Yes. Of course."

"Very well. We will be working on this from our end, my dear. As soon as we have any word of what's going on, either Will or myself will get a message to you."

"Is there anything you can do to help Father with this horrid misunderstanding about the mummies? They seem to think he's trying to steal them."

Wigmere shook his head. "I'm sorry. All the Brotherhood's movements must remain shrouded in secrecy. We can't risk making our presence known."

My heart sank. How was Father going to get out of this mess?

"I'm sure as more becomes known over the next day or two, your father's name will be cleared. Meanwhile, I suggest you read all the texts you can get your hands on regarding mummies and Osiris."

Of course! As god of the Underworld, Osiris ruled over the dead. And mummies were most definitely dead.

"Anubis, too, since he was god of mummification," Wigmere continued. "We'll comb our archives for anything that might explain what could cause all these mummies to be on the move. Hopefully one of us will find a clue as to what Chaos is up to."

"Very well, sir."

Wigmere gave a bracing nod. "Keep your spirits up. We've defeated the Serpents of Chaos before—we can do it again."

"Thank you, sir." However, last time we hadn't been dealing with the forces of the Underworld, which put a rather new spin on it.

Wigmere rapped on the carriage door and Will opened it so quickly that I couldn't help but wonder if he'd been eavesdropping. "She's ready to go back," Wigmere said. "Is the coast clear?"

Will shifted his eyes to the left, then the right. "I reckon so."

Wigmere winked at me, but it was lacking its normal enthusiasm. "We'll use Will here to keep in touch."

I nodded, then hopped out of the carriage and followed Will as he scurried across the street, his eyes darting everywhere. When we reached the museum, he stepped partway into a hedge before opening the door and fairly shoving me inside. Surely he was overdoing this whole lookout bit? Before I could bring it to his attention, he disappeared down the street and I was alone in the museum's hallway.

Everyone was most likely still in the foyer, talking to the police. Hopefully, no one would have noticed my absence. I locked the door, then stepped farther into the hallway—

Directly into Clive Fagenbush! And I do mean directly. I bounced off him like an Indian rubber ball, nearly losing my balance and landing on my bum in the process.

"Watch where you're going," he snarled, then brushed off his suit, as if I had dirtied it somehow.

"How was I to know you'd be skulking around down here?" I said, mirroring his gesture by brushing off my pinafore.

"I wasn't skulking. I've come to show Constable Biggs here the east entrance, as he asked me to." That was when I noticed that he did indeed have the constable with him. "What are *you* doing here?" Fagenbush asked suspiciously.

"I . . . came to see if the door had been tampered with." I turned to the constable. "But it hasn't been. It was locked up tight when I found it."

Before either of them could question me further, I hurried down the hall.

Once I reached the foyer, the familiar sensation of beetles marching down my spine overtook me for a moment. How could I have forgotten? I had work to do.

But as I looked around, I saw that I was nearly too late. Strangers—a small army of them—were swarming everywhere. Unfamiliar porters and workmen toiled side by side with Dolge and Sweeny, lugging the mummies down to Receiving, where I assumed carts were ready to return them to their owners. Weems was trying to direct traffic but just kept getting in the way.

There were a couple of other men, too, although they were younger and dressed in suits. One was talking to Stilton and writing things down on a pad, while another was trying to set up some photography equipment. More policemen, perhaps? I inched closer to overhear their conversation.

"Oh, yes," Stilton was saying. "Tales of mummy curses have been around for ages."

The stranger scribbled something furiously on his notepad. "Yes, go on. What are some of the most common effects of these?"

"Well, there are stories of people dying or having serious accidents, or horrible misfortunes befalling them after they'd disturbed a mummy."

The man stopped writing and looked up at Stilton. "What exactly do you mean by 'disturb'?"

Stilton's left shoulder jerked. "Move it from its rightful resting place. Or any resting place, I suppose. Or open the seal on its tomb . . ."

The fellow began scribbling again. "What can people do to protect themselves?"

"Well, not handle mummies, for one . . . and gold is supposed to be a powerful form of protection. . . ."

I was surprised at how well versed Stilton was in such mythology. I had thought him mostly a clerk.

"Gold?" the man echoed.

"Yes, gold represents the fierce power of the sun god Ra, which is said to drive the mummy away."

"Where on earth have you been?" Vicary Weems snarled.

I jerked as if I'd been burned, then realized he wasn't speaking to me. He was talking to Fagenbush. My enjoyment in watching Fagenbush squirm under Weems's questioning was distracted by a grunt off to my left. Dolge had just wrapped his burly arms around one of the mummies. Oh dear! He and Sweeny might come into contact with that vile curse.

I shoved a hand into the pocket of my pinafore and sauntered over to the mummies, as if wanting another look. When I got close enough to Dolge, I tripped and grabbed on to him for support—but of course it was actually so I could slip one of my extra wedjat eyes into his pocket.

"Watch it there, miss," he said. "I'd hate for you to bump up against one o' these mummies and get a curse." He winked, clearly thinking it a fine joke.

If only he knew . . .

I moved away to find Sweeny. He wasn't quite as good-natured as Dolge, so I'd have to be a little more clever with him.

While I was still puzzling over how to approach Sweeny, the man with the photographic equipment called out, "Over here, gents!" There was a loud *pop!* and a blinding flash, then Sweeny yelled out, "Ruddy 'ell! I can't see!"

At the same moment, Inspector Turnbull saw the photographer and began bellowing at the top of his lungs. "What's that reporter doing in here? Get him out! Out!"

I rushed to Sweeny's side while he was still batting the dancing dots away from his vision and patted his arm. "Don't worry. Your sight will come back in just a second." I slipped a wedjat eye into the pocket of his coveralls. "If you close your eyes, it makes the dots go away faster."

By this time two constables had reached the reporter and photographer and were none too gently escorting them out the front door. Weems rushed over to Stilton, clearly appalled. "Were you speaking with that . . . that *reporter?* I've a mind to give you a formal reprimand."

Oh, honestly. What did he call this—an *in*formal reprimand?

"I-I thought he was with the police. I had no idea he was—"

"Just get the mummies back where they belong," Weems scoffed. "I'll deal with you later."

As Stilton ran after Sweeny and another porter, a loud bellow erupted from the back of the museum, followed by a rapid thumping.

After a moment of startled silence, we all raced toward the sound, Turnbull in the lead, trailed closely by Father and myself. That is, until Vicary Weems pushed past me and nearly sent me careening into the wall. Beast.

When we reached the loading area, we found a bald porter lying on the ground, grimacing in pain, his leg twisted at a horrid angle. Dolge was struggling to balance the mummy they'd been carrying between them. Stilton trundled down the stairs to help.

"He tripped," Dolge explained.

"Broken leg, it looks like," Turnbull announced.

"Someone pushed me," the man gasped. "I didn't trip down no ruddy stairs. I was pushed."

"Who could have pushed you?" Turnbull asked, looking around. "We all arrived after your fall. There was no one else here."

The man set his jaw. "I don't know, but I *was* pushed. I *felt* it."

Turnbull reached up and scratched his head. "Very well. Let's get this man a doctor. Biggs! You and your men go find anyone else here who wasn't in the foyer with the rest of us. We'll want them for questioning."

But of course, I knew they'd find no one. Or no corporeal body, anyway. No. I was very much afraid that the push had been of a supernatural variety.

CHAPTER SEVEN
MISS CHITTLE

WHILE EVERYONE WAS BUSY SEARCHING for someone who might have pushed the porter, I decided to slip away to the reading room in order to begin my research. But before I could take more than half a dozen steps, there was an imperious rapping at the museum door. Now what? We weren't open for visitation today, and surely we didn't need any more policemen. (Or any more mummies—but I was pretty sure they wouldn't have knocked.)

Since everyone else was still sorting out the mess with the broken-legged porter, I called out, "I'll get it." I straightened my frock and quickly wiped my face in case any errant dirt or cobwebs had found their way there, then opened the door.

Grandmother Throckmorton blinked, her scowl deepening. "What are you doing opening the door? Don't you have studies to attend to?"

"Yes, ma'am." I dropped a quick curtsy. Not Grandmother Throckmorton! This was three days in a row. I wasn't sure I could take much more. "We've had a bit of excitement this morning and everything is off schedule."

"Yes," a cheerful voice boomed from just behind Grandmother. "So we heard! We thought we'd come round and see if there was anything we could do to help."

"Admiral Sopcoate, how lovely to see you again." With any luck, he would temper Grandmother's horridness.

"Well, don't leave us standing out on the stoop like common tradesmen. Let us in!"

I jumped out of the way and they entered, which was when I discovered they had brought a young woman with them. It didn't take an overactive imagination to conclude that she was most likely my newest governess.

"If that's more blasted police, don't let them in, Theodosia!" Father shouted from the far end of the room.

And how was I supposed to keep them out? I started to tell him not to worry, that it was only Grandmother Throckmorton and Admiral Sopcoate come to check on us, but Grandmother interrupted me. "Alistair! Such language!"

"Oh, hello, Mother. Admiral."

"Police?" the young woman with them repeated, her right eye twitching slightly.

"Miss Chittle—" Grandmother's loud voice had the governess flinching, and I wondered if she was related to Edgar Stilton—"this is my granddaughter, Theodosia."

"How d'you do?" I bobbed the most polite curtsy I could muster. It was hard with thoughts of mummies and research running through my head. A governess was the last thing I needed right now. "I'm very pleased to meet you."

She stared down her small, thin nose at me and gave a stiff nod.

The admiral moved forward to shake Father's hand. "Good morning, Throckmorton. We heard you had a dustup this morning."

Father ran his hand through his hair, making it stand up on end. "Yes, a bit of a pickle, I'm afraid. We've no idea how all these mummies got here and the inspector seems determined to find it our fault."

"Mummies?" Miss Chittle's pale white hand flew to her mouth, as if to hold back a scream. Honestly! What did she think was housed in a museum, anyway?

"That is inexcusable," Grandmother snapped. "I will not have the Throckmorton name dragged through the mud.

Give me this inspector's name and I will have the admiral look into the situation immediately."

Then the admiral did something quite astonishing. He reached out and patted Grandmother on the arm. "Now, Lavinia. I told you, your name is quite safe. I'll be sure of it."

I watched open mouthed, expecting Grandmother to bean the man with her cane for taking such liberties. But instead, her face softened and she patted him back.

Miss Chittle caught sight of the mummies lined up against the back wall, and she took two small steps backward.

"Don't worry. Father didn't steal them," I reassured her.

"Steal them?" Miss Chittle's gaze fluttered from the mummies to me, then to Grandmother. "You didn't mention anything about the police, ma'am. Or stealing."

Grandmother gave her a withering look. "You told me you had a strong constitution and nerves of iron. I would hope you haven't been lying to me. A woman in my position could make things very difficult for a governess who has lied."

Miss Chittle's throat bobbed as she swallowed once before speaking. "Of course not, madam. I never lie."

Grandmother gave a satisfied nod, then whipped her head around to me, as if she thought I'd been up to something while she wasn't looking. "This isn't *your* doing, by some chance, is it?"

"Now, Lavinia," the admiral said, "what could a young girl possibly do to create a mess like this?"

Have I mentioned I was growing rather fond of Admiral Sopcoate?

Grandmother relaxed a bit. "Very well. I suppose you're right."

Anxious to change the subject, I turned to my new governess. "What sorts of things will you be teaching me, Miss Chittle?"

"None of your impertinence now," Grandmother interjected. "Miss Chittle has been trained in the classics, so you won't suffer from an inferior education."

"Really?" My hopes grew.

Her eyes still on the mummies, Miss Chittle nodded absently.

"Plus," Grandmother continued, "she'll be teaching you all the things you lack. Etiquette, manners, comportment—"

Knowing better than to interrupt, I raised my hand to let Grandmother know I had a question.

"What?" she barked.

"What exactly is comportment, again?"

Admiral Sopcoate made a strange noise, then began coughing. Grandmother narrowed her eyes. "Comportment is how you behave, how you acquit yourself in public. It is something you are sadly lacking, as the disaster at Lord Chudleigh's illustrated."

I lowered my head. "Yes, ma'am."

Grandmother leaned closer to Miss Chittle. "Don't let her fool you. Butter wouldn't melt in her mouth."

It was quiet while I felt both of them studying me. After a long moment, Miss Chittle spoke. "Although I have no doubt I can teach your granddaughter, I would like to suggest we don't conduct our lessons here." She looked around the foyer, her eyes lingering briefly on the mummies before she continued. "There are far too many distractions, and it is quite unhealthy."

Grandmother thumped her cane. "We are in total agreement on that score."

"But Grandmother," I said, "the museum's reading room has so many scholarly texts for me to study. It's how I've learned Latin and Greek and hierogly—"

"None of which will do you a lick of good if you don't have the sense God gave you."

Did I not have enough sense to save Britain in her hour of need just months ago? I wanted to scream. But of course, I couldn't. I lowered my head and hoped Grandmother would think it was in shame instead of in fury. This would never do. I couldn't allow myself to be removed from the museum! Who would protect everyone from all the wretched curses floating around this place, let alone get to the bottom of this whole mummy fiasco? No. It simply wouldn't do.

Resolved, I lifted my gaze. "Very well. But don't you think it would be a good idea for me to show Miss Chittle around the museum so I can explain to her what I have been learning? That way, in addition to comportment and such, she'll know where to pick up in my studies?"

"I'm sure that's not necessary," Miss Chittle said quickly.

Grandmother waved her hand. "It can't hurt, and the admiral is still speaking with my son. So run along, but don't be too long."

I bobbed a curtsy at Grandmother, then turned to my new governess. "This way, Miss Chittle."

The woman sniffed, as if she really hadn't the time, but at least she followed. As we headed away from the front hall, my mind raced, trying to decide which of the exhibits I could use to shock her the most.

The answer was obvious: the ancient Egyptian exhibit, of course. Especially because the mummies already had her on edge. The Egyptian exhibit held many more gruesome delights to be explored. Plus, with any luck at all, she might be sensitive to the heavy, oppressive magic in the air.

I began outlining my education to date. "While I've spent

most of my time on ancient Egypt," I said, "I have also done quite a bit with the classics: Rome and Greece, as well as a smattering of ancient Babylonia, Assyria, and Sumer."

"Hm," was all she said as her eyes skittered from here to there, trying to take in all the corners and shadows of the hallway.

I paused at the doorway to the ancient Greek and Roman exhibit. "Would you like to take a look at our classical collection?"

"Very well," she said primly.

I stood back so she could go into the room first. Her gaze fell immediately on a life-size statue of Adonis, who wasn't wearing so much as a fig leaf. She jerked back from the doorway, her cheeks flushed bright pink. "I think I've seen quite enough," she said.

Honestly. Just how silly can a grown woman be? Without meeting my eyes, she continued. "Do you have a ladies' withdrawing room here?"

"You mean a lavatory?"

"There's no need to be vulgar, but yes, that is what I mean."

"Of course. This way, please." She didn't say a word as I led her to the restroom on the main floor. Since she was so prim and proper, I decided to wait for her outside.

It takes a surprisingly long time for an overly proper governess to visit the lavatory. When she finally emerged, her cheeks were still pink (was she embarrassed, perhaps?) and her eyes looked a little bright. I caught a whiff of something. Careful to be discreet, I sniffed again. It smelled like . . . sherry? But where would she have got hold of sherry? And at this hour! I knew for a fact there was none in the lavatory. Watching her more closely now, I asked, "May I show you the ancient Egyptian exhibit?"

"Yes, but only that. Then I think it will be time to go."

"Very well. This way, please." I led her from the main floor up to the third. On either side of us, statues of ancient Egyptian gods and pharaohs loomed. Isis emerged from behind one of the statues and began following us. I wondered how Miss Chittle felt about cats?

"Here," I said in my best museum-tour-guide voice, "is our most popular collection, ancient Egypt."

Miss Chittle stepped past me into the room. The electric lights flickered, and she flinched a bit. Of course, the lights did that all the time, but today the timing was perfect.

I led her to the large stone sarcophagus in the middle of the room. "This is the sarcophagus of an unknown priest from the Old Kingdom."

"A sarcophagus?" she repeated hollowly.

"Yes. A stone tomb. Where they placed dead bodies.

Although the priest's mummy wasn't one of the ones downstairs. It wasn't in the sarcophagus when Mum found it."

Miss Chittle swallowed nervously, then glanced at me. "It wasn't?"

"No." I pointed to the empty wall behind her. "That's where the mummies normally go."

Miss Chittle put her hand to her mouth and stepped back. It was hard to tell in the flickering light, but she looked a bit pale. "H-how do you think they got downstairs?"

I shrugged. "We're not sure. Someone probably carried them down. They don't weigh much, you know. Nothing but dried-up husks. All the important parts were taken out. Some through their noses."

She looked at me with an expression of horror. I stepped closer. "Did you know that the embalmers removed the deceased's internal organs, including their brains, during the embalming process?"

She shook her head, stirring up a faint cloud of sherry fumes.

I warmed to my subject. "They inserted long hooks up their noses and pulled the brains out through the nostrils." I flared mine at her, just for emphasis.

Miss Chittle placed her hand briefly on her stomach, then turned her back to me. Craning my neck, I watched her remove a small silver flask from her purse. She lifted it to her lips and took a few swallows, daintily dabbing at the corner of her mouth when she was done. She slipped the flask back into her purse, then faced me again. "Medicine," she explained briskly, not meeting my eyes. "For my nerves."

I refrained from snorting, but just barely. "Over here," I continued, "are Canopic jars. They're where they stored the deceased's liver, lungs, intestines, and stomach."

Miss Chittle moved away sharply and bumped into the sarcophagus.

"Careful there," I said cheerfully.

A faint hint of panic sprang into her eyes. She whirled around and headed toward the wall on her left. "Oh." Her voice was unnaturally high. "Here's a charming statue. A cat."

"Uh, no. That's not a statue. That's my cat, and she doesn't like to be—"

My words were cut off as Isis arched her back, hissed, then took a vicious swipe at Miss Chittle's gloved hand.

"—touched by strangers," I finished.

Miss Chittle squealed and jerked her hand back. Without another word, she lifted her skirts and ran from the room.

I looked back at Isis, who now sat as calmly as you please, licking her paw. "You didn't like her either, I take it?"

Ignoring me, Isis leaped off the column and streaked toward a floorboard in the far corner. Another mouse, probably. Well, she'd done her good turn for the day. I supposed she'd earned a hunting break.

Before I had a chance to dwell on my victory, Father's voice cut through the museum. "Theodosia Elizabeth Throckmorton! Get down here this instant!"

Oh dear. Time to face the music.

Reluctantly, I headed for the stairs. I wasn't dawdling. Not exactly. Just giving Father a bit of time to calm down.

CHAPTER EIGHT
A LONG SHOT

THERE WAS A SMALL CROWD IN THE FOYER—all waiting for me, apparently. Admiral Sopcoate was holding Miss Chittle's coat for her and she was trying to shove her arm into the sleeve—only, she was shaking so badly, she kept missing. "You didn't tell me the girl was mad as a hatter!" she said, making a final stab with her arm and managing to get it into the sleeve this time.

"Really, she's not mad, just very high spirited," Father said. I was heartened by his loyal support of me.

"Nonsense," Grandmother harrumphed. "The girl has far too much freedom, and her head has been stuffed with so much ridiculous learning as to make her useless."

Before Grandmother could get on a roll cataloging all of my faults, I interrupted her.

"Perhaps Miss Chittle should have some more of her medicine," I suggested sweetly.

Isis rubbed up against my ankles, but I kept my attention fixed on Miss Chittle as all the blood drained from her face. I felt a small twinge of guilt, but she did want me removed from the museum, something too dangerous to contemplate.

"Medicine?" Grandmother asked, her sharp gaze zeroing in on the younger woman. Miss Chittle had gotten both her arms into her sleeves by now and stood ready to bolt.

Grandmother sniffed. Her eyes widened, and then she sniffed again. Her eyebrows shot up. "Spirits, Miss Chittle?" Her voice rang out through the foyer.

As the governess blinked in alarm, Isis left my ankles and went over to comfort her. Perhaps Isis was trying to make up? But wait! What was that in her mouth? Before I could do a thing about it, Isis dropped a small, wet, bedraggled ball of fur onto the toe of Miss Chittle's lovely kidskin boot.

Eyes wild, Miss Chittle looked down at her shoe, shrieked, and, before I could explain it was a peace offering, kicked her foot and flung the poor mouse clear across the room. It struck one of the last remaining mummies smack in the middle of the forehead, then tumbled to the floor.

"I say, good shot, Miss Chittle!" Admiral Sopcoate called out, but she was already running toward the front door.

There was a long, uncomfortable silence, then Father snickered. Grandmother rounded on him, irritation snapping in her eyes. "Don't encourage her! She just chased off another governess—and drove her to drink in under an hour!"

Honestly! That was so clearly not my fault.

"Now, now, Lavinia," the admiral soothed. "Clearly the young woman had too nervous a disposition for this sort of job. You need to find a governess with a little more backbone."

Hear, hear, I thought but kept to myself.

Grandmother straightened her back and raised her chin a bit. "And I shall," she promised.

When everything fell quiet again, Father asked, "Theodosia, don't you have some work to do?"

"Yes, sir. I'll get right on that. It was very nice to see you again, sir," I said to the admiral. "Ma'am." I curtsied at Grandmother, then left. Really, there's nothing like Grandmother Throckmorton to put something as ghastly as catacombs into perspective.

I shivered when I opened the door that led down to long-term storage. The air was definitely disturbed. Something was afoot. I reached under the collar of my dress and pulled my three amulets out into the open, where I could clutch them in my hand. (I don't know if that actually made their protective magic any stronger, but it made me feel better.)

When I reached the bottom of the stairs, the sense of wrongness was overwhelming. Especially once I noticed that the entire right-hand wall was empty.

All the mummies that had been there the day before were gone.

I frowned. I was sure I hadn't seen them upstairs with the others. Still mulling over this puzzle, I turned to the left side of the room and squeaked.

All seven mummies from the right wall were now over by the left wall. But they weren't leaning up against it; they were standing free, looking down at the ground, as if paying homage to something on the floor.

CHAPTER NINE
WAKING THE DEAD

MY HEART THUDDING IN MY CHEST, I inched my way over to see what they were bowing to. When I finally worked my way around the last mummy (careful not to touch it), I saw the magician's staff I'd discovered the day before, still lying on the floor where I'd left it.

Keeping my eyes on the mummies the whole time, I squatted down and picked up the staff. As I rose, I heard a rustling and a creaking. One by one, each of the mummies' heads turned in my direction.

It was the staff that had called the mummies closer! The staff that had made the mummies upstairs leave their museums and private collections to gather here!

The realization struck me like a hammer.

I would have to get word to Wigmere at once. And I needed to figure out what exactly it was that I'd discovered. Something that had power over the dead, that was clear. But what? And why? And how much power?

And what was I to do with the wretched staff in the meantime? If I took it with me, would the mummies follow me up the stairs?

I took three steps forward to test it. Sure enough, every single mummy shuffled along behind me.

I nearly burst into tears. What did it all mean? Had their *ba,* or souls, returned to their bodies? Were they merely reanimated, such as the zombies of western Africa? The enormity of what I didn't know was staggering.

But it was clear that I would have to leave the staff down here with the mummies for the time being.

I hid the staff behind some shelving and backed away cautiously, half afraid the mummies would be attracted to my *ka* and follow me. But they had eyes only for the staff.

Once I was clear of the mummies, I gave in to the urge to run—not walk—up the stairs. When I reached the top landing, I breathed a sigh of relief.

It was time, definitely time, for a little research. Or rather, piles and piles of it.

I searched the reading room and quickly found what I was looking for on the shelves. My arms full of books, I headed for my small carrel, then shut the door with my foot. I didn't need anyone looking over my shoulder or surprising me. My poor nerves had had quite enough excitement already.

The first book I opened looked promising—*Mummies and Their Secrets* by Sir Lynn N. Bandage. He'd studied hundreds of mummies and conducted a number of mummification experiments of his own. The book contained a recipe for making a mummy (it took at least seventy days and either bitumen or natron salts) but nothing about what might have power over one. I put that book aside and reached for another one.

A Dark Journey Through the Egyptian Underworld by Mordecai Black talked quite a bit about all the demons one must safely pass before reaching the Egyptian afterlife, called Duat, along with spells and charms needed to pass them, but again, nothing that would serve my purposes and no mention of a staff.

Finally, I found a small tidbit in *The Rites of the Dead* by Sir Roger Mortis. *Anubis, the jackal-headed god of embalming, sits at the right hand of Osiris.*

Now, of course I knew all about Anubis and Osiris, but I'd never heard it phrased that particular way before, that Anubis sits at the *right hand* of Osiris. What if that wasn't a figure of speech but a description? The staff did have a jackal's head and could be a representation of Anubis. So, what if the staff was something that Osiris held in his right hand?

Hoping that I had finally found some answers, I turned the page to read more, only to be interrupted by a knock on the door. "Theodosia?" It was Edgar Stilton.

"Yes?"

Edgar entered and glanced quickly around the room, a tic starting on the left side of his jaw. "Your parents are looking for you. They're getting ready to leave for the day."

Bother. Just when I'd caught the scent! "Thank you, Stilton. I'll be right there." I stood and closed the book so no one would be able to see what exactly I'd been looking up, then left the room. Just outside I paused, then plucked a hair from my head and inserted it above the door latch after I had shut it tight. If anyone snuck in and examined my study materials, I'd know it. I have to say I was greatly relieved that we wouldn't be spending the night here at the museum with a staff that literally had the power to wake the dead.

CHAPTER TEN

HERE, MOUSY, MOUSY...

WHEN WE ARRIVED AT THE MUSEUM the next morning to find no one waiting on the steps for us, Father's mood improved considerably. In fact, he was so cheered that he completely missed the racking shudder that ran through me the moment I stepped inside. Drat it all! The newest restless spirit had hopped off the mummy it rode in on and was now lurking in our foyer.

Of course, no one else noticed a thing. Mother and Father immediately headed up to their workroom, hoping to get in a full day's work and make up for lost time.

I, however, lingered in the foyer, hoping for the chance to

conduct a Level Two Test on the *mut*—the dangerous dead—left by the mummy. If I could pinpoint the restless spirit's location, I could remove it.

Except the foyer was bustling with activity. Dolge, Sweeny, and two other porters were still lugging mummies down to Receiving. Odd. I thought they had made better progress the day before. Perhaps there were simply more of them than I had realized.

I was glad to see they were wearing the same coveralls as before. With luck, the wedjat eyes would still be in their pockets, offering them protection.

Dolge grunted and lifted a linen-wrapped form while Sweeny grabbed the other end. "I swear these ruddy things are multiplying like rabbits," Sweeny said.

Dolge muttered, "Watch out. Keep yer head low. Here comes His Nibs."

Both he and Sweeny ducked their heads and got very busy moving the mummy into the hall, only just managing to miss Vicary Weems as he came storming around the corner, a cowed Stilton and defiant Fagenbush trailing after him.

"See?" Weems thrust out his arm toward the wall. "This is what I'm talking about. I distinctly told you to return them to their exhibits yesterday, yet here they remain. Which leads me to ask, what *were* you doing with your time yesterday, if not attending to the tasks I'd set you?"

What rubbish! Surely the idiot was just making up excuses to reprimand them—I myself had seen both of them the day before, returning the mummies to their exhibits.

Except when I looked, I saw that, indeed, *all* our mummies were still in the foyer. How suspicious! Unless . . .

Unless they had been moved yesterday, but they'd returned this morning by the power of the staff? That would explain why no one had made any progress . . .

My musings were interrupted by a knock on the front door. "See who it is, Stilton," Weems ordered.

Stilton flinched, tugged on his ear, then went to go open the door. It was Inspector Turnbull. I slipped into the shadows behind one of the marble pillars.

The inspector took one look around the foyer. "Can't you lot hurry it up? I've got irate keepers and private collectors breathing down my neck."

Weems stepped forward. "I'm sorry, sir. I've told the men to hurry, but you know how employees are."

Turnbull shot him a look from under his thunderous eyebrows. "Where's Throckmorton? I've got a few more questions for him."

"No doubt," Weems said in a way that made me want to slug him. "I'll send Stilton along to find him. Won't you have a seat?"

"No, I think I'll go find him myself. Lead the way," he said to Stilton. Stilton shot a questioning glance at Weems, who shooed them along.

While I would have loved to have heard Turnbull's conversation with my parents, the returning mummies gave renewed urgency to my research. I hurried to my stack of books.

I planned to focus that day's research on Osiris, looking specifically for any mention of his staff. Before I opened the door to my carrel, I checked to see if my single hair was still above the door latch. It was. My studies were undisturbed.

The first book I opened was *Osiris: Lord of the Underworld*. The author, Anatole Quillings, wrote, *Osiris is not only the god of the Underworld and afterlife, but also of resurrection. It is to him that the Egyptians direct their prayers, hoping they will be resurrected in the afterlife.*

Hmmm. Were mummies getting up and walking the same as being resurrected? If not, surely it was very close.

I read the next paragraph and nearly squealed in excitement. *In addition to the crook and flail, Osiris possessed a staff that wielded great power over the dead.* I leaned in closer to look at the picture in the book. It showed Osiris sitting in judgment during the Weighing of the Heart ceremony. The staff he held in his right hand *could* have been the same one, but it was an old book and the etching was rough.

Sighing in frustration, I turned to a new book I'd discovered just last month: *Myths of the Egyptian Underworld*. I was thrilled to find this book had an entire section on Osiris. Perhaps now I could make some serious progress. I scanned the pages, looking for mention of a staff. Aha! Here it was!

The Staff of Osiris was one of his greatest treasures. The golden orb held in the jackal's mouth was fashioned by Ra himself and holds the power of life. This staff gave Osiris power over the dead by holding out the promise of life before them. This was the staff he used to resurrect those in the afterlife.

I gulped. How could I have in my possession one of the most powerful legendary artifacts in Egyptian history? It was supposed to be just a myth. However, a myth didn't explain all the mummies hovering over the staff in the basement. Or all the mummies congregating in our hallway. Well, there was only one way to get to the bottom of this.

It was time to conduct a test.

I had to be scientific about it. I had to see if I could use the staff to raise the dead. Of course, the only problem was where to find something dead. My parents most likely wouldn't be agreeable to stopping by a graveyard on the way home. Well, neither would I, for that matter.

There were the mummies, of course, but I already knew the staff worked on them. That was how they all got to our museum in the first place.

I slowly made my way to the catacomb stairs, wracking my brain to come up with a dead thing. As I passed through the foyer, I had a burst of inspiration. The mouse! With any luck, it would still be over against the wall among the mummies. (Flimp was a good watchman, but he wasn't very good at keeping things tidy.)

I lurked in the hallway, wanting to be sure all the others were off busily returning mummies. When the foyer was empty, I hurried over to the wall, my eyes glued to the floorboards. I was pretty sure the mouse had bounced off DjaDja Betuke, a Middle Dynasty mummy. She was supremely recognizable due to her watermelon-size head and I was able to pick her out immediately, relieved that she hadn't already been returned to her exhibit. Now the only question was, had she been standing in the same place the day before when Miss Chittle had launched the mouse at her?

"Excuse me," I muttered, trying to wedge my head between her and the mummy standing next to her. Their shadows puddled against the wall, making it hard to see, not to mention it had been a rather small mouse.

"What are you looking for, Theo?"

Edgar Stilton's voice startled me so badly that I jerked into DjaDja and nearly sent her plummeting to the ground. "N-nothing," I said, reaching out to steady her. "One of Isis's toys, actually. A stuffed mouse. You haven't seen it by any chance, have you?"

"No, I don't think so." His left eye began twitching so rapidly that he had to put his hand up to stop it, although he made it look as though he was just rubbing his temple. "Would you like some help looking for it?"

"No, thank you. I would hate for you to put yourself to any trouble. Besides, Mr. Weems would never approve."

Stilton made a faint grimace. "True enough."

Then Clive Fagenbush appeared and they began discussing which mummy to take up next. I continued making my way down the row, but it wasn't until nearly the end that I found a small shape huddled near the baseboards behind the mummy formerly known as Tetley. Any other mummy would have been preferable to this one. Mummies you had once known in real life were far creepier than ancient ones. Muttering "Forgive me," I bent down near his feet and reached for the mouse, grateful that I always wore gloves. They were excellent protection not only against magic, but also against dead furry things.

I stood back up and found Clive Fagenbush watching me

with his beady little eyes. "What on earth are you doing?" he asked, balancing the top end of a New Kingdom scribe in excellent condition.

Stilton looked up from the other end of the royal mummy. "She's just looking for one of Isis's toys. Oh! Found it, did you? Good job." He gently pushed his end, prodding Fagenbush with the other end. "Let's get moving, shall we? Before Weems comes round to clean our clocks again."

Sending a silent thank-you Stilton's way, I gingerly grasped the mouse by the tail and hurried for the catacombs.

I paused at the top of the stairs to listen. Hearing nothing, I decided it was safe to proceed. At the foot of the steps, I saw that none of the mummies had moved. Thankfully, it didn't look as if the Anubis statue had moved again, either. Which reminded me. I needed to research how to permanently remove the curse that had allowed him to spring to life the other day.

But first things first.

I set the little mouse down onto the floor, then retrieved the staff from its hiding place. Seven mummified heads followed it. Most eerie.

I pointed the head of the staff at the mouse, wondering

what I was supposed to do to get it to work. Shake it, maybe? Say something? But before I thought much further than that, the mouse twitched.

I glanced at the mummies, worried the staff might affect them somehow. But except for their painted eyes tracking the staff's movements intently, they seemed unchanged.

The mouse, however, twitched again. I leaned forward to see better. The mouse gave a shudder, then stretched his little arms and legs. He rolled over onto his feet, sniffed the air, and made a mad dash for the nearest shelf, which he disappeared beneath.

Well. I let out a long breath. That worked. It was indeed the Staff of Osiris.

A creak sounded behind me. My heart in my throat, I whirled around, terrified that one of the mummies had decided to come a little closer. But no, they were all lined up where they had been.

Anxious to get this most powerful artifact out of my hands, I shoved it under the shelf where the mouse had disappeared. It was still close to the mummies, but not out in plain sight.

I stood up and brushed off my skirt. My next order of business was to get word to Wigmere.

Immediately.

CHAPTER ELEVEN
FEELING THE PINCH

I HURRIED UP TO THE FOYER, anxious to get a look out the window and see if Will was waiting outside for a message as Wigmere had said he would be. Instead, I received a nasty shock. My parents were there, greeting Grandmother Throckmorton, who had just arrived with yet another governess candidate. Where *did* she find them all? And so quickly!

"Good morning, Mother," Father said.

Grandmother gave him a regal nod. "Alistair. Henrietta. I thought we'd best get here before another new scandal erupted."

"Now, Mother . . ." Father began.

But she caught sight of me and interrupted him. "Theodosia." She smiled, which was so startling, I forgot to curtsy. "I have found you the perfect governess. This is Miss Elizabeth Sharpe, and she's agreed to try to bring you to hand."

The young woman standing next to her blushed prettily, and I do mean prettily. She had pale gold hair and big blue eyes, and she smiled demurely at the compliment Grandmother had just paid her. Father stood staring at her stupidly until Mum elbowed him in the ribs. "Right!" he said, as if waking up from a short nap. "Well, we'll leave you to it." Mum gave a quick nod, then dragged him down the hallway and up to their workroom.

I smiled at Miss Sharpe. I would normally have been suspect at Grandmother's third choice, but Miss Sharpe was so lovely that I immediately wanted her to be my friend. "How do you do, Miss Sharpe?"

"Very well, thank you, Theodosia. I'm sure we'll get along splendidly."

In truth, so was I. For the first time ever, I had high hopes for a governess. She wasn't prune-faced or pinched or disapproving.

Grandmother looked very pleased with herself, and since

I was in such charity with her for picking such an appealing governess, I didn't even mind when she said, "You said you'd be able to mold and shape her?" That had Miss Sharpe sounding rather like a sculptor.

"Oh yes, madam. We shall have results." And this time when Miss Sharpe smiled, it felt vaguely like a threat and reminded me that a sculptor's tools were much sharper than a whip.

"Miss Sharpe—" I started to say.

"Ah, ah, ah!" She held up her finger. "I don't believe you've been spoken to, have you? And children must not speak unless spoken to. That is Golden Rule Number One."

Grandmother smirked in approval.

What a load of rubbish! I held up my hand, and Miss Sharpe graciously nodded her head. "Yes, Theodosia?"

"How am I to ask questions, then, if I can't speak unless spoken to?"

"You will find a proper lady has little need to ask questions. A proper lady is content with the explanations given and does not question her betters."

"But Socrates said that the best education is based on questioning. Surely you've heard of the Socratic method?"

She placed her hands on either side of her head. "Oh, my ears! How they burn with such impertinent talk." She turned to Grandmother. "Madam, I fear you have called me none too soon."

Grandmother gave a satisfied nod. "I thought so."

I raised my hand again, but this time both of them ignored me.

"How would you like to proceed?" Grandmother asked.

"I think it would be helpful if Theodosia and I took a little walk around the museum and got acquainted. You mentioned she's spent a lot of time here. I'd like to get a sense of what the unhealthy influences in her life have been so I can root them out." There was that small smile-that-wasn't-really-a-smile again.

"There's nothing unhealthy about our museum," I said hotly. Well, there was. But she didn't know about the curses. And that wasn't what she'd meant, anyway.

Miss Sharpe's eyes narrowed and she reached out and snagged my hand in hers. "Come," she said in a sickeningly sweet voice. "Let us begin our getting acquainted, shall we?"

And with that, she dragged me from the foyer into the hall.

"But Miss Sharpe," I began, then yelped in outrage when she pinched me.

"I don't believe you've been spoken to, Theodosia." Her eyes glittered with challenge.

"But you pinch—ow!" She'd done it again!

"And I will pinch you every time you fall out of line. I have many tools to help me mold young girls into proper young ladies."

I glared at her as I rubbed my arm. This would never do. And it was an excellent lesson on just how vile the most lovely package could be inside.

"So." She grabbed my hand again. "What would you like to show me first?"

It was all I could do to keep from yanking my hand from hers, but I really didn't want another pinch. I was already feeling black and blue. I shot her a sideways glance, not certain whether her question was a trap.

"You may speak now, Theodosia, as I have asked you a question. Stubbornness is most unattractive."

Ha! I thought. *Tell that to Grandmother Throckmorton.* My mind worked furiously. I had to think of something to get rid of her. But what? I led her down the hall, only to find myself yanked back by the arm.

"Ladies do not gallop," Miss Sharpe informed me. "They walk at a sedate pace."

"Yes, Miss Sharpe." *You wretched cow.* "Speaking of Socrates, would you care to see our classics exhibit?"

"Why, yes, Theodosia. That would be delightful."

When we reached the doorway, I stood back so Miss

Sharpe could poke her head into the room. Her gaze brushed past the life-size statue of Adonis that had so shocked Miss Chittle and scanned the rest of the statues. "Adequate enough," she announced.

I bristled. Talk about condemning with faint praise. "Very well. This way, then."

She was equally unimpressed with our imperial China collection, medieval display, and Assyrian and Sumer exhibits, barely sparing a glance for each of the rooms. When I took her to the ancient Egyptian room, she wrinkled her perfect little nose and said, "My, those bandages need a good washing, don't they?"

It had to be the shortest museum tour on record. Within no time we found ourselves outside the small family sitting room, where Grandmother had said she would wait for us. Pausing in the hallway, Miss Sharpe bent down and brought her face closer to mine. "Your grandmother says you're bright as a button." Before I had a chance to marvel over that, she continued. "But don't worry, I shall soon show you how to hide that light of yours under a bushel. You don't want everyone to know what an odd duck you are."

I gaped at her, unable to think of a reply. She gave me a charming smile, then, with a swish of her silk skirts, disappeared into the sitting room.

The room was full, as all the curators seemed to have decided to take a late tea right then. When they saw Miss Sharpe, they all got quite silly as Father introduced her around. It would have been highly annoying if I hadn't been so fooled myself when I had first met her.

It took forever for Grandmother and Miss Sharpe to leave. When they did, I insisted on walking them to the door. Both seemed impressed by my manners, which was just as well. If they'd known that the real reason I'd come with them was to keep an eye out for a street urchin in order to get a message to a secret organization, they might not have been so pleased.

As I waved goodbye to them, my eyes searched for a sign of Will, but the street was deserted except for a tall, thin man sitting on a bench, his top hat just barely peeking above the evening newspaper he was reading. Will must have decided I had no news to pass on today and given up.

Miss Sharpe could not have arrived at a worse time. It was clear she would be a formidable opponent.

But then, so was I.

CHAPTER TWELVE
SNUFFLES

THE MUMMIES RETURNED AGAIN the next day.

Our first indication was the huge crowd awaiting us at the museum entrance. Inspector Turnbull was there, along with Lord Chudleigh, Snowthorpe, and a number of other people I'd never seen before.

"Good gad!" Father said, leaping out of the carriage. "What is the meaning of this?" He was so distraught, he forgot to help Mother down.

Inspector Turnbull glared at Father. "I might ask you the same thing, sir."

"What are all these people doing at our museum?" Mother asked, alighting from the carriage.

Snowthorpe took a step closer to Father. "We want our mummies back, Throckmorton. This joke of yours has gone on long enough."

"What joke?" Father said. "What are you talking about?"

But I knew. I could tell from the way people were pressed up against the window, whispering and pointing. I tugged on Father's coat pocket. "I think the mummies are back, Father."

All the blood drained from his face.

Inspector Turnbull glanced at me sharply. "How'd you know that, then?"

"Why else would you all be here?" I asked.

Recovering, Father hurried to the door, but when he tried to open it, a muffled voice called out, "Go away! I ain't letting none of you in without the master here to answer your questions."

"It's me, Flimp," Father called out. "You can open the door now."

Flimp did, slowly, then peeked out at the gathered crowd. "Am I glad to see you, sir!" he said, but poor Father was so beside himself that he didn't hear him. Instead, he stared at the foyer in dismay. Or more accurately, he stared at the queue of mummies lined up against the wall, his whole body sagging.

"Throckmorton, this is preposterous," Lord Chudleigh said, shoving forward. "What are you trying to prove, anyway! I've half a mind to call for a meeting of the board and demand your resignation!"

"But sir—" Father began to protest.

"And I've half a mind to haul you in," Inspector Turnbull added.

"On what grounds?" Mother asked.

"Exactly!" Father echoed. "All I've done is arrive to find another crowd of mummies in my museum. It's not as if I had anything to do with it!"

"You haven't, have you?" Turnbull growled.

"Now, now, gentlemen. There's no need for any of that." Admiral Sopcoate pushed his way through the crowd. Behind him, Grandmother Throckmorton's carriage was parked up against the street, her thin nose poking out from behind the carriage curtains. For the first time that morning, I felt hopeful. Sopcoate always had a calming effect on people. Perhaps he could prevent Father from being hauled off or fired after all.

Inspector Turnbull nodded in deference to the admiral. "But sir, surely you aren't saying he had nothing to do with this."

Sopcoate put one arm on Turnbull's back and the other on

Chudleigh's. "What I'm saying is, we don't want to be arguing out here on the stoop where every news reporter and passerby can hear us, now, do we? Think of the scandal," he said to Chudleigh. Then to Turnbull: "Think of how that could compromise your investigation!"

Turnbull scowled at the truth of Sopcoate's words. "Don't let anyone else through that door until I get back," Turnbull instructed his constables.

"Of course not, sir!"

Turnbull nodded, then followed the admiral and the others toward Father's office, where they could have some privacy.

"Oh no you don't, boy-o!" A constable's raised voice caught my attention. "You heard the man. No one gets in here."

"But it's Open Visitation Day, guvnor, me only chance to see the museum!" a paperboy whined as he tried to push past Biggs. "Ye don't want me to have to wait an entire month, do ye?" Even though he was talking to the constable, the paperboy was looking straight at me.

Only, it wasn't a paperboy at all—it was Will!

I tilted my head to indicate he should go round to the side.

"I don't give a horse's hind end how long you have to wait. Now, off wi' you!" As I watched Will scramble away, I caught sight of an elegant woman standing toward the back of the crowd. It was Miss Sharpe, and she was attempting to work her way to the front door. She tried to catch my eye, but I ignored her and hurried to the side entrance instead.

By the time I got there, Will was waiting for me. "Wot took you so long?" he huffed, looking over his shoulder.

"I came right away," I huffed back, wishing he wouldn't get so put out just because of a few constables around. Although I supposed if I were in his trade, I would feel the same.

I heard a loud, wet sniffing sound. "Quiet," I warned Will.

He immediately froze. "Wot is it?"

"I don't know, but I think someone is skulking in the bushes." I squinted, having a hard time making out what exactly I was seeing.

"Oo is it?" Will asked, his voice tense.

"I'm not sure," I said. "But it looks like a bowler hat with ears. And a much-too-large morning coat."

Will relaxed. "Oh, don't worry 'bout 'im. That's me brother, Snuffles."

"Snuffles?" I echoed.

Will nodded. "On account of 'is nose always runnin' and 'im always snuffling it back up."

Another thick, wet sniff emerged from the bushes. "Right. Snuffles," I said. "But he doesn't have to hide in the bushes, does he?"

"'E's practicing, miss."

"Practicing what?"

"Why, 'is skills, of course. He's got to practice moving quiet-like and tailing people or he'll never make it in our family line of work." Will leaned in closer and lowered his voice. "Frankly, I think 'e's a bit 'opeless. Everyone can hear him sucking up that snot o' his from a mile away."

"We don't have time to discuss this right now. Come on." I grabbed Will's arm. "We need to go somewhere where we won't be overheard."

I thought about the reading room, but with nothing else to do until the inspector gave the curators marching orders, there was too big a chance they'd wander down there to do some work. Besides, Fagenbush seemed to be hanging around there a lot lately, and I most certainly didn't want to run into him.

Instead, I dragged Will into my small closet, the one small piece of the museum that I claimed as my own. When I pulled him inside and lit the oil lamp, his eyes went immediately to the sarcophagus next to the wall. "Wot is this place, anyway?"

I didn't think he'd understand about my need to sleep in the sarcophagus when I got stuck spending the night at the museum. It was the only thing I trusted to protect me against all the curses and restless spirits that roamed the museum at night. "My room, so to speak. Listen, we haven't any time to waste. I've got an important message for Wigmere, but I've got a governess now—"

"Whatcher got one of them for, anyway?"

"Believe me, it wasn't my idea. Now, I need you to tell Wigmere that I found out why the mummies are here."

His eyes grew wide. "Ye did?"

"Yes. Tell Wigmere that I think I found the Staff of Osiris. Here. In our museum. Can you repeat that to be sure you've got it straight?"

"Sure. You fink you found an Iris Staff—"

"No, no. The Staff of Osiris. Oh-sigh-ris. Say it for me."

"Oh-sigh-ris. Got it. What's that got to do wif the mummies, anyway?"

Even though we were all alone in the room, I couldn't help but lower my voice. "It wields power over the dead, and that's what's calling the mummies. Although . . . they seem to only be able to move at night."

"The dead!" Will squeaked, glancing nervously at the sarcophagus.

"Shhh! Yes, the dead. And I think that's why Chaos wants the staff. Now, can you remember all that or do I need to write it down?"

"Wot's wrong wi' my mem'ry, I'd like to know?"

"Nothing! I was just checking, that's all. Now—"

There was a rap at the door. "Theodosia!" We both froze.

"I say, Theodosia? Are you in there?" Stilton called out.

"Yes, I am. Just a second."

I motioned Will toward the sarcophagus. He looked at me as if I were crazy. "I'm not gettin' in that thing!" he hissed.

"You most certainly are," I hissed back. "If you don't, you'll be found out. What if they turn you in to the police?"

Will paled but shook his head. "I ain't gettin' in no stone coffin."

"Oh, don't be ridiculous! I sleep in there all the time, and nothing's ever happened to me."

Will's eyes nearly popped out of his head. "You 'ave?"

Stilton rapped again. "Theodosia?"

"Yes," I said loudly, then whispered, "Now, get in!"

Looking none too pleased, Will gingerly scrambled over the side and settled himself in the bottom of the sarcophagus. "Now, keep quiet!" I warned, then turned to open the door. "Hullo, Stilton."

"I say, were you talking to someone?" he asked, trying to peer into the room.

I maneuvered myself so that I partially blocked his view. "No, why do you ask?"

"I thought I heard voices." Still not convinced, his gaze wandered to the far corners of the closet.

"Oh, that. Now that I'm to have lessons again, I was practicing my Latin verb conjugating for Miss Sharpe." Remembering how he had seemed stricken with her the day before, I added, "You haven't seen her, by the way, have you? She should be here by now."

He pulled his gaze from the walls back to my face, a frown of concern wrinkling his features. "Now that you mention it, I haven't seen her. I wonder if she's stuck up in that mess out front?"

"Most likely," I said.

"Perhaps I'd better go check." Eager to help the lovely Miss Sharpe, Stilton turned to leave, then stopped. "Oh, I almost forgot. Your father would like to see you in his office. Right away."

"I'll be right there. But do please see if you can find Miss Sharpe. I'd so hate for her to get put out with all this horrid business going on this morning."

"Yes, of course," he said, then hurried away. I closed the door and breathed a sigh of relief. "Okay," I whispered. "It's clear. You can come out now."

Shakily, Will climbed out of his hiding place. "I ain't never doing that again. That was downright creepy, it was."

"Never mind that! We've got to get you out of here and safely on your way back to Wigmere, and I've got to go see what my father wants."

Will was only too glad to leave my little closet and scurried out into the hallway. I led him back to the side entrance. "Now, you're sure you can remember everything I told you?"

"Yes, miss. I ain't going soft in the 'ead."

"Sorry. It's just excruciatingly important."

"So you said. More 'n once."

"Right. Well, goodbye." Will opened the door, looked out, then jerked back inside and slammed it behind him.

"'Ave you got another exit, miss?"

"Yes, of course. But what's wrong? You're as pale as a sheet!"

"Nuffink. Just want to go out a different way than I came in. That's all."

"Well . . . we've another entrance on the west side of the building. Or you can use the delivery entrance."

Will paused a moment. "'E prob'ly won't know about that one. Let's use the delivery one."

"Very well." I led Will across the hall, trying to think of a way to get him to tell me what was wrong.

"Theodosia!" Father's voice came from far away, and it didn't sound happy.

"Come *on*." I grabbed Will's hand and broke into a run.

"We've got to get you out of here before we both get in loads of trouble." When we reached the loading dock, it was empty. No doubt everyone was still in the foyer, being questioned by the police.

I led Will over to the exit, and he poked his head out to look around. "All clear," he announced, then slipped outside. "Good luck wiv your father. 'Ope you're not in too much hot water."

"I'll be fine. Now, remember! Wigmere needs to get that message as soon as poss—" But before I had finished my sentence, Will had disappeared.

I shut the door, then headed for Father's office. As I approached, I heard raised voices coming from within. One of them was Inspector Turnbull's.

"If you're not involved with these stolen mummies, Throckmorton, do you care to tell me why the Grim Nipper's been hanging around?"

"Who? I have no idea what you're talking about! Who is this Grim Reaper fellow?"

"Grim Nipper." Turnbull spoke slowly and loudly, as if addressing a deaf person. "He's only one of the most notorious kidsmen in all of London. Known for moving hard-to-fence stuff, too. My constable spotted him outside in the crowd this morning."

"Well, he's not here at my request, I can assure you of

that! Now, where is that daughter of mine? Theodosia!" He poked his head into the hallway. "Oh! There you are! What took you so long?"

I stepped into the room, only to find myself scrutinized by Grandmother Throckmorton, Admiral Sopcoate, and Inspector Turnbull. Luckily, there was no sign of Miss Sharpe.

"Where on earth have you been, child?" Mum rushed forward.

"I was on my way to the reading room, trying to keep out of everyone's way."

"And where is Miss Sharpe, then?" Grandmother asked.

"I don't know, Grandmother. She hasn't been in yet this morning." Which wasn't a lie. Exactly. She hadn't been *inside* the museum yet.

"Hmph," she snorted, and I must say, it was quite pleasant to have her snorting at someone else for a change.

"Yes, well, the admiral has invited us to tour his battleship, the *Dreadnought,* today," Father explained. "Obviously your mother and I can't go because of all this unpleasantness, but your grandmother wants you to go anyway—"

Grandmother interrupted him. "It will be an excellent educational opportunity. With or without Miss Sharpe," she added.

This felt like a most inopportune time to be away from the

museum, what with Inspector Turnbull breathing down Father's neck and Grim Somebodies being spotted outside.

At my hesitation, Grandmother brought her cane down on the floor, the effect somewhat muffled by the Turkish carpet. "Nonsense. Of course you're going. You'll not throw away an opportunity to see Britain's shining star firsthand. Now, what are you waiting for? Go get your things. We haven't got all day."

Knowing arguing would be futile, I said, "Yes, ma'am," then hurried to get my coat.

And my hat. I knew only too well Grandmother would just send me back for it if I left it behind.

CHAPTER THIRTEEN

The *Dreadnought*

ONCE WE WERE SETTLED in Grandmother's carriage, Admiral Sopcoate rapped on the ceiling, signaling the driver to be on his way. As we began down the street, we passed a small, familiar-looking figure racing along. With a shock, I recognized Will. I started to wave, then stopped myself. Grandmother would never approve. A short distance behind Will I spotted an even shorter figure nearly swallowed up in a too-large morning coat and an equally oversize bowler. Snuffles.

A furtive movement behind Snuffles caught my eye. It was a tall man in a tattered top hat wearing an . . . undertaker's coat! I peered more closely, not sure if the man looked vaguely familiar or it was just the second undertaker's coat I'd seen in as many days.

"We'll take the embankment route, shall we?" Admiral Sopcoate leaned back against the cab cushions, eyes shining. "The water levels from the recent flood have only now begun to recede back down the embankment. I'd like to see how they're coming along with the cleanup down there."

He sounded suspiciously cheerful about surveying something as grim as flood damage, I thought. I was willing to bet those who'd lost their homes didn't feel quite the same way.

At the look on my face, he quickly added, "Sorry. Can't take an appreciation for weather out of an old salt like me."

I supposed that made sense. Weather was an incredible force, capable of creating plenty of chaos on its own. Unfortunately, the recent downpours that had caused this flood had had help from the Serpents of Chaos. The severe rains would never have occurred if not for the damage done when the Heart of Egypt had been in Britain's possession.

"So, dear girl," Admiral Sopcoate said, changing the subject, "does the inspector have any theory yet as to why all these mummies keep showing up? He's had two days. You'd think he'd have figured it out by now."

"He hasn't, sir. In spite of your valiant defense, he is still inclined to think Father's behind it."

Grandmother thumped her cane on the carriage floor. "Nonsense."

"Of course it's nonsense, Lavinia. The inspector will figure that out soon enough. It hasn't helped any that there's been so much in the paper." He leaned forward, eyes bright with curiosity. "I say, is it true that one of the mummies was cursed and caused a porter to break his leg?"

"Sopcoate!" Grandmother barked. "I don't need you encouraging her in this poppycock. She gets quite enough of that at home."

"Quite right. So"—he clapped his hands together in a jolly manner—"what is it you do all day in that museum of yours? I imagine we saved you from a day of boredom, eh?"

"Well . . ." I glanced cautiously at Grandmother. "I study ancient Egypt and Greek and Latin and hieroglyphs. Sometimes Father lets me help out with maintaining the exhibits and whatnot. Right now, he has me cataloging the museum items down in the basement."

"Sounds very dry and dusty to me," he said.

I felt Grandmother's steely gaze boring holes clear through my forehead. "Yes, well, I do very much appreciate this chance to see your boat," I said politely.

"Ship," he corrected. "I bet you're looking forward to having a new governess to study with. The one your grand-

mother's found for you sounds like just the ticket." I wanted
to ask which governess that would be—the prune, the one
reeking of sherry, or the pincher—but all I said was, "Yes, sir."

Grandmother gave a small nod of approval.

Admiral Sopcoate frowned, as if something had just occurred to him. "Have you just been teaching yourself, then?
All this time?"

"Well, mostly—"

"If you can call that teaching," Grandmother interrupted.
"I think she's just been stuffing her head full of nonsense
that no healthy girl would want to know about."

"But Grandmother," I asked, "why is it okay for a girl to
know about battleships but not Egyptology?"

Grandmother's nostrils flared. "Because battleships have
to do with the pride and glory of Britain. Every British subject ought to be well informed on that score. But no one
needs to study a bunch of long-dead heathens."

So *that's* what she thought of Egyptology. I'd always wondered. "Thank you," I said. "I understand now." She studied
me to see if I was being impertinent, but I wasn't. I just finally understood her views on the subject.

Satisfied that I wasn't being disrespectful, she turned back
to the admiral. "Well, I think this is an amazing achieve-
ment, Sopcoate. It's not many members of the admiralty

who would have the foresight to put our crown jewel on display for all Englishmen to marvel over."

The admiral chuckled and patted her arm. Honestly. These two were getting nearly as bad as Mum and Dad. "It would never have been possible without the recent floods, Lavinia. But once it was clear that the higher water line was here to stay for a bit and we could get her through, I realized what a fine opportunity it would be."

"I'm sorry, but I don't quite understand why a ship would be a crown jewel."

Grandmother flinched at my words. She looked as though she was going to remind me that children should be seen and not heard, but the admiral spoke first. "Why, of course you wouldn't! You're only a child. And a girl, at that. I bet you your younger brother, Henry, could tell you all about the *Dreadnought*."

Oh, how Henry would have crowed if he could have heard this! If it had been anyone other than the admiral who had said it, I would have taken great exception. But he'd been so kind and jolly, and helped Father with the police, and kept Grandmother from being too beastly, so I let it go. "Do you really think it's our crown jewel? Why?"

"Because it's only *the* greatest battleship ever built, young lady! Outclasses everything else on the ocean today and renders all other battleships obsolete. It assures Britain's position as the greatest naval power in the world."

"But I thought we already were the greatest?"

"Good girl," he said, looking quite pleased. "You're right. We were and are. But we like to be twice as great as any other two countries combined, so we mustn't rest on our laurels."

I supposed that made sense. Kind of like Father wanting not just to have a better collection than the British Museum, but a HUGELY better collection.

"Besides," Grandmother Throckmorton muttered darkly, "someone needs to keep that Kaiser Wilhelm in check. That dreadful man thinks to knock us from our pin, no matter what he says otherwise."

My ears perked up at the mention of Kaiser Wilhelm. Von Braggenschnott had talked about him, too. He claimed that the Serpents of Chaos were feeding the Kaiser's drive to compete with Britain in order to bring about chaos and disorder. And I must say, it had almost worked.

Which brought my thoughts right back to the Staff of Osiris. I desperately needed to find out more about its history, not to mention finding a better hiding place for it. If Wigmere was correct and the Serpents of Chaos were back in London, it wouldn't take long for them to discover the staff's location.

Especially if mummies kept showing up every morning!

I squirmed in my seat. I needed to find a way to keep the mummies from returning the next day. I was afraid Turnbull would arrest Father if they showed up again.

I rested my aching head on the cool glass of the carriage window and looked outside.

All sorts of rubbish littered the street where the floodwaters had spilled over. Driftwood, old leaves, rags—all were pitched up against the edges of the buildings. People's furniture sat out on their stoops, drying off in the brisk air. Even the sandbags were still up where they'd been piled high to prevent more flooding.

Looking at how much damage the Serpents of Chaos had accomplished with severe rains, I shuddered to think what they would do if they had power over death in their greedy, grasping hands.

As we arrived at the Royal Albert Dock and traveled past miles of docks and quays, cargo containers and pulleys, the *Dreadnought* came into view. She was larger than any other ship in sight, her hard gray lines etched darkly against the lighter gray sky, all masts and funnels, cabling and turrets. A long, thick-plated, armored beast that towered over everything.

We got out of the admiral's carriage, and he led Grand-mother and me toward a gangplank with thick rope rails. There were two sailors posted there, dressed in smart blue uniforms with white piping on the collars and smart sailor hats. At the sight of the admiral, they snapped to attention and saluted. "Sir!"

Their action startled me so badly that I found myself saluting back in reflex—only, I aimed too high and managed to knock my hat clear off my head. It rolled onto the dock, then fluttered along the ground for a second before going over the side into the water.

There was a moment of stunned, embarrassed silence in which I was afraid to even look at Grandmother. Then one of the sailors winked at me. "Don't worry, miss. I'll fetch it for you." He hustled over to the side, fished out the hat, and held it up to me with a flourish.

"Thank you, sir!" I said, taking the soggy hat from him and holding it gingerly between two fingers. I wasn't quite sure what I was supposed to do with it now, but it had been very kind of him to save it for me, even if he didn't know how much I loathe hats.

The admiral cleared his throat. "I've brought a couple of visitors with me today, as you can see. I've a mind to give them a tour of the ship."

"But of course, sir. Shall we call for an escort, sir?" the shorter one inquired.

"No, thank you. I can manage." Sopcoate held out his arm for Grandmother. "Do watch your step, Lavinia," he advised.

"I've got it. I'm not infirm, you know."

He winked at her. "I know that very well, madam," he said, his words causing her to blush slightly. And may I just say that old, wrinkled cheeks aren't made for blushing?

I brought up the rear, holding my soggy headgear behind my back, hoping no one would notice. Much.

I suppose visiting a battleship would be a lovely way to spend an afternoon, if one wasn't distracted by the threat of one's father being hauled off to prison. Or by wondering who on earth the Grim Nipper was. Or by worrying whether or not one slippery street urchin had managed to get a most urgent message to the head of a secret organization.

Or if one wasn't accompanied by one's grandmother.

Once we were on board, Admiral Sopcoate dropped us like a hot potato. After introducing us to Captain Bacon, the admiral went off with him to inspect some turbans or some such, and Petty Officer Tipton was in charge of our tour. He gave us a smart salute, and Grandmother leaned down and muttered in my ear, "Now, those are manners. You could learn something from him."

Honestly. Grandmother Throckmorton could ruin an afternoon faster than a bout of influenza. I wondered if she had been born with that skill or had to work at it.

I had to admit, the sheer size of the *Dreadnought* was awe inspiring. The deck spread out to either side as far as my eye could see, interrupted by turrets and towers and all sorts of lines and cables. Anchor chains as thick as my leg ran the length of the deck.

Tipton caught me taking in the enormity of her. "Over five hundred feet long, she is. And has an eighty-two-foot beam."

I wasn't sure what a beam was, but he was quite proud of it, so I murmured something properly awestruck.

As we continued to wander around the deck, we passed a group of sailors giving a section of the ship a lick of fresh paint.

"See how neat everything is, Theodosia," Grandmother pointed out. "How clean and bright that fresh coat of paint makes everything appear."

So what was her point? Did she want me to paint the museum white? Frankly, all the stark whiteness was quite blinding. It was giving me a headache.

Luckily, Petty Officer Tipton took over from there. "Did the admiral mention to you that the *Dreadnought* was put together in a year? A marvel of naval engineering, that. And speaking of engineering, the *Dreadnought* can go three knots faster than any other ship in her class, thanks to her two sets of Parsons turbines."

"Why would men wearing turbans make the ship go faster?" I asked.

Grandmother flushed. "It's turbines, you silly girl. Not turbans."

"Oh," I said in a small voice.

"An easy mistake," Tipton said with a quick wink at me.

Anxious to change the subject, I looked back the way we'd come. Hordes of seamen swarmed busily over the deck. "How many men does it take to run this ship?" I asked.

"Around seven hundred, give or take. Here, this way, please. I'll take you down and show you the gunroom."

He led us over to a narrow door, then down a very steep set of stairs. "Do watch your step, ma'am," he warned, holding out his arm for Grandmother.

"I've got it," she said with a huff of exasperation.

When we reached the lower deck, Tipton showed us to a set of double doors. "The gunroom," he announced. We stepped into a room with a number of tables and chairs, some of them set as if for a fine dinner. There was a gramophone in the corner, but no guns. However, after the turban blunder, I wasn't about to point that out.

We left the gunroom and continued on down the narrow aisle. On either side of us were scores of little doors. One of them stood open, and I saw it led to a tiny, cramped bedroom. "Who sleeps in there?" I asked.

"That's an officer's cabin. In fact, most of these rooms along here are officers' cabins."

"They're awfully small." In truth, they weren't much larger than my little closet at the museum.

"Well, they have to squeeze a lot of them on the ship to house all the men," he explained.

"I suppose they must be small if you have to fit seven hundred of them on the ship," I agreed.

Tipton chuckled. "No, no. Only officers get cabins. The crew just hangs their hammocks wherever they can find space."

"They don't get rooms of their own?"

"Hardly," Tipton said. "They're lucky to get twenty-four inches to themselves."

That seemed rather unfair, if you asked me.

Tipton led us back up the stairs to the upper deck and we emerged at the base of a large tower. As I looked up, I saw that enormous tubes stuck out of the tower. With a jolt, I realized they were the guns. Great big whopping ones.

"Here, have a look at this, will you?" I recognized the admiral's voice but couldn't see him anywhere. Officer Tipton pointed up, and I saw the admiral and Captain Bacon on top of the turret, next to one of the enormous guns.

"Come have a look at this twelve-pounder, why don't you?"

"But how do I get up there?" I asked.

"By the ladder, of course," was Admiral Sopcoate's reply. Officer Tipton pointed to the ladder bolted to the turret, and I glanced questioningly at Grandmother. I wasn't sure she'd look too kindly on my climbing ladders and risking exposing my knickers to the entire crew of the Royal Navy's finest.

Understanding at once the question in my gaze, she nodded. "Go ahead, but keep your knees together and don't dally. Besides, it's a rather short ladder."

It was all I could do to keep from gaping at her. Surely this change of temperament was due to Admiral Sopcoate's good influence.

Tipton led me to the ladder, and while Grandmother distracted him with conversation, I set my soggy hat on the ground, then scurried up as fast as I could. Admiral Sopcoate motioned me over to where he and the captain were studying what looked to be a very skinny cannon.

Captain Bacon was holding an enormous shell that was as long as my forearm and three times as thick.

Admiral Sopcoate indicated the loading chamber. "We just pop this in the tube here, add a powder charge, and the gun's ready to go."

I blinked as a realization hit me with the force of one of those artillery shells. Of course! The key to the staff was popping the Orb of Ra into place—that's what had triggered all the mummies! The power lay in putting the two together, just like a cannon was harmless until loaded with artillery!

And if I'd had a minute to think in the past forty-eight hours, I would have figured that out ages ago.

All I had to do was remove the wretched orb and the mummies would stay put. Excellent.

I glanced at Admiral Sopcoate, deep in conversation with Captain Bacon, then at Grandmother, talking with Petty Officer Tipton. Now I just had to get these two to quit jawing long enough to return me to the museum.

CHAPTER FOURTEEN

THE BLOOD OF ISIS

WHEN THE CARRIAGE FINALLY PULLED UP in front of the museum, it was nearly dark. It was all I could do to keep from hopping out and running inside, except I knew Grandmother would have taken that as a grave insult and very poor manners besides. However, instead of bidding me goodbye, she began to gather her things. "Oh, are you getting out, too?" I asked.

"Well, of course we are. We're not about to drop you off like a package."

My heart sank. I so needed to get to the staff and remove the orb! It would be dark soon, and the mummies would be on the march shortly after that.

I waited as patiently as I could while the admiral stepped from the carriage, then turned smartly to assist Grandmother. The way she smiled at him made me feel a little embarrassed for her, so I looked away. I would have thought grandmothers were much too old to get sweet on anybody, especially a salty old admiral.

Once Grandmother had finished her simpering and creaked her way out of the carriage, we all proceeded to the museum's entrance, where Flimp let us in.

"Mr. Throckmorton's in his office," he told us.

"Excellent," the admiral replied.

"Thank you very much for taking me to see your ship. It was most impressive, and I think you should be very proud." Not to mention it may have given me a very important clue to halting the mummy exodus.

"Not at all, not at all," the admiral said, patting me on the shoulder.

"Come," Grandmother said imperiously. "I want to check and see if Miss Sharpe ever made it here today. If she didn't, I'll want to know the reason why."

She strode off toward Father's office, Admiral Sopcoate and I lagging in her wake. Although I was very glad that Miss Sharpe appeared to have been taken down a peg or two in Grandmother's estimation, I was desperate to get back down to the catacombs and try my new theory for deactivating the staff.

We reached Father's office, and Grandmother rapped once on the door and marched in. Mother, who'd been talking to Father, jumped to her feet and came over to greet me. "Did you have a good time, dear?" she asked.

"It was very interesting, Mother. And educational."

"Wonderful!" She put her hands on my shoulders. I was beginning to think she did that whenever Grandmother was around just to steady herself. "Thank you so much for taking her, Admiral Sopcoate. It was an opportunity of a lifetime. I'm only sorry we couldn't accompany you."

Grandmother snorted. I asked her, ever so sweetly, "Would you like to borrow my handkerchief, Grandmother, dear?"

She stared at me, truly shocked at my vulgarity. "I beg your pardon?" she said in her frostiest voice.

"Eh, what?" the admiral said. "Here, you can use mine, Lavinia." He whipped out a starched white handkerchief the size of a flag from his pocket.

She slapped it away. "Don't be silly! I don't need a handkerchief!" Her face reddened, and I felt Mum's grip on me relax a bit. *Take that, you old bat,* I thought.

Grandmother glowered at me, as if able to discern my

thoughts. "Did Miss Sharpe ever show up?" she asked Father.

"Yes, she did. She arrived about a half an hour after you left. When I explained Theodosia would be out for the day, she said she'd see her tomorrow."

The scowl on Grandmother's face told me she wasn't happy, so I decided to press my advantage. "Grandmother, don't you think it would be best, given Miss Sharpe's missed appearance this morning, if we plan to meet here at the museum for at least the first week? That way, if she is unavoidably detained again, I won't be left home alone. At least here at the museum, if Miss Sharpe doesn't show, I have my parents nearby to supervise me."

"If Miss Sharpe is unavoidably detained again, she'll have to answer to me," Grandmother muttered. She studied me for a long moment, then said, "Very well. I suppose the idea of you left home alone to wreak whatever havoc and damage is too much of a risk. I'll send a note around to advise her of the change."

I glanced down at my feet, trying to hide the glow of victory from her. "Thank you, Grandmother. May I please be excused now?"

"What do you have to do that's so important you must leave?" Grandmother asked.

"Nothing—I was just going to . . . write an essay! For Miss Sharpe. Discussing Britain's supreme naval power."

"I say, what a good idea, that," the admiral said.

Grandmother blinked, and then her face softened. "I agree. An excellent idea. Get to it, then."

Mother followed me out into the hall. "Theo? Can I have a word with you before you start on your essay?"

"But of course, Mother." She beckoned me to follow her a short way down the hall. When we were far enough away from Father's office, she leaned down closer to me. I could plainly see the exhaustion and worry on her face: the fine lines around her eyes, the slight crease of worry on her brow, the pale shadows under her eyes. Poor Mum!

"I just wanted you to know we'll be spending the night here tonight. Your father is determined to camp out and see for himself who is bringing all those mummies here and what their purpose is. I've sent around for some supper, but I wanted to let you know."

"Oh, excellent! What time shall I meet you and Father in the sitting room?" A nice, cozy family dinner was just the thing I needed to bolster my spirits.

"I don't think we'll have time for that, Theo. This whole mummy fiasco has put us too far behind. We'll just all eat on the run tonight, shall we?"

"Very well, Mum." I refused to allow myself to be disappointed. This would give me plenty of opportunity to take care of our staff problem, after all.

By this time, it was well past dark. I'd never been down to the catacombs after dark before. Who knew how many spells and curses down there came alive at night? Hundreds, probably.

Which meant I needed to wear as much protection as possible. There was only one amulet I knew of that would keep me safe in these circumstances, but it belonged to the museum. I normally didn't use it, but this time it seemed warranted. The Blood of Isis.

After the goddess Isis tricked the sun god Ra into giving her his real name, which she used to learn all available magical knowledge, she was attacked by Seth as she tried to protect her husband Osiris's body. The Egyptians believed that where her blood hit the ground, it formed jasper, a semiprecious stone they revered for its magical properties. According to them, jasper and carnelian both held all the magical power that ran through Isis's veins. So, between all the new *mut* and *akhu* (not to mention mummies) invading our museum, I wouldn't mind a little of Isis's power right now. One could never have too much protection against restless spirits. Besides, being Osiris's consort, if anything would have a calming influence over the dead, it would be her.

As I headed across the darkened foyer, I heard it. The

rustling and groaning of the *mut* and *akhu*. Only, it was louder tonight. My mind flew back to the rows and rows of mummies that had been in the museum earlier that day. Who knew how many of them had been the victim of a violent death?

I quickened my steps. Even if they hadn't died horribly, surely their spirits were highly disgruntled at being paraded around London and disturbed from their resting places again and again. And once spirits became disgruntled, they became restless, and once they were restless, they might not be interested in returning to the realm of the dead until they felt they'd been avenged.

Out of the corner of my eye, I saw a dark shadow. My hand had crept halfway to my amulets before I recognized it as the mummy formerly known as Tetley. All the other mummies were gone, except him. Lord Chudleigh had most likely instructed Dolge and Sweeny to leave him here for Father to deal with, rather than have to take care of his own mistake.

Besides, what did one do with a fake mummy, anyway? I must say, I felt rather sorry for Tetley. Sorrier than I'd ever felt for him when he was alive.

However, that was not my problem. Not tonight, anyway.

Eager to be away from the restless dead and the mummified Tetley, I took the stairs up to the Egyptian exhibit two at a time. Once there, I hurried over to the low glass display table. The Blood of Isis amulet lay on a black velvet backing. The flickering electric light gleamed off the burnished gold, making the red stone glow like an ember from a fire. Just looking at it made me feel safer.

I went around to the back of the case, removed the pin, then slid the door open and reached inside the cabinet.

Was it just my imagination, or was there a warmth emanating from my hand where I touched the amulet?

I pulled it out and closed the display case so no one would see that it had been opened. I planned to have the amulet back by morning, so hopefully no one would ever know that I had borrowed it.

As I worked to string the amulet onto an old bootlace, I felt a faint draft across my face, then heard a soft rustling and creaking sound. I froze and forced myself to look up, very glad I had the Blood of Isis amulet clutched in my hand. My gaze fell on the mummy nearest me, and I saw that it didn't look as stiff as usual. Then the one next to it, Henuttawy, an unwrapped mummy from the New Kingdom, shifted on her discolored, bony feet. The creaking and popping and rustling grew louder and I realized the moon must have risen. The mummies were beginning to answer the call of the staff! I had to deactivate it now, before they all began marching downstairs.

I shoved the bootlace back into my pocket and, clutching the Blood of Isis in my hand, made a mad dash for the catacombs.

I stepped into the stairwell to the basement and paused. Faint whisperings rustled through the dark air below me. Quickly, I reached out and turned up the gas lamps, which did a surprisingly poor job of penetrating the shadows. Still grasping the Blood of Isis in one hand, I made my way down the stairs. The air grew colder, my arms and back prickling with the chill.

Or maybe something else was causing my uneasiness—best not to think about that right now.

When I reached the bottom stair, I paused. Everything felt so different in the dark, which made no sense, because it was dark down here even during the daytime. But that was Egyptian magic for you. The truth was, the *mut* and *akhu* down here were thick enough to spread on toast. (When I was lucky enough to get morning toast, that is.)

I took another step into the room and felt something watching me. I peered into the gloom and found the jackal statue staring straight at me. I froze, afraid he might leap off the shrine.

After a long moment during which he didn't twitch so much as a whisker, I decided he would stay put. I made a mental note that once I got the mummies under control, I really had to remove the curse on the jackal and return Vicary Weems's coat to its peg.

Putting the jackal out of my mind—well, as much as I could, anyway—I crept over to the mummies, keeping my movements as quiet as possible.

They were all still gathered near the hidden staff, staring at the bottom shelf as if it were the most interesting thing in the world. Perhaps it was, especially if it held a staff with the power to grant them life.

I gently squeezed through the bandaged crowd in order to reach the staff, whispering pardons as I went. It was actually quite horrid, squeezing past a mummy. One must have absolute discipline over one's mind to keep from thinking about touching a long-dead thing that had once been a person and was now a . . . what? I shuddered and pushed my way between the last two mummies.

I knelt on the ground, gritted my teeth, and shoved my hand under the shelf to begin groping for the staff. I sincerely hoped the resurrected mouse was long gone and would not mistake my fingers for a bit of sausage.

At last my hand made contact with something sleek and hard. I grasped my fingers around the staff and pulled it from its hiding place. When I stood, all the mummies' faces followed me. It was horribly disconcerting.

I reached down to pluck the golden Orb of Ra from the

jackal's mouth, then stopped. How was I going to lug a half dozen full-grown bodies across the room? Perhaps I should use the staff first to get them over against the wall where they belonged, then turn it off.

I cleared my throat, then jiggled the staff in front of their noses. That seemed to get their attention. As I slowly backed away toward the opposite wall, the mummies parted to let the staff through. "Come on, now," I whispered, waving the staff some more. "Follow me."

Much to my delight, they did.

Keeping their eyes on the staff, they slowly shuffled their way across the room. Behind me, I felt things fluttering around, getting out of my way as I approached. Was the staff driving the evil spirits away? Or was it the Blood of Isis? I wasn't sure, but I was grateful all the same.

When we reached the far side of the room, I had no clue as to how to get everyone to line up. As an experiment, I rapped the wall twice with the staff. Immediately, the mummies fell into place. Brilliant!

With them safely back where they belonged, I reached into the jackal's mouth, grasped the golden orb, and tugged. It popped out into my waiting hand as easy as you please.

There was a sighing sound. I looked up to find the mummies all rigid against the wall, no longer staring at the staff but looking straight ahead.

A footstep creaked on the stairs. Gasping, I whirled around, barely managing to bite back a scream at the shadowed form lurking on the stairs.

Tetley. It was only Tetley, I told my galloping heart. His mummified form must have responded to the pull of the staff.

Well, he couldn't just stand there on the stairs for all eternity! Setting the staff against the wall, I wrestled Tetley down the rest of the steps and next to the other mummies. Hopefully no one would come looking for him.

The shadows began to thicken, and the rustling sound grew louder. Had it been the power of the staff that had kept the restless spirits at bay until now? Fighting down panic, I secured the golden Orb of Ra safely in my pinafore pocket, then hurried up the stairs, not one bit careful how quiet I was.

As I slammed the basement door, a shudder ran through me. That had been close. Would the restless *mut* have come closer? Surely not with the Blood of Isis in my possession. Trying desperately to believe that, I headed toward the family room.

A tall figure stepped out of the shadows, blocking my path and pointing a shotgun directly at my chest.

CHAPTER FIFTEEN
MIDNIGHT WANDERINGS

"THEO? IS THAT YOU?"

I nearly wet my knickers in relief. "Father! Yes, it's me! Who did you expect?" And then I remembered—he was lying in wait for the mummies. I glanced at the stairs that led up to the Egyptian exhibit, wondering if any of the bodies had begun to make their way down before I had turned off the staff's power.

He lowered his shotgun. "Well, not you, that's for certain. Whatever are you doing?"

I looked at him in exasperation. "My chores! You're the one who assigned me to organize the basement, aren't you?"

"Oh, yes. How's that coming, then?"

I can't even begin to tell you how odd it is to carry on a conversation with your father when he is holding a shotgun. "It's coming along very nicely," I lied. "Now, if you don't mind, I thought I'd see if there's anything to eat."

"Of course. There are some meat pies in the family room."

And so I left him, standing guard in the foyer with his shotgun. I could only hope he wouldn't seriously hurt someone. Least of all himself.

I ate the last two meat pies, then retired immediately to my closet. It had been a long day, and I was exhausted. I turned down the blanket, crawled into the sarcophagus, and fell fast asleep with the Blood of Isis clutched firmly in my hand. There would be time enough to deal with the other problems tomorrow.

I was awakened some time later by a sharp prickling against my scalp and something rough and warm scratching my face. Whatever was doing the scratching and the prickling vibrated loudly, like a Hoover or perhaps a motorcar engine. It took me a moment before I recognized the sound as Isis. Purring.

Even though she had been undemonized months ago, she'd never gone back to being quite as cuddly as she used to be, so anytime she was up for a purr and a snuggle, I was happy.

"Hello there, miss!" I reached out to scratch her between the ears, which she enjoyed a moment before batting my fingers away and giving me one last rough scratch with her tongue. Then she hopped out of the sarcophagus, went over to the door, and waited.

When I didn't follow immediately, she rubbed against the doorjamb and gave a faint meow.

I sat up, all drowsiness chased completely away. She meowed again, and I clambered out of the sarcophagus, slipped into my shoes, then went to light the oil lamp on the desk. Holding it out in front of me, still clutching the Blood of Isis with my other hand, I followed the cat into the darkened hall. I paused and heard no noise coming from anywhere. Puzzled as to what Isis was up to, I let her lead me. As we passed the sitting room, I popped my head in. Mother was crumpled up on the couch, sound asleep, but Father was nowhere in sight. Isis kept walking.

I rushed to catch up, but she disappeared into the great yawning darkness of the foyer. Remembering the shotgun, I took a few cautious steps forward. "Father? Are you still here?" I whispered out into the blackness. But there was no answer.

Then I heard it. A low rumbling gargle, as if one of the sphinxes that flanked the staircase was giving off a warning growl. I froze, unsure what to do. I hadn't thought to check the sphinxes for curses in ages. They'd always been clean, so I'd given up worrying about them. Far too soon, it looked like.

The noise came again, then stuttered.

Maybe that stutter meant the magic had gone dormant again? Besides, Isis had ventured forward. Surely she wouldn't have braved any black magic.

I tightened my grip on the amulets and walked firmly (but quietly!) into the foyer. The sphinxes looked as placid as ever, but Father was propped up against the haunch of one of them, fast asleep, his forgotten shotgun laid across his lap.

I jumped slightly when the rumbling came again, relief mingling with annoyance when I realized it was only Father —snoring. Honestly! He could have given me a heart attack.

Feeling slightly foolish (but much braver), I squared my shoulders and hurried over to where Isis waited impatiently. As soon as I drew close, she galloped off into the darkness again. I wished she'd learn to wait up for me.

She led me past Flimp's office. He was also asleep—and snoring as well. I reached out and closed his door as quietly as I could, cutting off the grating sound.

And that was when I heard it. The soft *snick* of a latch. I paused, wondering if it might be the echo of Flimp's door closing, but the sound of quiet footsteps moving rapidly across the floor disabused me of that notion.

My heart lodged in my throat, I turned down the oil lamp and set it carefully on the floor, then headed toward the sound.

It was very disorienting trying to follow footsteps in the dark. The large, cavernous rooms of the museum gave everything a slight echo. Just as I was certain I was coming upon the footsteps, I heard the distinct click of another door being opened, then closed again.

Isis shot out of the dark past me toward the noise, and I followed. It had been the side entrance!

When I got there, I tried to open it, only to find it was locked. How could the intruder have gotten in if it was locked?

Shoving the question aside, I reached out to unlock it, then jerked my hand back at the sharp tingle of magic buzzing along my gloves. Desperately wanting to catch at least a glimpse of the intruder, I reached for the knob again (this time ignoring the disturbing sensation), opened the door, and cautiously poked my head outside.

A tall, cloaked figure was just disappearing around the corner of the building, and he'd been carrying something. Something long and . . . *no!*

I scampered back inside—making sure to lock the side entrance—then hurried to the basement. *Please don't let it be the staff, please don't let it be the staff,* I chanted to myself.

Panic won over caution and I bolted down the steps to the catacombs. At the bottom of the stairs, I peered through the gloom to the west wall. All the mummies were still lined up like determined soldiers, but the staff was gone. I glanced to the floor, hoping it might just have fallen over, but of course it hadn't.

Whoever that intruder had been, he'd stolen the Staff of Osiris.

Well, a part of it, anyway, I thought, patting the pocket of my pinafore where the heavy gold orb lay safely hidden.

Even so, he'd come very close to getting the staff *and* the orb! Only a matter of hours, really. And he was bold enough to strike when there were so many of us here in the museum. What if Father had awoken, or Mum? Or even poor dear Flimp? Think of what danger they would have been in.

I had to get word to Wigmere right away. He needed to know that they had the staff and how bold they'd been in getting it.

Whoever *they* were. I was guessing it was the Serpents of Chaos, but really, it could have been anybody! The Grim Nipper fellow that Inspector Turnbull had been talking about. Clive Fagenbush, the beast, or even that prig Vicary

Weems. Perhaps he was in cahoots with Lord Chudleigh. What if he was trying to get Father fired so he could become Head Curator, as he probably thought he deserved?

I moved to go back up the stairs, nearly tripping over Isis, who was sitting on the first step waiting patiently for me to get going. I reached down and gave her a good scratching. "Excellent work, miss," I told her. She began to purr.

The next morning I was awakened by a loud pounding that seemed to shake the very walls of the museum itself. I scrambled out of the sarcophagus, scrubbed my face with my hands, and hurried out to see what was going on.

When I reached the foyer, I saw that it was quite late. All the curators stood huddled in a small group, whispering among themselves, seemingly ignoring the pounding at the door.

Mum appeared at the foot of the stairs, the heightened color in her cheeks the only sign she'd just woken up. How does she manage to sleep without wrinkling her clothes, I'd like to know. "Where on earth is everyone, and why haven't they opened the door?" she asked.

Fagenbush shoved his hands into his trouser pockets and deferred to Vicary Weems with a sneer. Weems cleared his throat. "It's his lordship, ma'am. He's, um, asleep."

"H-holding a gun," Stilton added.

I stepped forward. "Shall I let them in, Mum?"

Mother reached up and patted her hair. "Perhaps we'd best see who it is first," she suggested, visions of Grandmother no doubt running through her head.

I was halfway through the foyer when Father woke up. "What's all this racket?" he demanded, working out the kinks in his neck.

"Someone's here," I called out over my shoulder. When I reached the front, I peeked out the window, nearly squealing when I found myself eyeball to eyeball with Inspector Turnbull, who was peering *in*. "It's Inspector Turnbull, Father. And he has three constables with him. A small crowd, actually. It looks like some of those newspapermen who were here the other day."

"What in the ruddy hell do they want?"

"We'll find out, won't we?" I muttered to myself. I took a deep breath and put on my most innocent face before opening the door. I was terrified that somehow the inspector had heard of the break-in last night—it wouldn't do at all to have the police dragged into the matter of the staff. I had to get word to Wigmore first thing this morning!

"Good morning, Inspector. It's rather early in the morning for calling, don't you think?"

"This isn't a social visit, young lady." He squeezed his way inside while his constables held back the clamoring crowd of reporters.

"Is it true one of the mummies is cursed?" one of them shouted.

"Did one of the men who touched the mummies really break his leg?" another one called out.

"What happened to the photographer who took the only known picture of the mummy?"

"Is it true that gold is the only way to protect ourselves from the mummies?"

Inspector Turnbull slammed the door shut on that last question, then took his handkerchief out of his pocket and mopped his face. "I thought I'd come by here first thing this morning rather than get all the way to my office, then have someone call me back here. Seemed more efficient some-how."

"But why would anyone have called you here this morning?"

The inspector skewered me with a glare, then looked pointedly at the foyer wall.

Which, much to his surprise, was empty.

Except for Father, who was struggling to his feet, his shot-gun dangling from his right hand.

"What do you want?" Father boomed.

The inspector eyed the shotgun warily. "You wouldn't be threatening an officer, now, would you?"

"Heavens no, Inspector Turnbull!" Mother hurried forward, anxious to smooth things over. "He was keeping watch last night, hoping to find who was bringing all the mummies to the museum."

"Except they didn't have the nerve to show their faces," Father said, clearly put out.

The inspector glanced again at the blank wall. "So I see," he said. "And it's a good thing, I might add. I came here fully expecting to find the mummies again, and if I had, I'd have arrested you, Admiral Sopcoate or no."

I thought it very foolish of the inspector to taunt Father when he was holding a shotgun.

"However," he continued as he eyed Father's reddening face, "since they're not here, there's not much I can do. Just remember, I've got my eye on you." He turned his gaze toward the curators. "Which one of you is Weems?" he asked.

"I am, sir." The new First Assistant Curator stepped forward, looking very self-important.

"Good. I need to have a word with you." Weems paled a bit but otherwise gave no sign that he minded as he followed the inspector down the hall.

I glanced around to make sure everyone else was occupied. Mother was brushing Father off and Fagenbush was bossing poor Stilton about something, so I slipped off after the inspector, walking on quiet feet.

Yes, eavesdropping is a vile habit. Luckily, I wasn't eavesdropping. I was spying. Spying is noble, especially when doing it for a good cause, such as my parents.

"So, Lord Chudleigh says you're an upstanding sort of chap," the inspector said.

Weems puffed up a bit at this. "I like to think so."

"So tell me, have you seen anything suspicious the past couple of days?"

"Well, this whole place is a bit more dodgy than I was led to believe during the interviews."

Dodgy? How dare he! We weren't the slightest bit dodgy.

"The Third Assistant Curator seems a very nervous sort. Always twitching and clearing his throat."

"Go on," the inspector encouraged.

"Then, there's that Fagenbush fellow. He has a very guilty feel to him, even though I can't pinpoint why. Seems like he's always skulking around."

I wasn't sure how I felt being in agreement with Weems, even on Fagenbush.

"And," he continued, "no one can quite explain what happened to their former First Assistant Curator, at least not to my satisfaction."

"What about the Throckmortons?" Inspector Turnbull pressed on. "Have you noticed anything strange about them?"

"Well, Throckmorton is brilliant, there's no doubt about that. However, sometimes brilliant isn't too large a step from mad, if you know what I mean."

I clenched my fists. Beast.

"Yes, yes. I know exactly what you mean. Do continue."

"He works the oddest hours. Never seems to go home and is always muttering to himself. And that child of his? What's her name? Theodosia? Most unnatural child. Always underfoot and watching me."

With good reason, I might add.

"By the by, did I mention that my greatcoat was stolen?"

"Yes. Three times now."

"Well"—Weems's voice became defensive—"have you found it?"

"Can't say as we have, sir, since we're a little distracted BY ALL THE BLOOMING MUMMIES RUNNING AROUND," the inspector hollered.

There was an awkward silence, and then Weems spoke, much more circumspectly this time. "Well, I thought they might be related, that's all."

"I doubt it. One last thing." There was a rustle of paper as

Turnbull pulled something from one of his pockets. "Have you ever seen this man before?"

"No," Weems said primly. "I haven't."

"Are you sure? You've never seen him hanging around the museum? Or talking to Throckmorton?"

"No, no. I'm quite sure. I'd remember someone as disreputable looking as that. Who is he?"

Inspector Turnbull grunted. "The Grim Nipper. And if you see him, or anything else fishy, let me know. Here's my card."

Weems took the small white card from the inspector. "Thank you. I'll be in touch if I find anything else out."

The rotten little snitch! He was going to blab everything he learned straight to the police!

He continued, "I'm glad to do whatever I can to help. I must say, this isn't nearly as respectable a museum as I'd hoped."

The inspector bid Weems good day, and I flattened myself against one of the columns, hoping he wouldn't see me as he moved on to Edgar Stilton's office. I realized that this would be a good time to get away to see Wigmere. Everybody was busy and no one would notice if I slipped out. Pleased with my plan, I hurried to the west entrance and opened the door.

And immediately spotted the tall man in the undertaker's

coat and battered top hat leaning up against the building across the street. When he saw me, he quickly glanced down at the newspaper he was pretending to read. Then it hit me. *This* must be the Grim Nipper! And he had been skulking around the museum for *days*.

My mind whirred with possibilities, as I clearly couldn't exit here. I could try to sneak past Dolge and Sweeny in the loading area, but there was a good chance Turnbull would work his way down there to question them, and I really wished to avoid running into him.

Which left the east entrance. Not to be deterred from my visit to Wigmere, I ran to that side of the museum. Unfortunately I didn't have enough money on me for a cab, which meant I would have to walk—very quickly. I opened the door, my mind full of all that I needed to tell Wigmere, only to run smack into Miss Sharpe, who was standing just outside, trying to catch her breath.

CHAPTER SIXTEEN
FOILED AGAIN

"MISS SHARPE!" My heart sank all the way to my toes.

She smiled at me. "That's right. Have you forgotten we're to start our lessons today?"

Of course I had, but I didn't want to say so. "Not at all. In fact, I was coming here so I could greet you when you arrived." How on earth was I going to get word to Wigmere with Miss Sharpe hanging around my neck like an albatross all day?

"That was very kind of you. And I'm sorry I'm late, but I thought we were to meet at your house this morning and do our lessons there, as your grandmother had wanted to get you out of this stuffy old museum."

Well, she was exactly right. Grandmother *had* planned for us to conduct our studies at home, until I'd persuaded her otherwise.

"May I come in?" Miss Sharpe asked.

"Oh, I'm sorry. Of course!" As I stood aside to let her in, a movement in the bushes caught my eye. Surely the Grim Nipper couldn't have made it over here already? But no. I could tell by the reddish brown jersey and waterproof cap it was only a public sweeper. Although what he was sweeping over there in the bushes, I had no idea.

The sweeper caught me watching him and winked.

Embarrassed, I started to turn away, then caught sight of the bright blue eyes hidden under the lip of the cap.

Will. In yet another disguise.

As Miss Sharpe shrugged out of her wrap, I motioned frantically at Will to let him know I had a message for Wigmere. He jerked his head in Miss Sharpe's direction and shrugged.

He was right. He couldn't approach me while she was around. This was getting more complicated by the minute.

"Theodosia? What are you doing?"

"Oh, I was just enjoying the feel of the morning air."

"Well, do close the door before one of those hideous newspapermen finds his way over here."

"Of course, Miss Sharpe." I resigned myself to a long, frustrating morning.

"Is there a place for us to begin our lessons?"

There was only one place, really. "Yes. The reading room should be perfect. Hardly anyone ever goes in there."

"Excellent. Will you show me the way? Your grandmother mentioned something about an essay you were writing."

"Yes, but I've only just started it."

"Even so, I look forward to seeing it. I would like to examine a sample of your writing skills and penmanship."

Bother. I'd have to be more careful about tossing Grandmother excuses in the future.

When we reached the reading room, I turned up the lights and stepped aside. Miss Sharpe looked around the room. "I think over in that corner will do nicely," she said.

I followed her over and took a seat. She gave me a quick, fierce perusal, then frowned. "Come here, Theodosia. Let me get a better look at you." She grabbed my hand and pulled me directly into the light, her eyes widening in faint horror. "Oh, my! This will never do. It looks as if you slept in your clothes! Look how wrinkled and mussed they are."

Her eyes moved from my frock up to my face. She shook her head. "You look like a beggar child! Has no one ever taught you to wash in the morning? Or to run a comb through your hair? I'm afraid your grandmother doesn't understand how dire your manners and behavior truly are."

I was very hot under the collar by this point, and my cheeks were burning. I started to explain that I had indeed slept in my clothes, but something about Miss Sharpe's pursed mouth bade me hold my tongue. She'd already made it clear that she thought my parents were severely lacking, and I'd no wish to give her any additional ammunition on that score.

"Have you nothing to say for yourself, Theodosia?"

"Our maid is ill," I lied, "and the ironing isn't getting done."

"But how does that explain your shocking filth?"

Shocking filth? I'd just forgotten to wash my face, for goodness sake. "I was in a hurry?"

"Lazy is more like it. Well, excellent. This presents us with our first opportunity for a good lesson. Come with me." Once again she grabbed my hand and began pulling me along behind her.

"Where are we going?"

She looked back over her shoulder at me. "Ah, ah, ah! You have not been spoken to." She held up her thumb and index finger as a reminder, and I clamped my mouth shut.

Moments later we reached the lavatory, where Miss

Sharpe dragged me over to the sink. She snatched one of the coarse hand towels from the shelf and thrust it at me. "Now wash."

Resentment at being treated like a four-year-old bubbled inside me. It made it worse that I did indeed need a wash, but when one is woken up by police pounding on the door, one doesn't really have time for such niceties. I glared at Miss Sharpe.

Faster than I could have blinked, her wretched hand darted out and pinched me on the arm. I bit my tongue, refusing to make a sound no matter how much it had hurt.

Miss Sharpe dimpled and shook her head. "I would so hate to have to contact your grandmother about this, Theodosia. I don't think you realize how dire your situation is. If I can't bring you to hand, you will be shipped off to Miss Grimstone's School for Wayward Girls. Is that really what you want?"

I felt all the blood drain from my face. Even I, with my limited knowledge of schools, had heard warnings of that place. Trust Grandmother to have picked the most wretched school available. And she would make sure my parents did it, too. Recognizing defeat—at least for the moment—I wet the towel and scrubbed at my face. As horrid as Miss Sharpe was, it *did* feel good to have a wash.

When I was done, I folded the towel and went to place it on the sink.

"Again," Miss Sharpe said.

"I beg your pardon?"

"Again. You will wash your face twenty times this morning so you will not forget again."

Not believing my ears, I stared at her.

She reached out and delicately straightened one of her cuffs. "I hear at Miss Grimstone's they have to break a layer of ice on their basins before they can wash in the morning."

I gritted my teeth and picked the towel up once more.

When we returned to the reading room half an hour later, my face was red and raw. Miss Sharpe did not realize it yet, but she had just edged Grandmother Throckmorton off the top of my Most Disliked People list.

I spent the next several hours studying grammar and being told my handwriting was atrocious. This agony was made worse by the fact that there seemed to be an unusual amount of activity in the reading room that morning. Every single one of the curators managed to make an appearance. I found myself hoping they would think my face was red from exertion—or even embarrassment—rather than guessing it had been scrubbed to death.

Miss Sharpe pointedly ignored both Stilton and Fagenbush but simpered sweetly at Vicary Weems. The attention from her caused him to puff up so thoroughly that he could hardly fit through the door on his way out.

At long last, Miss Sharpe checked the watch pinned to her dress and announced it was time for a lunch break. Excellent news—I hadn't had time for breakfast and I was starving.

"Where do you normally eat your lunch?" Miss Sharpe asked.

"On the fly" was the truthful answer, but I'd learned not to tell Miss Sharpe the truth if I could help it. "In the family sitting room."

"Very well. You'll have to show me the way." She picked up her small satchel and followed me down the hall.

So much for my hope of slipping away to pass a message to Will.

When we reached the sitting room, she sat at the table and began unpacking her lunch. She pulled out an apple, some cold roast chicken, and a piece of cake. My mouth watered and my stomach grumbled loudly. I hurried over to the cupboard, took down a new jar of jam, and unwrapped the day-old loaf of bread. With the smell of roast chicken filling my nose, I resolutely made myself two jam sandwiches, then went to sit down at the table across from Miss Sharpe.

Watching someone else eat lovely food when one is

making do is horrid. Especially when one wants to smash one's jam sandwich into the self-satisfied face of that person. Miss Sharpe ate her lunch in silence. I inhaled my two sandwiches before she even finished her chicken, so then I was forced to just wait. The cake smelled of butter and vanilla and looked very moist, and Miss Sharpe managed to eat it without leaving so much as a crumb behind. She carefully rewrapped her napkins, then returned them to her satchel. She looked up at me and smiled. "Time to get back to our lessons."

Once back in the reading room, Miss Sharpe instructed me to work on my essay concerning the visit to the *Dreadnought*. It was very hard to concentrate on a boat when my mind kept reminding me that I simply had to get a message to Wigmere as soon as possible.

Miss Sharpe sat nearby, serenely reading her copy of *Mrs. Primbottom's Guide to Raising Perfect Children*. Every once in a while, she would share a choice little tidbit with me.

"Ah, here we go. 'A lack of cleanliness must be discouraged as soon as possible, as it is impossible to properly love filthy children.'"

I did my best to ignore her and tried to determine if a turban engine was spelled the same way as the turban one wore on one's head.

"'Penmanship is a sign of virtue, and sloppy penmanship reveals a disorderly soul.'"

I gritted my teeth and bore down on my pen nib. I really had to do something about her. And soon.

A short while later, Miss Sharpe put aside *Mrs. Primbottom's Guide to Raising Perfect Children* and picked up a copy of *The Staff of Duty: A Governess's Tales from the Trenches*. Fortunately, she did not appear to be inclined to share these tales with me, for which I was eternally grateful.

Mum stuck her head inside the reading room. "Excuse me."

Miss Sharpe turned a cool glance her way. "Yes?"

Mother raised an eyebrow. "Actually, I was speaking to my daughter."

Miss Sharpe sniffed. "Very well, but I normally prefer to have no interruptions when working with my pupils."

Mother glanced pointedly at the book Miss Sharpe had been reading. "It won't take but a moment. Theodosia, I just wanted to let you know that Father and I have been called to an emergency board of directors meeting at Lord Tumsley's." In spite of the strong face she was putting on for Miss Sharpe, I could tell she was worried. "We won't be back until five o'clock."

"Very well, ma'am," Miss Sharpe said, even though Mother

had been talking to me. When she looked back down at her book, Mum blew me a quick kiss, which lifted my spirits a small bit. I loathed the idea of Mother and Father being grilled by a bunch of stuffed shirts who clearly had no true knowledge of anything important.

Two long, painful hours later, Miss Sharpe looked at her watch, an expression of disapproval on her face. "Your parents aren't back yet. They did say five o'clock, didn't they?"

"Yes, they did, but perhaps the board of directors had lots to talk about."

She frowned. "I'm afraid I've a meeting I must go to—"

At last! A chance at freedom!

"—and I can't let you stay here all alone."

"Oh, but you can! Besides, I won't be alone. Most of the curators stay until seven o'clock, and Flimp is here all night. I'll be fine." Not that any of that mattered, since I planned on escaping to Somerset House immediately in order to report to Wigmere.

"Well, if you're sure. Perhaps I should ask Mr. Weems."

"Certainly," I said, folding my hands in my lap. "If you have another fifteen minutes to track him down."

She glanced at her watch again. "Oh, dear," she muttered, and I briefly wondered what kind of meeting she had. Finally, she seemed to make up her mind. "Very well." She pulled a book from her satchel and handed it to me. "But I'll give you something to do while you wait. We're going to work on your Latin next. You can begin by translating this. I expect pages one through ten to be done by tomorrow morning."

I took the volume of Virgil's *Bucolics* from her. "Very well, Miss Sharpe." I would have said yes to just about anything to get her on her way at this point.

Miss Sharpe bundled into her things and left. Five minutes later, I did the same. I patted my coat pockets, only to find them empty. Drat. I would need money. Even I wasn't so foolhardy as to walk clear across town in the dark.

I hurried to the sitting room and over to the settee. Wrinkling my nose, I shoved my hand between the back of the cushion and the seat. My fingers met with crumbs and lint and mysterious bits of all kinds. Ignoring them, I shoved my arm in farther and groped toward the sides. There— something hard and flat. *Please let it be a coin!*

It was! I did this twice more, scraping together enough for cab fare, then rushed downstairs and out the west entrance. I hadn't wanted Flimp to see me leave, as he would have most likely tried to stop me or at the very least sent someone after me.

You'd be surprised at how difficult it is to get a cab to take notice of an eleven-year-old girl. You'd think they'd stop just because they realized I shouldn't be out after dark, but they seemed to look right through me and drive on past. Finally, a hansom dropped a gentleman off two doors down from the museum. Before the cabby could take off again, I darted forward and put a hand on the side of the cab.

"Eh, wot's this? Let go of me cab, miss!"

"No! I mean, please. I need a ride. I've got the money!" I said, holding up the coins.

His eyebrows shot up, disappearing into his cap. "What's a young bit like you doing out by yerself, eh?"

"My parents . . . let me come visit the museum today . . . and now I'm to take a cab back to meet them. At Somerset House."

He shook his head and reached for the coins. "I can't very well let you stand around out here all by ye'self wif no one to watch over you. Climb in."

I thought he muttered something about parents who didn't mind their offspring properly, but I ignored it. Of course Mother and Father minded me properly. They were just busy right this minute. Getting a good drubbing, I was afraid.

Luckily the cabby kept his mouth shut for the rest of the ride and got me to Somerset House in good time. As he dropped me off, he said, "I've a good mind to go in there and give yer parents a stern talking-to."

My mind scrambled quickly, trying to think if Wigmere would catch on in time to pretend he was my father. Well, grandfather, more likely. But the cabby just shook his head. "It's none o' me business, but you watch yerself, miss. Lots of unpleasant things lurk in the city after dark."

And didn't I know *that* better than most. "Thank you so much. I will be careful." I waved goodbye, then made my way across the large courtyard to the front door of Somerset House. The doorman raised his eyebrows when he caught sight of me. "I'm here to see Lord Wigmere," I explained. His face cleared a bit, as if he were used to odd comings and goings on Lord Wigmere's behalf.

Come to think of it, he most likely was, given the nature of the Brotherhood of the Chosen Keepers.

When I reached the third floor, I saw Sticky Will still in his public sweeper disguise, lurking just outside Boythorpe's partially open office door.

Will heard my step on the landing and whirled around. His face relaxed when he saw it was only me, and he motioned me to be quiet and come closer.

"I been waiting for someone to come along all afternoon. Go ahead, now—knock on 'is door."

"I don't want to knock on his door," I hissed. "He'll only stick his annoying nose in my business and try to keep me from seeing Wigmere."

Will's face fell. "Ah, come on, miss. I promise you, 'e won't be able to bother you this time. Just knock. Please."

Well, he did say please. And by now, my curiosity was piqued. He clearly had something up his sleeve. I sighed. "Very well."

I sidled up against the doorjamb and rapped smartly.

Boythorpe looked up, his eyes narrowing when he saw me. "Yes?" he said without getting up. A sure sign of his lack of respect. Pulling out my best Grandmother Throckmorton impersonation, I said, "I'm here to see Lord Wigmere. I'll be happy to show myself to his door."

"I don't think so," he said, then planted his hands on the desk and pushed to his feet.

Or tried to.

But he seemed rather stuck to his chair, so he only made it halfway up. The seat clung to his bottom like a half-laid egg.

He frowned, trying to get a glimpse of the firmly stuck chair behind him, looking for all the world like Isis when she decides to chase her tail. His face turned pink as he realized he'd been the butt—literally—of a practical joke.

"Never mind, Boythorpe. Really, I can find Lord Wigmere all by myself." Unable to contain myself any longer, I moved a few feet down the hall, where I erupted in a fit of laughter. Will joined me, clutching his sides. "What on earth did you do to him?" I asked when I could speak.

"'E's boxed me ears one too many times," he said. "So I smeared a layer o' treacle on 'is chair."

"Aren't you afraid he'll tell Wigmere?"

"Nah. I caught the sniff trying to read Wigg's mail one day. If 'e tries to tell on me, 'e knows I've got that up me sleeve."

I frowned. "Reading Lord Wigmere's mail seems rather serious. Don't you think you should report that?"

"Nah. I caught him before he got anything opened up. Now, come on—Wigmere will want to see you straightaway."

CHAPTER SEVENTEEN

The Orb and I

I DID MY BEST TO COMPOSE MYSELF. It wouldn't do to waltz into Wigmere's office giggling.

"Miss Theodosia to see you, sir," Will announced.

"Send her in."

Will stood aside so I could enter. The solemn weight of Wigmere's office chased any thought of giggling clean away. It had the same heavy silence that a church or library might have had.

Wigmere looked up at me, his eyebrows drawn together in concern. "Something must be dire indeed to bring you here at this hour. Is it your parents? Are they all right?"

"Oh, they're fine, sir. Well, as fine as possible, considering they're attending an emergency meeting of our museum's board of directors. I suspect they are getting a good raking over the coals about the mummy situation right about now."

If I was hoping he would offer to keep them out of their predicament, I was sorely disappointed. "Well, come in. Sit down." He looked back at Will. "Thank you. That will be all." Will tugged his cap, then bowed out of the room, closing the door behind him.

"Now, what've you come all this way to tell me?"

"Did Will tell you about the Staff of Osiris? Did he explain that's what called all the mummies to the museum?"

"Yes, he did. But I wouldn't mind hearing it straight from you."

I quickly told him of finding the staff in the basement and returning the next day to find all the mummies gathered round. Then I explained about my experiment with the dead mouse, but stopped when Wigmere's mustache twitched. He wasn't laughing at me, was he? "Is something wrong, sir?"

"Nothing, nothing. Carry on."

When I'd finished, he leaned forward. "You didn't bring the staff with you, by any chance, did you?"

Honestly! What did he think I'd done with it? Hidden it in my skirts? "I'm afraid that wasn't possible."

He sighed in disappointment. "Rather difficult to carry around, yes?"

"Well, not only that . . ."

"Well, what, then?"

Steeling myself, I drew a deep breath. "I'm afraid the staff has been stolen, sir."

"What?" Wigmere nearly leaped out of his seat, which was rather extraordinary given that he normally needed a cane.

"Someone broke into the museum last night and stole the staff."

"Good gad! D'you have any idea who it was?"

"None, sir. But no one knew about the staff except you and Will and me."

"There are many who pay attention to magical comings and goings in this town, Theodosia. Most likely they've been watching the museum ever since the first wave of mummies showed up on your doorstep. And of course, we now know that Chaos is back in the game."

I got a rather sick feeling in my stomach.

"We've checked all von Braggenschnott's last known addresses but have come up empty-handed. Chaos has gone to ground, I'm afraid. Have you had a chance to do any research on the staff?"

"Yes, a bit. I'm afraid it's rather grim news. As far-fetched as it sounds, the staff is rumored to actually have belonged to Osiris, which is nonsense, don't you think?"

He didn't immediately agree, which made me nervous. Instead, he pursed his lips. "We've been researching down on Level Six, and they came up with similar information. Mostly myth and legend, nothing concrete."

"Can you tell me?"

"Of course." He settled back in his chair. "Way back in the mists of time, probably in the Early Dynastic Period, a staff came into being. Its exact origins are unknown. Some of the earliest writings of the time claim that it was created by Egypt's most powerful early magician, Menhotep. Other sources claim that it was forged by Osiris himself, during the short period he walked this earth before taking up his reign in the Underworld."

"But I thought he was only a myth!"

Wigmere shook his head. "Some sources claim he was actually the fourth pharaoh of Egypt. Anyway, throughout Egypt's Old Kingdom, the staff was held by the highest magician in the land, waiting in readiness for the pharaohs' use. Different pharaohs wielded the staff with different results, depending on their nature and their need. But eventually the staff passed from human awareness, hidden in some temple or pyramid tomb, forgotten by many, if not all.

"The next rumors of the staff's existence came to light during the Middle Kingdom. Some claim its power is what allowed Egypt to conquer Nubia and forge alliances with Syria and Palestine. During the rule of Akhenaten, the pharaoh who introduced the worship of the sun god Aten, the staff was feared destroyed, but it turns out it was hidden from sight by priests who served Osiris, waiting until it was safe again.

"There is one more mention. Rameses III is said to have used the staff to create a Fog of War, which succeeded in defeating the Sea People who threatened Egypt. Then once again it fell off the historical map. Everything written after that point is pure rumor and speculation. A number of sources claim that somehow Alexander the Great got a hold of the staff, and that is what allowed him to conquer Egypt. It was assumed to be in possession of the Ptolemies up until the Romans conquered the land. Some say Cleopatra lost the staff, others that she gave it over in secret to the Romans, then, consumed by remorse, killed herself.

"The most concrete evidence we have of its actual existence is a copy of a papyrus attributed to the scribe Itennu, cataloging a collection of Egyptian national treasures housed in the Library of Alexandria."

"But then, wouldn't it have burned along with the library?"

Wigmere leaned forward. "Here's where it gets interesting. Rumors of the staff's existence began to appear in some of the early medieval grimoires. No one had actually seen

it—it was just a wisp of a rumor among other rumored artifacts of power. However, some of the grimoires and other
medieval magical texts whispered of its continued existence,
asserting that it did not burn with the library.

"There is a curious historical footnote that mentions a
small but dedicated group who had vowed to protect the
pharaohs and their treasures until the end of time. It is
thought that they managed to smuggle a cache of Egyptian
treasures out of the Library of Alexandria before it burned.
We are still trying to follow that trail."

"And somehow one of the treasures ended up in our museum?"

"Precisely."

The room fell quiet as we both pondered the full implications of this.

"But sir, why would the Serpents of Chaos want to have
power over the mummies? What would they possibly gain
from that?"

He met my gaze with his deep, troubled eyes. "I don't
know. We haven't figured that part out yet. But I have no
doubt that London will soon be terrorized by a mob of mummies."

"But wait—I completely forgot!" I pulled the Orb of Ra
from my pocket and laid it on Wigmere's desk.

He stared in wonder at the golden orb. "What is this?"

"It's the orb from the staff! I removed it last night so that the mummies wouldn't return to the museum. I was afraid if they showed up again, Inspector Turnbull would arrest Father. So I deactivated the staff. Without the orb, I believe the staff has no power. It was only after I put the orb into the jackal head of the staff that the mummies became active."

His eyes shone in admiration. "Excellent work, Theo. Just excellent!"

I squirmed in pleasure. "Thank you, sir. I thought I'd leave it here for safekeeping."

At my suggestion, Wigmere's face settled into a concerned frown.

"What? What is it?"

"I think you will need to keep the orb, Theodosia."

"But why? Wouldn't it be safer with you?"

"It would, but *you* wouldn't."

Unease worked its way down my spine. "What do you mean?"

"It won't take Chaos long—if they are indeed the ones in possession—to figure out that the staff isn't working, and what do you think they will do when they discover the orb is what's needed to make it work? They will come looking for it, my dear. And if you don't have it to give to them, it could go very badly for you."

"But I thought we didn't want the orb to fall into their hands?"

"True. But if I have to choose between the orb and you, I prefer to keep you safe. You're already mixed up in things that are far too dangerous for a girl of your age. The least I can do is try to ensure your safety. No, you must keep it for now. Furthermore, if they come after it, you must give it to them, Theo. Your safety is more important than keeping the orb out of their hands."

"Yes, sir," I said as I slowly returned the orb to my pocket.

"How did you get here?" he asked.

"I took a cab. But I'm rather out of funds now."

He grabbed his cane and rose to his feet. "That doesn't matter. I want you to be escorted back to the museum by one of my men. It will be safer that way."

I followed him out of his office and waited while he arranged for transportation. He assured me that they would continue their research and he urged me to continue mine. We agreed to keep in touch through Will.

When I went downstairs, Will was waiting to escort me to the carriage that Wigmere had ordered to take me home. Right then seemed as good a time as any to find out what was going on with him. Once we were out of the building and free from being overheard, I spoke up. "So, exactly what kind of trouble are you in?"

"Wot're you talkin' about, miss?"

"That tall, greasy-looking fellow with the hooked nose and undertaker's coat," I whispered fiercely. "I've seen him hanging around the museum. Inspector Turnbull called him the Grim Nipper. Is he following you?"

Even in the dim light, I could see Will's face grow sickly pale. "Shhh! Don't say that name out loud! Not if'n ye want to keep yer skin."

"Then tell me why he's following you! Every time you come to the museum, he's hot on your tail. Is he part of your old life? An old professional acquaintance?"

"No one's following me, miss," he said, his face set in stubborn lines. "Here's yer carriage, now."

"Well, you be careful," I said in a low voice. "And don't do anything to give Wigmere cause to mistrust you. He wouldn't be happy you were mingling with someone like the Grim Nipper."

"Course I won't. Off wi' you, now."

I hesitated, wondering if I should press him further, but the horses were stomping in impatience. The driver looked down. "Is there a problem?"

"No. No problem," Will called back.

With a last warning look at Will, I climbed in. The driver clicked his tongue and slapped the reins.

As I settled back onto the seat, I had to admit I felt much better now that I'd told Wigmere everything. The entire Brotherhood of the Chosen Keepers would be on it. Surely it would be only a matter of time before they found a way to outmaneuver the Serpents of Chaos.

But I was a little disturbed at Wigmere's worries for my safety. Earlier I had only thought of keeping the magic of the staff from the Serpents of Chaos. Now the orb was an ominous weight against my leg. I pushed that unpleasant thought aside and pondered what else Wigmere had told me.

To think that the Egyptian gods may have once upon a time walked the earth! And that they'd left such powerful artifacts behind. Artifacts that had power over death. But, I reminded myself, that was the nature of myths. They grew larger and grander over time.

Although the staff *did* seem to prove that there was some kernel of truth in them.

It was quite dark now. My stomach growled. What time was it, anyway? Could I talk the driver into stopping for something to eat on the way back to the museum? Then I remembered my lack of funds. Bother. Looked like jam sandwiches *again*.

There was a loud rattle of carriage wheels coming up behind us, the thundering of hooves growing louder and louder. The driver steered our carriage over toward the side to make room. However, instead of passing, the other vehicle drew up even with us. I heard a shout, and then two loud thuds overhead caused our carriage to dip wildly and lurch to the side. The driver cried out and then fell silent, but the carriage kept going.

With Wigmere's warnings echoing in my head, I scooted over to the window, pulled the curtain aside to see what was going on, and found myself face to chest with a black-cloaked form. Before I could so much as squeak, the large, threatening figure yanked the door open and swung himself in, landing on the seat across from me.

Heart pounding, I scrambled back into the far corner.

The intruder shut the door behind him, then turned to face me.

In the dim light of the carriage lamps, I could just make out that one side of his face was horribly scarred.

"Hullo, Theodosia." The familiar voice raised chills along my arms. "Fancy meeting you here."

I forced myself to meet the man's gaze. The skin of his left eye was pitted and red, the eye itself a useless milky white.

But even with all those scars, I would have recognized Nigel Bollingsworth anywhere.

CHAPTER EIGHTEEN

Old Friends, New Enemies

THE LAST TIME I'D SEEN our ex–First Assistant Curator was right after I'd beaned him on the head and he'd collapsed in an annex of Thutmose III's tomb. To say I wasn't expecting to see him in London was an extreme understatement.

"What? Cat got your tongue?" Bollingsworth asked. "Hard to imagine you at a loss for words." He tilted his face into the carriage light. "What do you think of your handiwork, Theo? Would you call it an improvement?"

Refusing to cower, I lifted my chin. "Is that why you've paid me a visit?" My voice sounded far too high and wobbly. "To show me your scars?"

He reached up and ran his fingers over his ruined face.

"No, Theo. I'm here because once again you've been far too clever for your own good."

"What do you mean?"

His hulking form swallowed up all the space in the carriage. "Where is the Orb of Ra?"

"I-I don't know what you're talking about. What's an Orb of Ra?"

"You little fool! You are in no position to play games with me." Long gone was the friendly First Assistant Curator who used to be kind to me. "We knew you had it, along with the staff—otherwise all the mummies in London wouldn't have shown up on your doorstep."

"Wh-what makes you say that?"

"We have known of the staff for some time now. It is one of the many artifacts of power we've been searching for. All we were lacking was its exact location, which you so helpfully discovered for us. Now, give me that orb."

"It was you who stole it!" Of course! It all made sense now. Who better to know his way around our museum than the ex–First Assistant Curator?

"We want the Orb of Ra, Theo. The staff is useless without it."

"Was it you who mummified Tetley?"

A shadow of something—regret?—crossed his face. "No,

it wasn't me. And you're stalling. I am more than happy to force you to reveal the orb's whereabouts." He caressed his scarred cheek again. "They say that revenge is a dish best served cold. Would you agree?"

I gulped, trying to think of a way to gain more time. "It's back at the museum. If you take me there, I'll show you where it is."

"You're lying," he said.

How on earth had he known I was lying? I'm actually a rather good liar, when I need to be.

Bollingsworth leaned forward, his nose inches from mine. "Now, where is that orb?"

His voice rose on the word *orb*, and it was clear he was running out of patience. Just then, the carriage took a turn much too fast and pitched us both up against the wall. There was a *thunk* as my pocket made contact with the door.

Bollingsworth gave a chilling smile. Faster than a snake, his arm darted forward and grabbed a handful of my frock. He pulled me away from the door toward him. I struggled, but there was nowhere to go and he was much stronger than I.

He thrust his hand into my pocket and pulled out the orb, letting go of me as soon as he had it. I tumbled back against the seat feeling sick and filthy, as if his touch had corrupted me in some way.

He held the orb up in the carriage light. "Beautiful," he whispered. "You're so good at finding things we need, Theo." He glanced at me, our eyes meeting. "It's a pity that won't save you." He shoved the orb into one of his pockets but made no move to leave the carriage.

"Y-you have the orb. Why don't you go now?" I said, rather desperate for him to be on his way.

"Ah, but you and I have some unfinished business, do we not?" His eyes glittered at the promise of vengeance.

"No, no. I think we're quite finished," I said, hoping my voice didn't quiver too much.

"I owe you, Theo," he whispered. "Even the Bible says so. An eye for an eye, is it not?" His hand crept inside his cloak.

Deciding I'd rather take my chances on a tumble from the carriage than with Bollingsworth, I felt along the carriage wall behind me, groping for the handle. Call it a hunch, but my chances of survival seemed much better outside the carriage than inside.

The carriage swerved again, and I tumbled away from the door.

The sound of another carriage reached us, and Bollingsworth peeked out the back window. *Please let it be the Chosen Keepers*, I thought. *Please, oh please.* Stokes. Bramfield. Thornleigh. Any one of them would be sorely welcome now.

Our carriage was racing along recklessly and it was all Bollingsworth and I could do to hang on. Then there were three loud thuds, and once again the vehicle dipped and swayed dangerously as new bodies climbed aboard. Bollingsworth drew a long, sharp knife from the folds of his cape. He wouldn't have done that if he were expecting his fellow Serpents of Chaos. That could only be a good sign. Or so I hoped.

The door of the carriage jerked open. A man in a hood and cape stood balanced on the running board, blocking my view of the streets outside rushing by. He took one glance at Bollingsworth and the knife, then reached in, wrapped his arm around my waist, and pulled me from the careening carriage.

The last thing I saw was the opposite door bursting open and another cloaked figure hurling himself into the carriage, ramming into Bollingsworth and knocking him back against the seat.

Then I was dangling from the stranger's arm, my heart pounding wildly as the cobbled streets churned below in a dizzying rush. While I was most glad to get away from Bollingsworth, I had no desire to be crushed beneath racing hooves or carriage wheels. But the fellow had the grace and balance of a cat. He kept a firm grip on me while the second carriage drew closer, another man braced against the doorway.

Before I could so much as say, "I think not!" I was lugged like a bag of potatoes from one man to the next. The second man caught me with a slight *oomph,* and then we both tumbled back into the carriage.

I lay on the floor for a moment, trying to catch my breath and hoping I wouldn't be sick. Our carriage turned down a side street, leaving Bollingsworth and the other man racing off into the night.

I was torn between thanking the stranger who'd caught me and asking him what in the world he'd been thinking. Although I most fervently appreciated being rescued, I wasn't overly fond of the method. Surely the Chosen Keepers could have rescued me in a little less terrifying manner? I would have to speak with Wigmere about this.

The man who'd caught me reached up and removed his hood. "Hello, Theo. Sorry it took us so long to get to you."

I gasped. It wasn't one of the Chosen Keepers I'd been expecting.

It was Edgar Stilton!

CHAPTER NINETEEN

The Little Stilton That Could

"STILTON!"

"Yes. Sorry about the hood and all."

I was truly and utterly speechless. "But how . . . why . . . ?"

"Here, why don't you climb up off the floor and get comfortable. We'll be there in just a few moments and we will explain everything to you then."

"We? Who's 'we'?" I pushed myself up off the carriage floor and perched on the edge of the seat opposite Stilton. "And where's 'there'?"

"You'll see. I'm not allowed to explain it to you."

Well, surely if Wigmere had sent him, he could have told me, so that ruled out the chance that he worked for the

Brotherhood. I'd so been hoping they had been the ones to rescue me. Well, I was assuming it was a rescue. "Thank you for coming to my aid back there."

"Glad to do it, Miss Theo. We wouldn't want anything to happen to you."

We? Really, who was this "we" bit? "Did you, um, recognize the fellow in the carriage?"

Stilton frowned. "I'm afraid I didn't get a good look at him. Is he someone I'd know?"

I had no idea if I should tell him it had been Bollingsworth or not. How much did he know of Chaos, if he knew anything at all? "Not necessarily. I just thought, since you were rescuing me and all, you might have had an idea as to who you were rescuing me from."

"No," he said. "Just keeping you safe." And that was all I could get out of him until the carriage turned up Tottingham Court Road. Was he taking me back to the museum? Why hadn't he just said so?

However, the carriage trotted on by the museum, and with a sinking heart, I realized we weren't going there after all.

"I'm afraid I have to blindfold you," Stilton said apologetically. "Orders from higher up."

"Blindfold me? Why ever for?"

"The location of our temple is highly secret."

Temple? I didn't know of any temples in this neighborhood. Even so, surely I was better off with Stilton than with Bollingsworth. But when Stilton pulled a long strip of black cloth from his pocket and held it out to me, all my reassurances flew right out the window. "Turn around, please."

"Really. I won't breathe a word—"

"It's not my decision, Theo—otherwise I would never insist."

Not having much choice, I did as I was told. Stilton *had* rescued me, even if it had been for unknown reasons.

However, just because I was blindfolded didn't mean my mind had stopped working. I did my best to count turns and pay attention to the direction the carriage went in. Perhaps later, with a map in front of me, I could re-create our route.

With a jingle of a harness, the carriage pulled to a stop. "Here we are," he announced. There was a rustle of movement as he left his seat, then a click and a rush of cold air. The carriage rocked as he hopped out. "Put your hand in mine, Theo. I won't let you fall."

"Really—I promise I won't tell anyone where your temple is." I began grabbing at the blindfold, hoping to rip it off. "I can't possibly climb out of a carriage if I can't see."

A firm hand caught mine and pulled it back. "I'm sorry,

Theo. I can't let you do that. We'd both be in trouble then. Here." Stilton's hand grasped my elbow as he guided me gently out of the carriage. "Watch your step there—one more. There you go," he said as my foot finally connected with terra firma.

We shuffled across the sidewalk, and when we stopped abruptly, I bumped into Stilton. He grabbed my shoulders to steady me, then knocked on something solid. An odd knock, really—it had a strange little pattern to it, almost as if it was . . . code. But of course!

With a creak of a hinge, a door swung open. "What took you so long?"

"There was a bit of trouble, but Gerton and Whiting are taking care of it. Watch your step," Stilton warned me. "There're three stairs down."

Feeling helpless, I groped my way along the steps, my nerves strung tight. Then I was led down a maze of corridors —left, then right, then left twice more. I was hopelessly turned around, and just as I thought I was going to come unglued, someone yanked the blindfold from my head.

I blinked. I was standing in a long corridor, lit with black candles in sconces on the wall rather than gaslights.

"Are you all right?" Stilton asked, sounding concerned.

"Yes, just disoriented is all."

"Come along and we'll get you some explanations." He led the way down the hall. I followed, while two hooded men brought up the rear.

We went down a flight of steps that opened up into a huge chamber. It was also lit with candles, but still felt very gloomy. Once my eyes adjusted to the dimness, I noticed that there were a dozen cloaked, hooded figures standing in a semicircle up against the wall. One man stepped out from the shadows. He didn't have a hood, and the candlelight glinted off his shiny bald head.

"Were there any problems?" he inquired.

Stilton bowed low. "None that couldn't be handled, Supreme Master."

Supreme master? Oh, for goodness sake! What rubbish was this? "Who are all these people, Stilton?" I asked.

Ignoring my question, the bald man studied me with his rather wild-looking eyes. "You're quite sure?"

"Positive," Stilton said, his voice full of certainty.

Honestly! If he were half this confident back at the museum, he would have made Second Assistant Curator by now.

"But she is so young. Unmarked in any way."

Stilton shrugged. "Isis was young once, too."

"Isis? The Egyptian goddess? What has all this got to do with her?" I asked, my impatience growing.

"Do you know who we are, child?" the bald man asked.

I nearly stamped my foot in frustration. "How could I? Stilton hasn't told me a thing!"

He nodded in approval at Stilton, then threw his arms in a sweeping gesture. "We are the Arcane Order of the Black Sun." He paused dramatically, as if that should mean something to me. When I said nothing, he continued.

"We are the most secret of societies, dedicated to studying and understanding the wisdom and power of the ancients."

Another secret society? Honestly. Didn't anybody belong to a good old-fashioned club anymore? "Wisdom and power of the ancients?" I repeated. "Exactly which ancients are you referring to? There's so many of them, really."

He frowned at me. "The gods of the pharaohs, of course. We seek to discover their sacred doctrine and divine natures. To approach the temple of their ancient truths."

"Are you off your pins?" I asked.

The bald man looked at Stilton. "Are you sure you aren't mistaken?"

Stilton shook his head. "No, Supreme Master."

Some of the supreme master's fanatical glow faded. "I expected someone older. Taller. With more seriousness about her." He didn't even try to mask the disappointment in his voice.

And I had expected someone thinner, with more hair, but

was too polite to say so. "I'm very serious, Mr.—er, what did you say your name was? I never joke about Egyptian magic."

"My mundane name is Aloysius Trawley."

"It is true, Most Elevated Leader. She takes her magic very seriously."

I whirled around to face Stilton. "What do you know about me and my magic?"

"I know that you perform strong magic to keep the museum safe from the evil spirits who live there. I know you can raise the dead."

"Raise the dead?" Trawley's buggish eyes nearly popped out of his head.

"That creak on the stairs! That was you! Spying on me!"

Stilton had the good grace to blush. "I knew you were doing magic."

"How?" I demanded. "How did you know?" Was he like me, then? Able to detect magic?

But his supreme master interrupted us. "Will you show us your magic?" he asked, rubbing his hands in eagerness.

"No! Of course not. I don't do magic. I only remove curses."

"Perhaps you could do just a tiny bit of magic for us?" Trawley looked very much like my brother, Henry, asking for a second helping of Christmas pudding.

"No. I'm sorry. It's quite impossible." Especially because I no longer had the staff or the orb. "Is that why I'm here? Because you want me to do magic?"

Trawley bowed his head. "No, no. We only want to worship you, O Light Giver of Heaven."

Light giver of heaven? What *was* he jawing on about?

Seeing my perplexed look, he tried again. "We want to sit at your feet and learn of your wisdom, O Maker of Sunrise."

"Wisdom? What wisdom are you referring to? I'm only an eleven-year-old girl, and I've been told that wisdom is not my strong point."

Stilton stepped forward, threw himself onto his knees in front of me, and bowed low. Horrified, I backed up until I bumped into the wall behind me. "O Queen of All Gods, we will protect your secret. We will tell no one of your identity and only ask that we may serve you so that your light and wisdom may shine down upon us."

"Stilton," I hissed. "Get up! Get off the floor!"

But instead of Stilton getting to his feet, the others in the room began to drop to their knees as well. The last to do so was Trawley, and when he got to his knees, he didn't bow his head but instead looked me straight in the eye. "It is our greatest wish to serve you, Lady Isis."

"Isis," I echoed, my brain too stunned to work properly.

Stilton looked up from the floor. "Yes. We know your secret, but our lips are sealed. Unto death if it must be."

"My secret? What secret?" My voice squeaked and I cleared my throat, trying to fight the rising panic.

"Why, that you're Isis reincarnated, of course."

My jaw dropped, and I gaped at the Third Assistant Curator on his knees in front of me as I realized he was utterly, barking mad.

Any scholar knows that the Egyptians didn't believe in reincarnation!

CHAPTER TWENTY
THE SCORPION TAIL

THERE WAS A COMMOTION coming from the corridor. Trawley and Stilton jumped to their feet, then stepped in front, as if to shield me.

Three more cloaked figures came into the room. One of them seemed familiar. I was fairly certain it was the fellow who had hauled me like a sack of turnips from the carriage.

When the others saw who the newcomers were, they relaxed. "Report," Trawley said.

The tallest man stepped forward. "They got away. The driver leaped off the coach, and in the ensuing crash the other fellow gave Gerton the slip."

A broad, heavily muscled man spoke next. "He was right handy with a knife, O Great One, and it was close quarters."

Trawley looked at me with concern. "Who were these men, Divine Mistress? Do you know why they wished you harm?"

Did these men know about the Serpents of Chaos, I wondered? Did secret societies know about one another? Best not to risk it. "No, I don't." I decided to stick as close to the truth as possible. "I think the man in the carriage was a former employee of my father's. Someone he had to fire. Perhaps he held a grudge?"

"Ah," Trawley said. "Perhaps you don't trust us yet. Very wise, for one so young. But you may rest assured, we will not compromise you in any way. We shall not reveal your secrets. We wish only for the chance to worship Your Greatness and perhaps share a little in your wisdom."

Why did I think Trawley meant "magic" when he said "wisdom"?

"As a symbol of our trust, we will offer you protection against those who wish you ill."

"No, thank you. Really, I do much better on my own. I'm used to it."

"No, no. It is we who insist. We wish for nothing more than a chance to serve you. The least we can do is offer you some small protection against whoever it is that wishes you harm. In fact, we will assign seven scorpions to guard you, as of old."

"Yes," Stilton said, his face eager. "I'm Tefen and will walk by your side."

The three figures that had helped to rescue me from Bollingsworth stepped forward, too. "Ned Gerton at your service, miss. Me code name's Befen."

"I," said the tallest of the three, "am Basil Whiting, otherwise known as Mestafet. This gentleman here is Petet."

The man who had driven the carriage while the others whisked me to safety bowed low. "Peter Fell reporting for duty, miss."

Three other figures hopped up from their knees, like deranged jack-in-the-boxes, all shouting their scorpion names at me.

The seven men had, in fact, named the seven scorpions assigned to Isis by Thoth to be her bodyguards. Except I was *not* Isis. And Trawley was most certainly not Thoth.

They had to be joking. Didn't they? But they all stood at the ready, willing to obey my slightest command. I was beginning to get a headache.

"Tell us how we may prove ourselves to you," Trawley murmured. "How may we servest thou?"

"Look. You have it all wrong. I am not Isis." I turned to Stilton. "Whatever gave you that idea, anyway?"

Stilton raised his head. There was a smudge of dirt smack in the middle of his forehead. "I saw you raise the dead with my own eyes."

I paused. "You mean the mouse?" I asked.

He nodded eagerly. "Yes. The mouse, but the mummies, too."

I started to explain, then stopped. What if I managed to convince them I wasn't Isis—what then? They were willing to worship and adore me now, but that was only because they thought I had loads of power. What would they do if they thought me a fraud? Well, I wasn't really a fraud. But I certainly wasn't Isis. They might feel rather duped. Or tricked. Or just plain foolish if I managed to convince them I wasn't the ancient goddess.

Even more worrisome, how would they feel about having shared their secrets with a stranger? Especially an eleven-year-old stranger?

Their security was fairly tight, and they seemed to place great value on their secrecy. How would they treat me if they felt I had breached all that?

The truth was, I might not even make it out of here. I'd always trusted Edgar Stilton, but that had been before I knew he was off his nut.

My best course of action lay in letting them believe what they wanted to believe, commit to nothing, then get away as quickly as possible. I sighed. "Very well. I would be honored to accept your most, er, esteemed offer of help. And security." Besides, with the Serpents of Chaos about, one could never have too many friends on one's side. "But really, I must be getting back to the museum. My parents will be worried."

"She has been gone a long time," Stilton confirmed.

"Very well. Perhaps next time we meet, you will trust us enough to instruct us in the ways of Egyptian magic?" Trawley asked, his jowls trembling in excitement.

"We'll see. It may be difficult to get away. I do have a governess and parents who watch over me, you know. They might have something to say about this whole thing."

"Don't worry. We will be most discreet, O Illuminated One. And we will work at your convenience. Use Tefen here as a messenger and we will answer your calls at once."

The minute Stilton and I were alone in the carriage headed for the museum, I turned on him—or at least where I thought he'd be. It was hard to tell through the blindfold. "Just how long have you been spying on me, anyway?"

"Not spying, Theo. It's just that sometimes when I walked by the reading room, I saw you reading the ancient texts. Once in a while, you would even mutter the words out loud."

There was a short pause, then he continued. "At first I just wondered what you were up to, but then I began to realize that you were actually using the information, doing magic of your own."

"Not magic. Removing curses. Really, that's all I do."

Stilton nodded. "Removing curses, then." I felt him move forward on his seat, then blinked as he plucked the blindfold from my eyes. "You do realize it's more than that, don't you? I mean, not just anyone could look that stuff up, then read it out loud and have it work. That takes years of study, hours and hours of practice, to master."

"But why did you have to tell that man Trawley all about it?"

"Why, Theo, he's the grand master! He was the one who initiated me into the greater mysteries. I couldn't keep such knowledge to myself. I owe it to him to tell him whenever I encounter something of this nature."

My shoulders twitched. Somewhere out there in the dark, the other six scorpions were following us, trying to ensure my safety. I wondered who would protect me from *them*? Especially once they realized it was the staff that held all the power, not me.

The carriage pulled up in front of the museum and dropped me off. I waved goodbye to Stilton—or Tefen, as he insisted I call him when we were alone—and wondered how on earth I was going to face him in the morning. Did he have any idea how silly he and his fellow Black Sunners appeared?

Oh well. Best to think about that later. I had plenty on my plate for the rest of the evening—such as trying to come up with an explanation that would satisfy Mother and Father as to where I'd been for the past few hours.

All was quiet when I let myself into the museum, with no one wandering about calling my name. That was a good sign, at least.

I tiptoed down the hall to the foyer, which was also empty and quiet. My stomach growled, reminding me I was famished. I hadn't eaten since noon that day. I suppose it's a miracle I'm not stunted in my growth.

As I made my way to the sitting room, I rummaged around for a good excuse. Perhaps I'd just tell them that Miss Sharpe and I had gone out. But where? Where on earth would a governess have taken her student this late at night? Still no excuse at hand, I stopped outside the family room and listened. I didn't hear anything. No Mum humming, no Father regaling her with his most recent research news. Nothing. I sniffed. I didn't smell anything, either, which meant they'd not brought any dinner back with them.

I went into the sitting room and made myself two jam sandwiches, then began eating them in an appalling rush. There was so much to be *done*.

Halfway through my meal (although I wasn't sure two jam sandwiches properly qualified as a meal), I saw a crumpled newspaper tossed up against the hearth. Curious, I went and picked it up, brought it back to the table, and smoothed it out so I could read it.

LONDON PEPPERED WITH GOLD THEFTS

A number of thefts were reported last night, all claiming varying amounts of gold had been taken from the premises. From White Chapel to Hyde Park, people are missing their gold. As Cyrus Bentwillow told this reporter, "That gold was all I got. I bought it to protect me family from the mummies prowlin' the streets, and some blighter went an' stole it from me! What's this world coming to, I'd like to know."

Now I knew why the paper had been discarded. Father hated reading about the mummy situation!

Thinking of my father had me wondering if my parents had made it back yet. What if the horrid board of directors had had them hauled off to jail?

I shoved the last bite of sandwich into my mouth and hurried upstairs to the workroom on the third floor. Relief trickled through me as I heard the sound of Mother and Father talking.

"They're idiots, that's what the problem is," Father was saying. "None of them has the slightest interest in true history or scholarship. It's all a hobby to them. A game."

"Yes, it is," Mother agreed. "They clearly have no idea what's involved or why you wouldn't be hungering after their wretched mummies. Just how many times do you have to tell them that we already have so many, you've forbidden me to bring any more home?"

Father grunted. "Far too many."

"Hopefully this will be the end of it. I shudder to think what this has done to my chances with the Royal Archaeological Society."

"Well, if those mummies show up here one more time, Henrietta, I won't be held accountable for my actions."

That was easy for him to say now, I thought. He wasn't locked up tight in a jail cell as Inspector Turnbull had threatened. Which only confirmed the fact that I had lots to do in very little time in order to make sure Turnbull wouldn't have any reason to lock him up.

"Did you know Weems was a friend of Lord Chudleigh's when you hired him?" Mum asked.

"Gad, no," Father exclaimed. "That reference wouldn't have cut the mustard with me."

"Chudleigh seems to think very highly of him." I could tell by Mother's voice that she was reluctant to point that out.

"Chudleigh also thought very highly of his fake mummy."

"True," Mum said. "But still, I rather loathe the idea of Weems keeping Chudleigh apprised of our every move and decision. Especially under such trying circumstances."

Weems was an insufferable prig! With his intention of running the entire museum, the more trouble Father was in, the better things looked for Weems. Well, we'd have to see about that.

I listened for a few moments longer, disappointed when it became clear they'd never even realized I was gone. But this served my purpose perfectly, I assured myself. It was silly to feel put out that they didn't notice I was missing.

I made my way back past the Egyptian exhibit to the stairs, my mind churning. Now that the Serpents of Chaos had the staff and the orb, they would have the power to call all the mummies. Even if the mummies weren't gathered at our museum, Turnbull would still most likely suspect Father, not to mention we'd lose our entire collection. Which meant I had to find a way to protect our mummies from the powerful call of the staff.

Of course, the real trick was to figure out what on earth Chaos planned to do with a hundred mummies, but first things first.

My initial stop was the reading room. I needed to read over Archimedes's *The Power of Amulets: A Lost Art.*

When I arrived, who should I find there but Clive Fagenbush. And he was studying the back corner of the shelves, the very ones where I'd found all my information on mummies and Osiris.

I tried to retreat down the hall until he was done, but the old floor squeaked and gave me away. I winced as Fagenbush whirled around. "What are you doing here?" He scowled.

"Finishing up an essay for Miss Sharpe. What are you doing here?"

His scowl grew even deeper. "Researching something for one of the collections, of course. It is my job, if you recall."

"Yes, very well. Carry on."

But before I could leave, Fagenbush called out, "Wait! This section is missing quite a large number of books. You wouldn't happen to know where they are, would you?" he asked.

"No. But there are quite a lot of other curators around. Perhaps one of them was a little quicker in his duties and beat you to it."

Fagenbush's eyes narrowed at the insult. "Perhaps you've squirreled them away in your little *office*," he snarled.

"Oh, no. Those are just some books in Latin that Miss Sharpe wanted me to translate. Surely you don't need to practice your Latin, do you?"

I was half afraid he was going to barge in there and search my office, but my father being Head Curator must have held him back. "Very well," he said at last. Then he picked up the three books he had set aside. As he passed me, I craned my head, trying to get a look at the titles he was carrying, but he managed to cover them with his arm. Because I'd done that a hundred times myself, I knew he was doing it on purpose. The rat.

Clearly he was up to something. I wished I could have understood why Wigmere was so certain Fagenbush wasn't behind any of this. I would have to ask him again, next time I saw him.

But for now, I had some research to do. Wigmere had said that they'd found mention of the staff in old medieval grimoires. We had a few of those around here. Perhaps I should start with them.

I headed straight for the farthest, darkest corner of the reading room, where the oldest and most forgotten texts were jumbled together. These tended to be the ones Father and the other curators took the least seriously, but I found them invaluable.

There were a number of grimoires there: *Opus Majus* by Dr. Mirabilis, *The Black Pullet* by Johannes Faust (yes, *that* Faust!), *An Occult Philosophy* by Henreich Cornelius Agrippa, and *De Umbris Ideaum* by Bruno. But none of them touched on any magic of the pharaohs or ancient Egypt.

I picked up the last book. It was extremely old and bound in black leather that had faded and cracked with age. The pages were brittle and covered in a spidery Latin script.

Even though I'm much better at translating Greek and hieroglyphs than I am at Latin, I managed to muddle through the introduction. The author was Silvus Moribundus, a medieval occultist who was translating an ancient Egyptian papyrus written by Nectanebo II's head priest and magician, Sephotep. The name brought me up cold.

Sep was the name of the god of chaos. And the suffix *hotep* meant "pleased." So if a priest was named Sephotep, then it wasn't good. Not at all. It meant he was very adept at creating chaos. A small shiver of apprehension ran through me. The only good thing was that if anyone would have the answers as to what would make mummies walk in this world again, it would surely be the god of chaos.

My fingers tingled in anticipation. This book could well possess secrets not found anywhere else! What on earth had it been doing stuffed in a forgotten corner?

However, I had more urgent business to attend to right then. I slipped the grimoire inside Miss Sharpe's copy of Virgil and got to my amulet research.

Nearly an hour later, I pushed the volume away with a sigh of disgust. There had been nothing in there on how to protect mummies against the Staff of Osiris. I guess this made sense, now that I thought about it, as none of the books even acknowledged the staff's existence.

Even more disturbing, all of the normal amulets of general protection could actually end up making things worse! The healing eye of Horus, for example, could very well end up healing the mummies, and what if it "healed" them back to life? Disastrous!

And my other trusty favorite, the ankh, was just as useless in this instance. It was the Egyptian symbol for life, and I most assuredly did not want these mummies any more lively.

This meant I would have to improvise, and that was always a tricky business. In the end, I decided the best course was to use a simple Blood of Isis amulet for each of our mummies. Whoever possessed the amulet was said to be protected by Isis from all other magical influence.

However, the Blood of Isis amulet required a red stone,

either carnelian or jasper. Even red glass would do in a pinch. But could I find enough for all the mummies? Thirteen on display, plus seven in the catacombs. That made twenty—well, twenty-one counting Tetley.

I quickly jotted down the recipe, then dashed to my closet to check my supplies. I knew I had some carnelian and jasper in my curse-removal kit, as well as a length of gold wire.

Unfortunately, there were distressingly few bits of red stone in there: nine tiny pieces of carnelian and only four pieces of red jasper. Which meant I'd have to hunt something up for the other eight amulets. In the middle of the night, no less.

Honestly! I deserved a fancy medal like the one Admiral Sopcoate wore pinned to his chest.

The best selection of stones was bound to be up in the workroom on the third floor. Unfortunately, so were Mother and Father, who would ask all sorts of awkward questions. That left short-term storage down by Receiving. Hardening my resolve and trying very hard not to think of Nigel Bollingsworth skulking through the museum in the dark, I stood up.

Isis, who'd been wrapped around my ankles, meowed in protest. Remembering her excellent stint at guard duty the night before, I whispered, "Is there anyone else out there?

Care to check for me?" Although really, what was the point? It wasn't as though cats ever did anything you asked them to.

But Isis blinked her golden eyes at me, then sauntered out into the hallway. Brilliant! I followed cautiously as she led me down the hall toward the stairs.

When we reached the short-term storage area, I turned up the gaslights, the familiar hiss of gas filling up the eerie silence.

While Isis began prowling around the corners looking for mice, I went over to the old, battered Canopic jar on the shelf where I stored stray bits. There were two more pieces of jasper in there. Excellent. That made fifteen—only six more red stones and I'd have enough.

I crossed over to the worktable, wondering if anything from Amenemhab's tomb would work. There was a lovely spread-wing pectoral amulet, but it was in good condition, and as badly as I needed those red stones, I wasn't going to destroy a perfectly good artifact.

I knelt down to examine a crate under the worktable and began picking through the contents. An old silver mirror, an eye-makeup palette, six little scarabs (none of them red), and a flint-bladed knife. Then, far in the bottom corner, I found something.

It was an elaborate falcon-headed collar made up of rows and rows of cylindrical faience beads. Red faience beads, to be exact. But many of them were loose. Usually things in these crates were items that were of a low priority, either too broken or damaged or unimportant to be worked on until the rest of the dig's artifacts had been prepared for exhibit. Which meant I could most likely borrow six of the beads to make the Blood of Isis amulets, then return them once the Staff of Osiris had been . . . what? Returned? Located? Well, I could return the beads later.

I worked the loose beads free from the setting, then slipped them into my pocket. Just then Isis meowed, and I heard a squeak on the stairs. I froze as a beam of torch light flashed on the wall. "Hello? Who's down here?"

It was Flimp!

"It's just me! I was looking for Isis!" I reached down and picked her up for emphasis. She began purring and rubbing her head against my arm.

"Oh, sorry, miss. Gave me a scare, you did, what with all the strange goings-on lately."

"I'm sorry, Flimp. I didn't mean to."

"You'd best scamper back up to the sitting room and wait for your parents. Until the police find out who's behind all this recent mischief, you shouldn't be wandering around alone so late."

"Excellent point, Flimp! Thank you. I'm coming up right now." Holding Isis firmly in my arms, I scurried up the stairs, not liking one bit Flimp's reminder about how unsafe the museum was at the moment. As if battling the normal everyday *mut* and *akhu* weren't enough, now I had evildoers to contend with as well!

Back in my carrel, I quickly settled down to make the amulets. I had no idea how long it would take Chaos to activate the staff and start using it, but I was guessing not long.

Ideally, I would have liked to have carved the stones into the shape of a *tyet*, which basically looks like a knotted rope. However, I wasn't much good at carving and didn't have the time. Instead, I cut twenty-one small pieces from the last of my gold wire and fashioned them into the *tyet* shape.

Next, using sticky sap from a silver birch (it should really have been the sap of a *nh-imy* plant, but I didn't have access to one of those, whereas we had plenty of birch trees at nearby parks), I dabbed a bit on the red stones, then pressed the gold wire *tyets* into the sap, making sure they were secure and wouldn't fall off.

When I was done, I had exactly twenty-one amulets. Perfect. Now I had to invoke the spell that would make these work.

I glanced back at the book and committed the ancient words of power to memory. Then, not wanting to repeat any unpleasant incidents such as the one that had happened last winter, when I accidentally directed a foul curse into *her*, I checked to see where Isis was. She was safely curled up by the door. Certain she was out of harm's way, I began to chant.

"For you who wear this, the power of Isis shall be the magical protection of your limbs and Horus the son of Isis shall rejoice. The way will be blocked against you, and you shall be protected against any who would do you harm or cause you an abomination."

There. That ought to do it. All I needed now were pieces of bast to string them around the mummies' necks. Once again I had to substitute what I had on hand, which was quite a bit of raffia from two summers ago when my best straw bonnet fell apart. (In spite of what Father claimed, I had had no idea that fiddling with the loose end would have caused the entire thing to unravel!)

Once all twenty-one amulets were strung onto raffia, I placed them in my pocket, careful not to tangle them. Now I just had to put them on the mummies, and my night's work would be done.

I left the reading room, trying to decide whether to begin with the Egyptian exhibit or down in the catacombs. It seemed best to get the most unpleasant part out of the way first, much like eating one's Brussels sprouts before pudding.

As I stepped into the foyer, there was a faint rustling, as if the shadows were sighing. Reminding myself that I had twenty-two Blood of Isis amulets on me, not to mention my normal three, I glanced overhead at the skylights and saw that thick cloud cover had thoroughly hidden the moon. That cinched it. Best to visit the catacombs now while the moonlight was as dormant as possible, lest it wake any spirits. Although it was true that none of the actual moonlight shone in the catacombs, sometimes curses didn't need the light itself, only the power of the moon.

Isis was still avoiding the catacombs, so I descended the stairs alone, relieved when I didn't hear any restless stirrings. At the foot of the steps, I turned on the gaslight, grateful for even that feeble light.

The mummies were where I'd left them, which was a good sign. Apparently Chaos hadn't activated the staff. Yet.

I pulled the first amulet from my pocket and wrapped it around the neck of Rahotep, a powerful Third Dynasty priest, murmuring the spell once again just for good measure. I moved to the next mummy and the next, murmuring the spell each time until I finally came to the last of them.

Done with the scary part, I went up to the Egyptian exhibit and paused when I came to Statuary Hall. All the shadows looked darker somehow, and the air felt more restless. I was convinced that at least one of the visiting mummies had left their severely disgruntled *akhu* behind. I was going to have to do a *mut* sweep and see if I could trap it.

But that would be for another day. Taking a deep breath, I said a little prayer, then hurried down the hallway, looking neither to the left nor the right. The rustling grew louder, and at the very edges of my vision, I could see shadows detach themselves from corners and begin to follow me.

I picked up my pace, nearly breaking into a run to get to the exhibit room.

Not that it was much better. There was creaking and groaning going on in there, too. It was the sort that grownups brushed off as the building settling, but if you listened carefully enough, you could hear the rise and fall of murmured voices in chant, as if beseeching the gods or reciting a prayer—or a curse.

Well, the sooner I was done, the sooner I could leave. Starting with the New Kingdom mummy of Ipuki, an official during the reign of Seti I, I tied the raffia string around his neck so that the Blood of Isis amulet sat against his throat, then slipped the amulet under the edge of the linen wrappings so it wouldn't be immediately visible. When I was happy with the placement, I moved down to the next mummy, Suten-Ahnu, royal scribe to Sensuret I. And so I worked, trying not to think about what I was doing and moving as quickly as I could.

The unwrapped mummies were the most difficult to work on, their glassy eyes staring at me from old, dried-up skin, their mouths pulled back into leering grimaces. *Don't think about her, don't think about her*, I chanted as I strung an amulet around Henuttawy, an Eighteenth Dynasty priestess from the temple of Sekhmet. When I finally got the amulet around her neck, I pulled away quickly and shuddered, hoping if her *ba* was still hovering about, it wouldn't take offense.

When I reached Heneu, vizier to Queen Sobekneferu, I caught wind of voices. I paused in my work, trying to hear better.

Relief spurted through me when I realized it was only my parents, and I returned to my duties. As I placed one of the amulets on Meri-Tawy (royal architect and priest who served the god Ptah), I realized my hand was shaking. Thank goodness he was the last one.

Exhausted, I hurried back to my closet, hoping to catch a bit of sleep before morning came.

CHAPTER TWENTY-ONE
A TEST OF WILLS

FAR TOO EARLY THE NEXT MORNING, I was awakened by a soft rap on my closet door. "Who is it?" I asked, sitting up and rubbing my eyes.

"It's Miss Sharpe, lazybones."

The sound of Miss Sharpe's voice woke me up as thoroughly as a pitcher of cold water poured over my head. Come to think of it, that might just be what she was planning.

I hopped out of the sarcophagus and hurried to the washstand. "Coming!" I called out.

When I heard the door open, I fumbled for a towel and

ended up using my extra pinafore in my haste. "Theodosia, why on earth aren't you up yet? Oh my!"

Miss Sharpe studied my small room with a look of marked distaste. "This will never do," she announced. "Everyone knows that a bedroom should be spacious, dry, and airy. Not some small, dank corner like this." She put her hands on her hips and shook her head. "We simply must get you out of this museum before it's too late."

I wanted to ask, "Too late for what?" but was certain I wouldn't like the answer. Instead, I followed Miss Sharpe to the reading room, where I was forced to begin my lessons without any breakfast. ("No breakfast for lazy girls who can't bestir themselves from their slumber!" were Miss Sharpe's exact words.)

The only good thing about the morning was that I was able to pretend to be working on translating Virgil's *Bucolics* while I was really translating Moribundus's grimoire.

Even with my familiarity with Latin, it was fairly slow going. Moribundus did have a tendency to ramble on and on about ancient secrets accessible to only a learned few. But finally, halfway through the morning, I came across the word *baculu*—the Latin word for staff. At last he was discussing the Staff of Osiris. Farther on, my eyes caught the word *necro*.

I didn't need my dictionary for that one! I recognized the prefix *nec* from the words *necropolis* and *necromancer*. *Necro* meant "death." My sense of discovery heightened, I kept going, excitement mounting. *To extinguish the flame of eternal life, turn the jackal on his head and let Nun swallow him whole.*

Was he really saying that the staff could be used to kill as well as to resurrect? The idea was so shocking, I was half afraid Miss Sharpe would sense me reading it. I cast a furtive glance her way, but she was still reading about womanly virtue.

Nun was the Egyptian god of the primordial waters from which all life sprang. Suddenly, I remembered Wigmere's tale of Rameses III using the staff to create a Fog of War that prevailed over his enemies. I flipped back to the page and double-checked my translation.

Not only was I correct, but Moribundus was giving veiled instructions as well. If one turned the staff upside down and submerged it in water, it could be used to kill.

And frankly, killing sounded much more up Chaos's alley than resurrecting!

This wasn't good. Not good at all. Chaos had had the staff for only one day now, but from what I knew of the Serpents of Chaos, it wouldn't take long for them to put it to use.

I had to get this information to Wigmere.

Once again I glanced at Miss Sharpe. How could I get free of her long enough to get a message to Will?

If she thought I wanted a walk, she'd be certain not to give it to me. Therefore, I had to be rather sneaky. "Excuse me," I said around a yawn.

"Cover your mouth," Miss Sharpe instructed without looking up.

I refrained from pointing out that I *had* and if she'd bothered to look, she would have seen it. Instead, using my most pathetic voice, I said, "I'm so sorry, Miss Sharpe, but I'm afraid my head has begun to ache terribly. Could I possibly go lie down?"

Miss Sharpe laid her book down on the table and studied me. "I think not. No, Little Miss Lazybones does not need extra sleep. What she needs is exercise. I think it's time for a walk. Let's get our wraps, shall we?"

"If you say so." I tried to look disappointed, but in truth, I was ecstatic. If we went out for a walk, there was a good chance Will would spot us and I could signal to him that I had a message to be delivered.

Miss Sharpe stood up. "Come along, then."

I shoved to my feet and followed her to the coat rack.

"How is that Latin text translation coming?" she asked, putting on her wrap.

"Very well, thank you. I should be done in another day or two."

"Excellent. I can't wait for you to read it to me so I can enjoy the fruits of your labors."

But of course, I had no intention of sharing Moribundus's treatise on ancient artifacts of power with her. And not just because she would think it was ancient Egypt's version of a penny dreadful—the grimoire was too full of ugly, dangerous magic to even think of uttering aloud.

When we stepped outside, we were met by a brisk if biting wind. I noticed there were quite a lot of people milling about in the square. It took me a moment to recognize Will, who was masquerading as a chimney sweep, his face half covered in soot. When our eyes met, he doffed his cap.

To the right of the museum entrance, a wide, stocky man in an ill-fitting morning suit sat on a bench under a beech tree. He looked vaguely familiar, and I finally realized it was Ned Gerton, code name Befen. Loitering in the doorway across the street was Basil Whiting (Mestafet), and Peter Fell (Petet) manned a pie cart.

Just what I needed—a troop of occultists following me about.

I glanced back at Will, wondering what he'd make of all the extra gentlemen, as I hadn't had a chance to explain yet about the scorpions, but my pulse quickened at the tall, lean form lurking against a lamppost a few feet behind him. The Grim Nipper!

"Theodosia? Are we going to walk or loiter?" Miss Sharpe's voice called my attention back to the matter at hand, and together we began to walk toward Cavendish Square. I couldn't help but wonder if Will even knew the Grim Nipper was there. It was clear that drastic action on my part was called for.

Grateful for the barrier of my heavy woolen coat between my arm and Miss Sharpe's pincher fingers, I took a deep breath, skipped ahead a few paces, then spun around to face Miss Sharpe. Walking backwards allowed me to keep an eye on all the goings-on behind me.

"What are you doing, Theodosia?" She glanced around, worried that someone would see my odd behavior. "Turn around before you trip and fall."

"Oh, I won't, Miss Sharpe! This is very good practice for balance, you know. In fact, it was my Grandmother Throckmorton who taught me this trick. You see, if a girl can walk backwards without tripping and stumbling, then she can certainly walk gracefully when doing it in the normal way." The whole time I chattered, my eyes darted behind Miss Sharpe, trying to locate all the players. Gerton had just gotten up from his bench, folded his paper under his arm, and begun sauntering behind us.

Will had pulled his cap low over his head and put the chimney broom over his shoulder. He walked slowly but purposefully, as if he were on the way to a job.

"Your grandmother never taught you any such thing," Miss Sharpe said. "Now we must add lying to your list of faults."

Miss Sharpe may have been a horrid cow, but she was nobody's fool, I'd give her that. "Oh, really she did! She said it was a good way to prepare oneself for . . . dancing! That's it! Dancing is quite a lot like walking backwards, isn't it, Miss Sharpe." I paused. "You *have* been dancing before, haven't you?"

"Of course I've been dancing. But this ridiculous game of yours will do nothing to prepare you for that."

The Grim Nipper moved out of the shadows and slunk forward a few paces before scuttling into a doorway, just like a greasy shadow. Will seemed oblivious, but that could have been to keep the Grim Nipper off-guard.

Another figure appeared, this one quite small and sporting a large bowler. Snuffles was trailing behind the Grim Nipper. Thankfully, someone had Will's back. Although what an undersize eight-year-old could do to fend off the Grim Nipper, I wasn't sure. Perhaps he could sneeze at him.

As we neared the park, I noticed the Nipper drawing closer to Will. As I was wondering what Miss Sharpe would do if I called out a warning, the Grim Nipper put on a burst of speed. Just as I opened my mouth to yell (I'd decided to risk Miss Sharpe's curiosity), the Nipper grabbed Will's collar and yanked him into an alley. I squeaked.

"Theo? Are you all right?" Miss Sharpe asked.

Then, almost without conscious thought, as if my body had come up with the idea all on its own, I pretended to get my feet all tangled up and tripped. "Ow!" I said, screwing my face up tight and clutching my ankle.

Miss Sharpe stopped walking, folded her arms across her middle, and pinched her lips in disapproval. "I warned you nothing good would come of walking backwards."

Honestly! Can no grownup resist saying, "I told you so"? I groaned as if in pain.

Miss Sharpe looked around, clearly unsure what to do. Finally, she knelt down and gave my ankle a sharp prod.

"I think I may have sprained it," I said.

She sniffed. "That is what happens to odd ducks who waddle backwards."

For a moment I was seized by an overwhelming desire to quack at her. Odd duck, indeed. Instead, I said meekly, "I'm sorry, Miss Sharpe."

"Do you think you could hobble back to the museum?"

I shook my head.

"I suppose you could lean on me," she suggested with a look that said she'd rather clean chamber pots without her gloves.

"I don't think so," I rushed to say. "I'm much heavier than I look." The whole point was to get rid of her for a few moments so I could go find out what had happened to Will.

She glanced around the square. "I can't very well just leave you here."

"Oh, but you can! Don't forget—my parents let me go out and about on my own as long as I don't cross Oxford Street, and we're nowhere near Oxford Street. Besides," I said, playing my trump card, "it's hardly *your* fault, what with me being an odd duck and all." I hung my head humbly for good measure.

"Well, you're right about that part, anyway."

Would the beastly woman never leave? Will was in danger.

"Very well. I'll return to the museum and see if I can get one of the servants to bring round a cart."

"That would probably be best," I agreed. "I'll be right here when you get back," I assured her. But as soon as Miss Sharpe was out of sight, I leaped to my perfectly fine feet and made a mad dash for the alley down which I'd seen Will and the Nipper disappear.

Basil Whiting was just nearing the entrance when I reached it. "Stay there!" I hissed at him. I did not need to involve the Black Sunners in Will's problems. Whiting gave a curt nod as I slipped past him.

At first the narrow brick alley seemed empty, but then halfway toward the far end I saw the Nipper leaning into a doorway with Will pressed up against the door, shaking his head.

As silently as possible, I made my way toward a large pile of rubbish. I squatted down behind it so I wouldn't be spotted, then strained my ears to listen, but it was hard to hear over the pounding of my heart.

"You ain't been avoiding me, 'ave you, Willie, me boy?"

"N-no. Course not. Just been busy, that's all."

There was a loud, wet sniff somewhere off to my left. Snuffles must be nearby.

"Busy wif that new job o' yours, eh?" the Grim Nipper said. "Them fancy pants keeping you too busy for your old gig, then?"

Before Will could answer, the Nipper twisted the bunch of Will's collar he held in his fist, cutting off his reply. "These fancy pants of yours have led me to a right sweet gig now, they 'ave. People are taking their gold out of all their hidey places so as it'll protect 'em against these mummies, see. I'm tellin' you, Willie boy. There's plenty o' work for someone with fingers as light as yours."

"I-I got a new job, Nip! All the work I can handle."

"That's too bad, now, Willie, 'cause I'm needing an extra pair of hands to pluck with."

"Sorry, Nip."

He shoved Will against the door so hard, I heard the thunk as Will's head connected with the wood. "That's not the answer I was looking for, Willie boy. I'll give you another day or two to think on it. And next time, you won't let me down again or you won't like the consequences."

Then the Nipper shoved his hands into his pockets and left the alley, walking right by the rubbish heap. I shrank back against the turnip tops and ashes and made myself as small as possible.

The Nipper was trying to pressure Will into returning to his pickpocketing ways. That's why Will had been wearing disguises and keeping a low profile. He wasn't hiding from the police—he was hiding from the Grim Nipper!

I stood up, wanting to talk to Will, but he was already at the far end of the alley, making a quick getaway in the opposite direction.

To make matters worse, just then I heard Miss Sharpe's voice calling, "Theodosia?"

Drat and bother! I scurried back to the main street, being sure to hobble convincingly. Luckily, when I reached the sidewalk, she was looking the other way. "Here I am, Miss Sharpe."

She whirled around. "You're walking," she said, her tone accusing.

"Yes! Isn't it grand? It appears it was only a twist, not an actual sprain."

She didn't look as though she thought it grand at all. She seemed quite disappointed that I wasn't writhing in pain.

"Dolge said he'd be over as soon as he was free, but now it's clear you've just wasted everyone's time. Come along." She turned her back to me and began walking to the museum at a brisk clip, never looking over her shoulder to be sure I was following.

Even so, I made sure to limp all the way back to the museum, just for good measure.

We spent the rest of the afternoon doing sums. I loathe sums. Not because they're hard. In fact, they're quite easy. But governesses always make you do scads and scads of them—for practice, they say. Honestly. It's not as if the numbers have changed their values since the last time you did sums! The answers still work out the same way. Besides, I was anxious to meet up with Will. Hopefully, he and Snuffles had made their way back to the museum and were waiting for me to get them a message.

I had to find another way to get free of Miss Sharpe, at least for a few minutes. Deciding desperate measures were required, I cleared my throat. "Miss Sharpe? Could I be excused for a bit? I have to . . . use the facilities."

She blushed slightly at my indelicacy, as did I. It was mortifying to tell someone I needed to go to the loo, but it was too important that I speak to Will. I was willing to suffer the pangs of embarrassment (just one of the many sacrifices I had to make). "I might be a while," I added, patting my stomach. "Last night's dinner didn't agree with me." Then I disappeared out the door so she wouldn't see the mortification flaming in my cheeks.

And unfortunately, I came nose to nose with Stilton, who was lurking right outside. No doubt trying to protect me.

Had he heard my miserable excuse? I was afraid he had— he stepped away rather hastily and let me pass. The requirements for covert operations weren't for the faint-hearted or overly modest, let me tell you.

Once I was away from the prying eyes of curators and scorpion bodyguards, I rushed over to the west entrance, where, just as I'd hoped, Will was waiting.

I scanned the area to be sure we were alone. No Grim Nipper, no watchful scorpions—only Snuffles a short distance back, wiping his nose on his sleeve. "It's clear," I whispered.

Will popped up like a bobbing cork, then followed me inside.

"Am I glad to see you!" I said. "Although I haven't much time. I'm expected back at my studies in a moment or two."

"Well, quit jawing and spill it, then."

I blinked. Will wasn't normally this prickly. "Very well. There's some information you must get to Wigmere. Tell him according to a Dr. Moribundus, the staff not only has the power to raise the dead, but to kill as well. When it's submerged in water, I think it creates the Fog of War."

Will whistled.

"Exactly! Now you see why I was so desperate to meet up with you!"

"I'll get this news to him right away, miss."

"Good. Hopefully he'll know what our next move should be. Were you followed this morning?"

His face went immediately blank. "Followed?"

"Yes. By that Grim Nipper fellow who's been at your heels all week."

Will's face paled at the name. "I don't know what yer talkin' about, miss."

"Oh, don't be ridiculous! I saw the two of you arguing earlier today, over by Cavendish Square."

Will narrowed his eyes. "'Ave you been followin' me?"

"Of course not! But when you're following me, and someone else is following you, I can't help but see. And you are most definitely being followed. And then today I accidentally overheard you two talking."

Will snorted. "Accidentally, my bum. You're a blooming eavesdropper, you are!"

I gasped. "Am not," I said automatically. (Although, of course, I am. But only for the best of causes. Like a friend being in trouble.)

"Are too. A wretched busybody, you are. I'll thank you to keep your nose out o' my business."

"But I was worried about you! I heard Inspector Turnbull talking about the Grim Nipper. He sounds like a horrid person, and I hate the idea of him jeopardizing your new job with Wigmere."

"I can take care of me own self. You just stay out of my business. Now, you got anything else for Wiggy?"

"No, but—"

"That's all, then. I gotta go," he huffed.

"Wait!"

"What?"

"I wanted to give you this. It's for Snuffles."

Will looked down at the clean white handkerchief in my hand. "We don't take no 'andouts."

Stung by his rejection of my gift, I shoved it at him, snatching my hand back just as he closed the door, leaving a tangle of bad feelings in his wake.

I heard a grunt and a scuffle. "It's mine!" a muffled young voice said. "She gave it to me! I 'eard!"

"Oy—if'n you want it that bad, you can 'ave it," was Will's equally muffled reply, and then all fell silent.

Well, at least Wigmere would get the message about the staff. Will wouldn't be so mad that he'd ignore his job duties, would he?

I lifted my chin. I wasn't going to let one prickly hedgehog of a pickpocket get under my skin. I'd simply have to deal with this alone, as I had most of the problems I'd encountered in my life.

And my next step was to find out what Chaos had planned for the staff. No matter how I looked at it, I simply couldn't come up with a decent explanation as to why they needed so many mummies. No, their reason for wanting the staff had to be tied up with its darker, more evil powers. It was all too easy to accept that Chaos would have occasion to use the staff to kill. The problem was, I couldn't be expected to provide all of London with Blood of Isis amulets, now, could I? Of course not.

As I passed the medieval exhibit, I heard Miss Sharpe trilling for me. Remembering how much she loathed raising her voice due to its not being ladylike, I kept quiet, hoping to force her to screech.

"Theodosia! Your presence is required in the reading room at once! We've lessons to attend to!" The tone of her voice promised immediate retribution. I glanced longingly at the chain-mail shirts hanging nearby. Wouldn't those provide lovely protection against Sharpe's pinches! Unfortunately, Father would be most irate if I began wearing six-hundred-year-old chain mail. I did, however, snag my coat off the rack as I passed. It was thick, sturdy wool and would help dampen any vicious little reminders from Miss Sharpe's bony fingers.

I really needed to find a way to get rid of her. Right after I discovered what Chaos was up to.

CHAPTER TWENTY-TWO
A JACKAL ON THE LOOSE

THE NEXT MORNING I got up extra early, even before our maid knocked on my door. Although I usually slept much better in my own comfortable bed than in the sarcophagus, I'd ended up tossing and turning the whole night. Trying to put the time to good use, I'd come up with a couple of plans of action.

I loved having plans. They gave me hope.

Plan #1: Rid museum of newest vile spirit before it settled in for a long stay.

Plan #2: See if Wigmere assigned spies to Chaos to determine what their next move would be. I simply couldn't do it all by myself, and I was stuck until I executed . . .

Plan #3: Get rid of Miss Sharpe as soon as possible, as she was sorely getting in the way of my truly important work.

It was my most sincere hope that my parents and I would arrive at the museum before Miss Sharpe did so I'd have a chance to tackle the new angry spirit. But first I needed to conduct a purification ritual—just like the priests of ancient Egypt had done before they performed serious magic. Ideally, one should do this every time one is going to do any magic, but the truth is, one can't always predict this sort of thing. But on this day, I planned to be as ready as possible.

THEODOSIA'S QUICK AND SPEEDY PURIFICATION RITUAL

1. Remove any wool or leather clothing. Wear nothing that has come from an animal of any kind.

2. Wash face, neck, hands, and behind the ears with fresh water. (It should really come from the Nile, but because that was impractical when living in London, I used fresh water from the pitcher on the washstand.)

3. Put on clean linens. (Just for the record, I did put on clean linens every day. Well, every day when I was home and had access to them.)

4. Rinse mouth with natron. (Only, I substituted salt— it was wretchedly difficult to get a hold of natron.)

Once I was properly purified, I slipped into a heavy serge frock and combed my hair. Just then, our maid came into the room. "Oh! You're all ready, miss!"

"Yes, Betsy, I wanted to get a jump on the day. Are my parents up yet?"

"Yes, miss. They just sat down to breakfast."

Excellent. That meant Father was wanting to get to the museum early, which coincided nicely with my own plans and saved me from having to try to convince him.

At breakfast, I saw that Cook had prepared a rasher of bacon to accompany our eggs. In an act of fortitude rarely possessed by one as young as I, I did not put any on my plate, even though bacon was my favorite breakfast food. It was because of the wretched purification thing. Ancient Egyptians were prohibited from consuming the oxyrinchus fish. I didn't even have access to oxyrinchus fish, but it felt as if I had to substitute something. I knew many cultures considered pork to be unclean, so I figured it was the next closest thing.

With a self-pitying sigh, I heaped extra eggs onto my plate, grateful that they, at least, were not considered unclean. A girl couldn't be expected to face evil spirits and curses on oatmeal alone.

Mum glanced at my plate as I sat down. "No bacon, dear?"

"Not this morning, I think. I'm not all that hungry."

Father peeked out around his newspaper. "Then why have you put a small mountain of eggs on your plate?"

Father did pick the most inconvenient times to become observant. Thankfully, there was a timely pounding at the front door.

Father scowled, my eggs quickly forgotten. "Who on earth could that be?"

Mother picked up her napkin and gently dabbed her mouth. "I have no idea," she murmured.

I began shoveling eggs in as fast as I could. A visitor during breakfast was not a good sign. There was a very good chance the meal would be over within minutes.

We all listened as Betsy went to see who it was. Shouting ensued. I bolted down my eggs even faster. Seconds later, our harried-looking housemaid reappeared. "There's an Inspector Turnbull to see you, sir. I asked him to wait, but he was most insistent on—"

"Throckmorton? Where are you?" Turnbull's voice boomed off the walls of the breakfast room. "By gad, you've gone too far this time."

Furious at this intrusion, Father stood up so fast that he knocked his chair over. "What are you doing here at this hour? And what are you blathering on about, anyway?"

"The mummies! You've taken all the mummies again!"

Father threw his napkin down onto the table like a gauntlet. "I have not!"

"Well, they've all gone missing again!" Turnbull shoved past Betsy, who looked undecided as to whether she should stand aside or try to block the man's entrance.

"What makes you so sure I'm the one to have taken them?"

"Because I headed for your museum first thing and forced that watchman of yours to let me in. Oddly enough, you're the only man in all of London who still has his mummies! That's too big a coincidence for me, Throckmorton."

The amulets! The very thing I'd done to protect our mummies was now incriminating Father! The eggs in my stomach wobbled unpleasantly.

"Nonsense," Father said. "We just have better security than the other places."

Turnbull snorted through his mustache. "I have half a mind to haul you down to headquarters right now."

"On what grounds?" Father thundered back. Honestly. It was like listening to a fight between two bull moose.

"I don't know yet, but I'll find them. Where were you last night?"

"Here in my own home with my wife."

Turnbull turned his hot, angry gaze to Mum, who nodded her confirmation.

He dismissed it with a brusque wave of his hand. "It's not

like you'd tell me if your husband snuck out for a couple of hours, is it?" he scoffed. With one final glare of disgust, he stormed out.

Father stared after him for a moment. "We're leaving for the museum. Now."

It was a tense, silent ride to the museum. When we arrived, we were greeted by an even bigger crowd than the last time.

"Perhaps it would be better if we went around to the side entrance," Mother suggested.

But Father was in high dudgeon. "I will not run from this rabble, Henrietta. I have nothing to hide."

A wall of constables lined up against the museum kept the crowd at bay. We alighted from the carriage and began working our way toward them. Lord Snowthorpe was in the thick of it, as were a few of the newspaper reporters who'd been here three days earlier. I spotted Peter Fell—Petet—and quickly looked away. I did not want to deal with my scorpion bodyguards at the moment, even though, if the crowd's mood was any indication, we might need them.

"What 'ave ye done wi' our gold?" a heavyset man in a butcher's apron called out.

"Burn all the mummies!" an older woman with a sour face

cried. She was dressed all in black and brandishing an umbrella.

Father began using his cane (none too gently, I'm afraid) to force the crowd to make way. With one final shove, we reached the entrance. Constable Biggs recognized us immediately. "Inspector Turnbull is waiting," he informed us.

Once inside, I saw Father look at the far wall, frowning when he saw it was empty of mummies. "Well, where are they, then?" he asked.

Vicary Weems stepped forward. "They're all still in the exhibit room, where they belong. Sir," he added as an afterthought. He looked suspiciously cheerful, almost as if he were calculating just how much his salary might be when he took over Father's position.

Interrupting Father's conversation with Weems, Turnbull addressed all of us in the foyer. "No one leaves until I question them, understood? Beaton! Kimble! Search the entire building. If there are any mummies that don't belong here, I want to know about it immediately. Biggs, you get everybody lined up for questioning. I'm talking to everyone personally." He glowered at us all from under his bushy eyebrows, as if daring us to disagree.

This was going to put a big fat crimp in my ability to sweep the museum free of evil spirits. The redheaded policeman,

Beaton, headed upstairs to conduct his search. The second man, Kimble, headed down the hall toward the loading dock. He paused when he came to the door leading to the catacombs. "What's down here, then?" he asked.

Weems and Fagenbush looked at each other while Stilton glanced over at Father before speaking. "It's the basement, sir. Where we store items not currently on display."

Turnbull narrowed his beady eyes. "Any mummies down there?" Turnbull asked Father.

Father glanced over at me. "Um, yes. If I remember correctly, there are . . ."

I sneezed.

"Bless you," Mum muttered.

"Go on," Turnbull said to Father.

I sneezed again. And again. And again. Then four more times.

"Eight!" Father said, his voice firm. "There are eight mummies in the basement." Excellent! He'd gotten my message. Sometimes Father wasn't completely hopeless. He tossed me a look that said, *Well done.*

Kimble gave a nod, then opened the basement door. I tensed. While I had been able to turn the Anubis statue back into stone, I had never gotten around to completely removing the curse from it. Kimble was a large, robust man, which meant he most likely had a strong life force. Not to mention he was carrying a very bright electric torch. All I could do was cross my fingers and hope for the best.

A moment later, a loud, sharp bark erupted from the stairwell, followed by a shout of surprise. Then there was heavy thumping as Kimble came racing up the stairs, the jackal close on his heels.

"There's a mad dog down there!" he cried, trying to close the door on the jackal, who was already halfway through. Giving up, the constable raced back into the foyer and joined the rest of us, possibly hoping that with a variety of targets the creature wouldn't zero in on him.

"What in the blazes . . ." Father began.

"A dog?" Mum shot me a suspicious glance, no doubt remembering the barking she had heard a week before. "Do you care to explain that, Theodosia?"

My rescue came from a most unlikely place. "It looks more like a jackal," Father muttered.

Growling and baring his teeth, the dog faced the constables. Turnbull bore down on Father, furious. "Is this your idea of a joke? Siccing a guard dog on my men? Why didn't you warn us?"

"Because I didn't know he was down there!" He paused a moment. "Did you know he was down there, Theodosia?"

Uh-oh. I could just imagine how well my explanation would go over with this lot. *Why yes, Father. The Old Kingdom statue we have of Anubis came to life when I was down there last.* So this meant, unfortunately, I had to lie. "Perhaps whoever let the mummies into the museum three nights ago left one of the doors open and a stray got in? Oh! And perhaps that's why our mummies are still here! Perhaps the dog chased away the mischief-makers!"

Father looked at me a moment longer, then nodded. "Makes as much sense as any of this," he said.

A loud growl exploded through the foyer and we all turned to watch as the jackal lunged for Kimble, who scrambled back out of the way. Everyone was staring at the animal now, except for Stilton, who looked at me with open awe. The dolt. Could he be any more obvious? He was going to give away all my secrets if he wasn't careful.

Beaton, hearing the commotion, came running back downstairs with his billy club out. Anubis glanced at him, then back at the men in front of him. Without warning, he leaped to the side, evading them all and heading straight for the front of the museum. When he reached the bank of windows, he launched himself up into the air and crashed through, shattered glass falling everywhere.

There was a moment of stunned silence, and then the front door opened and Miss Sharpe walked in. "What on earth was that?"

CHAPTER TWENTY-THREE
A *MUT* TRAP

I FOUND IT INCREDIBLY DIFFICULT to keep my mind on my lessons (and had my knuckles rapped a number of times for it—thank goodness I wore gloves!). My mind kept returning to the poor mummies from the other museums, wondering where on earth they were. The idea of them wandering around London, lost, was most distressing. However, I was certain we would hear of any reports of such a thing. Besides, it seemed to me that the mummies had always moved under the cover of darkness before. So perhaps they had gotten to wherever they were going the night before.

Wherever they had gone.

I sat bolt upright, startling Miss Sharpe. "What is it, Theodosia?"

"Nothing, Miss Sharpe. I just landed on a solution to this problem you gave me."

But what had jolted through me like a bolt of lightning was that wherever the mummies had gone was most likely where the Serpents of Chaos—and the staff—could be found. The mummies responded to the staff; they were drawn to its power—that is the only place they would head.

So if we found the mummies, we'd find the staff. Brilliant!

All I had to do was remove the protective amulet from one of our mummies. It would be drawn by the power of the staff, and someone from the Brotherhood of the Chosen Keepers could follow it straight to Chaos's headquarters.

There was a sharp rap on the desk. "Theodosia!"

I flinched. "Yes?"

"I thought you said you'd worked out that problem, but you haven't written a thing."

"Oh. Sorry. I was wrong. It wasn't the solution after all."

Miss Sharpe's nostrils quivered in frustration. "Very well. I want you to now write out one hundred times, *I will not be overconfident.*"

It was going to be a long day. The only thing that kept me going was the idea that soon Will would arrive and I could turn this all over to Wigmere.

By midmorning, I had excused myself to go to the lavatory six times in an attempt to pass a message to Will. Miss Sharpe had taken to pinching me whenever I announced my need, and Stilton had stopped looking me in the eye after my third trip. Although I should have been embarrassed by the sheer indelicateness of it all, I had much bigger problems to worry about.

Such as the fact that it was becoming clear that Will had no intention of showing up today. Was he put out with me and refusing to act as messenger anymore? Or had something happened to him? He had seemed quite worried about the Grim Nipper.

There was one possibility I refused to allow myself to contemplate: that he wasn't showing up because he'd given in and done what the Grim Nipper had asked him to do.

Without Will, I had to come up with an alternate plan. Of course, the simplest would be for me to follow the mummy myself, but I do have some sense (in spite of what Father says). Even I wasn't willing to wander around the streets of London by myself late at night. Taking a cab was one thing, but following a mummy on foot who was heading straight for the Serpents of Chaos? No. That was out of the question.

But what, then?

I heard a creak outside the reading room and looked up to find Stilton peering in. Time for his late morning check, apparently. It was enough to stifle a sardine!

But wait—the Black Sunners! They claimed to want to do my every wish and command. And they were grown men. I could have *them* follow the mummy. Of course, I'd give them the strictest instructions not to do anything—not to approach our mummy or the mummies they found or the Serpents of Chaos—but they could find the location for me. That would work.

I wiggled my eyebrows at Stilton, who still hovered in the doorway, then jerked my head in Miss Sharpe's direction. He nodded, then cleared his throat. "Miss Sharpe?"

She looked up from her book. "Yes, Mr. Stilton?"

"I believe the constable was asking for you."

A wrinkle of distaste crossed her face.

Stilton shrugged apologetically. "They're questioning everybody, you know. It's nothing personal."

An aggrieved sigh escaped from my governess. "Very well, but I must say, this is much more than I signed up for."

Once she had left, Stilton slipped into the room and closed the door behind him. "What is it, Miss Theo?"

"I have an assignment for you and the other scorpions."

His face lit up like a Christmas tree. "Yes, O Bringer of Light. We live to serve you."

"Yes, yes. So you've said. But here's what I need you to do . . ."

As I explained the plan to him, his eyes grew bigger and bigger and his face flushed with excitement. "So I was right, then. You can raise the dead."

"Well, no. Not really." But it still didn't seem smart to explain about the staff. I was fairly certain I trusted Stilton, but I most definitely did not trust Trawley. And if Stilton told him about the staff, Trawley would most likely want it for his own.

"I will get word to the grand master at once to ask for his permission."

"Permission? But I thought you were assigned to me?" I distinctly remembered hearing them jaw on about adoration and being at my command.

"Yes, Miss Theo, but we are assigned to watch *over* you. We will need permission if we are to leave your side."

This was beginning to sound more and more like a prison every day. "Very well. But let me know as soon as you find out."

He bowed low, but before I could tell him to stop that, he left the room and I was blissfully alone. Which lasted for exactly two minutes before Miss Sharpe burst through the door, looking most put out. "Where is he?"

"Who?" Although I knew perfectly well whom she meant.

"Mr. Stilton, of course! The constable had no idea what I was talking about. Said he'd never asked to see me. I looked a right fool."

"I'm sure it was an honest mistake," I said, wanting to keep Stilton out of as much trouble as possible.

She sniffed. "I shall have to report him to Mr. Weems, as he is the only one who seems to have any sense around here."

Which just went to show you how poor her judgment was.

It was a long, tortuous afternoon. Miss Sharpe was in a beastly mood for having been made a fool of in front of the police (and wouldn't I have loved to see that!). She took it out on me by making me copy all sorts of rubbish from *Mrs. Primbottom's Guide to Raising Perfect Children*.

It was all utter rot, and she was a fiend about my handwriting, which wasn't at its best because I startled at every little sound I heard, thinking it was Stilton come to report on Trawley's decision.

Imagine my surprise when Vicary Weems interrupted us.

I can quite safely say it was the first time I was ever glad to see him.

"Excuse me," he said, his chin high.

"Yes, Weems?" I asked.

"I wasn't talking to *you*," he said pointedly. "I was wondering if perhaps Miss Sharpe would like to share a cab ride home. To cut down on expense, you know."

Miss Sharpe reached up and patted her hair. Honestly! Had someone delivered a cache of Cupid's arrows that no one had told me about?

"That is very kind of you, Mr. Weems, but I don't think it's a good idea," Miss Sharpe said.

In spite of all the pinches and knuckle rappings, in spite of all the wretched lines I'd been made to do, I leaned forward and whispered, "Don't worry. I shan't breathe a word to Grandmother about this."

Her eyes grew round and she looked at me with charity for the first time since we'd met. "Oh. Well then, yes, thank you, Mr. Weems. That would be lovely."

I nearly danced a jig. Everyone was finally leaving. Even better, as soon as Weems had escorted Miss Sharpe from the room, Stilton arrived.

"Well?" I asked. "What did Trawley say?"

Stilton gave me a slightly reproachful look. "The grand

master said that he would allow us to perform this favor for you if you would in turn do him a favor."

"What? I thought it was just about giving you permission to leave my side?"

Stilton's left shoulder twitched, and he looked sheepish. "The grand master wishes you to perform a small bit of magic for him. If you will agree to that, he will allow us to follow your mummy."

"What sort of magic?" I asked, immediately suspicious.

"To be determined at a later date, but mutually agreed upon by the both of you."

If we had to mutually agree upon the feat of magic, that gave me some wiggle room. "Very well. If that's the only condition under which he will agree."

"It is."

These Black Sunners were shaping up to be far more trouble than they were worth. I checked my watch. "It's six thirty now. I'm fairly sure that mummies are only ambulatory when the moon is out."

"Moonrise is at five after ten."

I blinked. "How'd you know that?"

"The almanac. In our rituals, we pay very close attention to the phases of the moon."

"Yes, but you're called the Black Sun."

"It's a code name for the dark of the moon, when magic is at its most powerful."

"Very well. Let's meet at the top of the stairs leading down to the basement at ten o'clock, then. I've got something I've got to do beforehand."

The newest round of missing mummies had poor Father stretched to the breaking point. He was convinced our mummies would go missing any minute. In fact, Father was so nervous that he had sworn to spend the night in the museum again—with shotgun firmly in hand.

Which was why I needed to rid the museum of this most recent disgruntled spirit that had attached itself to us; to protect Father. Why couldn't it have stayed with the mummy it rode in on? It wasn't as if I didn't have enough to do, what with mummies running loose in London, Will dabbling in questionable behavior and being followed by the Grim Nipper, a wretched governess stifling my every move, an ancient Egyptian god in jackal form coming to life, and seven inept scorpion guards acting, quite frankly, mad as hatters.

But of course, that was the whole point of chaos, wasn't it? My life was absolute bedlam. If the Egyptian god of Chaos were watching, he'd be deliriously happy.

Well, as soon as I got rid of this vicious spirit, that would be one less chaotic element to deal with.

I just had to decide where to set my *mut* trap. Spirits tended to lurk close to the final resting place of their mummified bodies, so I had to assume that this spirit would lurk close to its mummy's last known location: the foyer. This created a bit of a complication, because I had to get the trap set before Father wandered down with his shotgun to post guard.

I had managed to remain fairly purified throughout the day. The diciest moment came when Mother sent Dolge round for meat pies for dinner. I was starving by then but didn't dare have one for fear of ruining all the purification bother I'd gone through that morning. I settled for two jam sandwiches instead and tried not to feel sorry for myself. (Have I mentioned the extreme amount of fortitude one must have for curse removal?)

I stood at the edge of the foyer, trying to determine the best place to set the traps. Ideally, I should set one in each corner, corresponding with the four points of the compass.

In order to prepare the area for the ritual, the first step was to sprinkle the area with holy water (which had been most difficult to obtain). Using as little as possible in order to conserve my supply, I sprinkled drops across the entire floor. Next, I was to sweep the room of any evil influences with a broom made from the branches of a persea tree. As London had none of these that I knew of, I settled for a broom made of willow twigs, the willow being sacred to Osiris and as such would hopefully have some authority over dead spirits.

Once I'd swept the floor with the broom, my next step was to cleanse the air with holy smoke or incense. This was tricky because I was specifically prohibited from using lucifer matches, but how else did one get holy smoke than by fire? It had taken me quite a bit of thinking to work out a solution to this one, but I finally decided a mist of perfume from my curse-removal kit would work, it being the next best way to fill the air with cloying scent. Of course, I couldn't afford the kind that smelled truly lovely. Instead I had bought something called "An Evening's Enchantment" (even the name was perfect!), which smelled like a combination of wood smoke, violets, and vanilla.

Once I'd sprayed that throughout the foyer, I was ready to begin.

According to T. R. Nectanebus, I could use either clap nets or lassos of rope to catch the evil spirit. The museum did have two clap nets, but it would certainly raise all sorts of questions if Father found them hanging in the foyer. Rope was a little less noticeable and could hopefully be explained away as building maintenance.

The trick would be getting the rope up into the corners of the ceiling. I was rather short (as most eleven-year-old girls are), and the two ladders we had in the museum were much too heavy for me to drag into the foyer.

Not to mention someone would surely notice.

I had to settle for leaving the lassos on the floor. In order to compensate for this, I made sure to place something inside the traps to attract the evil spirits: horehound candy. Now, I know that horehound tastes vile, and whoever thought to call it a sweet should have their head examined. However, the Egyptians believed that the demon and ghost worlds were upside down and backwards from ours, so whatever was sweet and tasty to us would be bitter to them and whatever was horrid to us would taste sweet to them.

Besides, how else was I going to get rid of this foul stuff that Grandmother had given me for Christmas?

After placing a piece of the horehound candy into the middle of each loop of rope, I also placed a small bit of wax. If it became discolored, I would know a disgruntled or cursed spirit had crossed into the loop.

"Good heavens!" Father's voice boomed from behind me, making me jump. "What is that foul stench?"

It was "An Evening's Enchantment" cologne mixed with horehound candy, of course, but all I said was, "What stench, Father? I don't smell anything."

(I must say, keeping as many secrets as I do is an awful burden. I don't like it one bit. It makes me feel sneaky, which I'm not. Not really. It's just that I've learned the need for caution when discussing magic with grownups. They simply refuse to even entertain the possibility! What's worse, they give you worried, squinty-eyed looks if you bring it up, and you can be sure a nice long stay in a sanitarium or boarding school out in the country is your next stop. So really, it's all their own fault I couldn't confide in them.)

"And what on earth are you doing here?" he asked. "You should have been asleep hours ago."

"Yes, I know. I was just coming to tell you and Mother good night."

"Oh, well, good night, then."

"Good night, Father."

I skedaddled off to find Stilton. It was time to let loose a mummy.

CHAPTER TWENTY-FOUR

TETLEY TAKES A TRIP

I THOUGHT LONG AND HARD about which mummy to send. In the end, there was only one choice: Tetley. I simply couldn't bring myself to desecrate one of the genuine mummies by making him wander around London at night. Tetley used to be a part of the Serpents of Chaos, so really, it was rather like releasing him so he could return home.

"Why are we going down to the basement?" Stilton asked.

"I don't want to defile an ancient mummy, so I thought I'd use Chudleigh's fake and it's down here."

"Won't that be defiling an Englishman, then?" Stilton asked, slightly shocked.

"Not really. He used to work with these men. It seems much more fair to have him do it rather than a royal scribe from the Middle Dynasty. Now, come on."

I started down the stairs, surprised at how comforting it was to have another person coming with me. I waited on the bottom step, listening for any sign of movement. There was none.

"I say, what's Weems's coat doing down here?" Stilton asked, breaking the silence. "He's been looking for that. Making a huge stink, too, he is."

"Oh, sorry. I snagged it because I was cold. I mistook it for Father's." I did not want to tell Stilton about the Anubis statue. The more I learned about Trawley and his organization, the less I wanted them to know about me and the magic around here. "Come on. Tetley's over there."

Tetley stood where I had left him, propped against the wall in his desiccated combination suit.

"So, how are you going to get him to move?"

I took a deep breath and tried not to look into Tetley's face. "By removing this." I plucked the Blood of Isis amulet from Tetley's skinny, sunken chest. The air around us gave a shudder, as if an invisible wall of some sort had come down.

"I say, what was that?" Stilton asked in a hushed voice.

"The protection being removed."

Tetley slowly turned his head to the sound of my voice. My mouth went dry.

"It appears to be working," Stilton said.

I said nothing but watched as the mummy formerly known as Tetley straightened away from the wall and took one step forward. My hands crept up to the amulets around my neck. Tetley took another step forward and another. I quickly backed out of the way so I wasn't between him and the staircase. As he passed Stilton and me, his empty gaze lingered on us, a faint look of puzzlement crossing his mummified features. "Go on," I whispered. "The staff is calling you."

Tetley turned toward the stairs and, lifting his legs in a disjointed manner, made his way up. Halfway to the top, he looked back at me. Goose bumps rippled across my arms. I rushed forward to follow Tetley up the steps, realizing he'd need me to open a door for him or we'd risk his punching straight through a window as the jackal had. "Come on," I told Stilton.

"Coming," he said. "I just want to get Weems's coat. Perhaps if he had it back, he wouldn't be so foul tempered."

When we reached the top of the stairs, there was a dicey moment when Tetley really wanted to go through the foyer to the front entrance. I had to prod him rather grimly to redirect him to the west one.

When we reached the side door, I hurried around in front and opened it for him. Without so much as a pause, he stepped over the threshold and into the night.

Beside me, Stilton quivered in excitement. "I'll have a report for you first thing in the morning."

"Excellent! And do be careful, won't you? Don't try to stop Tetley or redirect him."

"I won't. Good night." And with that, Stilton exited the museum to follow Tetley. Three more scorpions detached themselves from the shadows and joined Stilton. I closed the door and hoped this would work. If not, I was out of ideas.

I was so lost in thought, trying to find holes in my plan, that I was halfway past Stilton's office before I realized there was a faint sliver of light shining from beneath the door. Odd. He must have forgotten to turn it off.

I stopped and retraced my steps, then opened the door.

Behind the desk, Clive Fagenbush shot to his feet. He'd been rummaging through the desk drawers! "What are you doing here?" he asked.

"Me? What are *you* doing here?"

"Museum business," he blurted out.

Of course I didn't believe a word of it. "Museum business requires you to go through Stilton's desk?"

Fagenbush looked down his nose at me. "Not that it's any

of your concern, but he was working on an assignment that he was supposed to have for me this afternoon. He left before he turned it in, so I hoped to find it here."

I narrowed my eyes. It sounded reasonable enough, but I didn't like to give Fagenbush the benefit of the doubt. I would ask Stilton about it in the morning.

"However," Fagenbush drawled, "it's clear I will be able to find nothing in this mess. It will have to wait until tomorrow."

He came around from behind Stilton's desk. "Coming?" he asked.

"Of course," I said, reaching to turn out the light. I followed him into the hallway, then firmly shut the door. "You might want to go out the front," I suggested innocently.

"And risk getting splattered with pigeon shot by your father? I think not, but good try."

Bother. He'd seen clean through that one, hadn't he?

CHAPTER TWENTY-FIVE
IF YOU GIVE A GOVERNESS ENOUGH ROPE...

I WAS UP EARLY THE NEXT MORNING, or perhaps it was more truthful to say I never really fell asleep. I spent the entire night wrestling with all my dilemmas. It was a relief to be able to get up, actually.

I immediately made my way to the foyer. Father was snoring loudly, sprawled up against the far wall and dangerously close to one of the lassos.

Saving that one for last, I checked the corner of the room closest to the entrance. The wax was white, which meant that no foul spirits had been near. Shoving the wax into my pocket, I kicked the rope behind a pedestal holding a bust of Nefertiti. Then I hurried on to the second corner near the big bay of windows at the front of the museum. The wax there was also still white.

The third corner was clean, too. Bother. I hated to think I'd gone to all that trouble and caught nothing! Cautiously, I approached the corner Father inhabited. Wouldn't it just cork it if his corner happened to be the one the spirit had gravitated to? Which made sense, really, as disgruntled spirits loved to make trouble for the living.

Tiptoeing as quietly as I could, I stepped around Father. The wax was a familiar green-black color, and I caught a whiff of sulfur.

Reaching out, I grasped the end of the rope in my gloved hands, then quickly tied a knot, then another one, then another, until there were seven knots in all. The knots would bind the disgruntled spirit to the rope until I could find a safe repository for it.

As I headed to my carrel, there was a loud knock.

"Hello? It's me, Miss Sharpe," she called out, her voice muffled by the front door.

Bother! Why couldn't she use the side entrance like the rest of the employees?

She knocked again, and Father's snoring was replaced with a sputter. "Wh-what? Who's there?"

"It's only me, Father. Miss Sharpe's here."

He got up off the floor and smoothed his hair down with his hand. "Well, don't just stand there. Let her in."

"That's what I was doing," I told him. Huffing over to the door, I opened it to admit Miss Sharpe, surprised to see a crowd out there again. Hadn't these people anything better to do? I scanned the faces, searching for Will, but didn't see anyone looking even remotely like him.

"Good morning, Theodosia," Miss Sharpe said.

"Good morning, ma'am."

Her gaze fell onto the rope in my hand. "What are you doing with that?"

I shrugged. "Oh, well, I—"

Her mouth flattened in disapproval, and she stuck out her hand. "Give it to me. Fun and games are over. It's time for our lessons."

"But it isn't a game," I protested.

"Theodosia," she warned with a glint in her eye. I recognized that glint. It was the one she got just before she pinched me, and I wasn't wearing my coat. I stared down at the rope in my hand, then back at Miss Sharpe, a rather evil thought occurring to me. "Why, certainly, Miss Sharpe," I said, then held the rope out to her.

She took it from me with a look of triumph, followed by a slight frown as she shivered delicately. "Goodness, it's chilly in here. Let's get to the reading room so we can begin your studies."

It was a long, horrible morning with policemen sniffing about in all the nooks and crannies of the museum and Miss Sharpe being her awful pinchy self. Because I was so distracted, I flubbed my lessons four different times and earned a pinch for each mistake.

And what, may you ask, was I so distracted by? The rope, that's what. Miss Sharpe seemed to have grown very attached to it, and as I worked on my lessons, she slapped it threateningly against her palm, like a whip.

"What is the square root of sixteen?" *Slap.*

"What is seven thousand two hundred seventy-seven divided by thirty-two?" *Slap.*

"What year did Queen Victoria declare India a part of the British Empire?" *Slap.*

And on it went. Luckily, she was cold enough that she had decided to keep her gloves on. But even with her hands protected, I was worried about what such prolonged contact with the corrupted rope would do.

Until she pinched me the third time. Then I decided I really didn't care.

And as if that wasn't bad enough, Stilton kept hovering nearby, almost bursting with his report from the night before, but I couldn't get him alone.

I was sure none of the Chosen Keepers had ever been tested as sorely as I.

Around midmorning, the sun finally reached our side of the building.

"It's finally beginning to warm up," Miss Sharpe announced. "Which reminds me, when did your grandmother say we could begin conducting lessons at your home?"

"As soon as you proved you could be consistently punctual," I said sweetly.

Miss Sharpe pressed her lips together and two spots of bright color appeared high on her cheeks. Deciding to ignore me, she draped the rope over the back of a chair and began to tug off her gloves. I held my breath, wondering if she was going to slap them across my face, but she merely laid them onto the table.

When she saw me looking at the rope, a calculating gleam appeared in her eye. Her naked hands closed around the rope and she resumed whacking it against her palm.

The horrid woman! She was doing it only because she could tell the constant slapping was irritating me. Thoroughly distracted now, I kept looking up every couple of minutes or so until she finally said in exasperation, "What? What are you looking at, you rude child?"

That's when I saw it. A bright red boil had appeared on her forehead. And there was a pinkish spot on her left cheek where another one was beginning to rise up. "Um, I think you have a spot," I said, tapping my cheek.

"What?" Horrified, she let the rope drop to the floor, then reached for her purse and rummaged around until she found a little mirror. Ducking her head to see better, she peered into the mirror, a look of horror on her face. "Excuse me," she muttered. "I have to use the facilities."

As soon as she was out of sight, I grabbed the rope and stuffed it behind one of the bookcases until I could deal with it later.

"Miss Theo?"

At Edgar Stilton's voice I jumped away from the bookcase, hoping he hadn't seen me stash the rope. "Stilton!"

"Tefen," he corrected.

"Tefen," I repeated. "We have to hurry because I don't know how long Miss Sharpe will be gone. What did you find out?"

Stilton came fully into the room, rubbing his hands. "Well, Befen, Petet, Mestafet, and I followed the mummy—"

"Tetley. His name is Tetley."

"Oh. Right. We followed Tetley down to the docks."

"The docks!" I echoed stupidly. This was odd. Last time Chaos had been in London, they'd been housed at Carleton Terrace. "Go on."

"Unfortunately, the mumm—er, Tetley—was seen by rather a lot of people. He created quite a panic whenever he was spotted."

"I should think so," I muttered. "Which dock?"

"The East India docks," Stilton said. "There was a small, rundown tavern there, and the mummy went right up to it and smacked into the door. A rough voice called out, 'Here's another one, mates!' There was a burst of laughter, and then a man opened the door, grabbed Tetley by the waist, tossed him over his shoulder, and pulled him into the tavern."

There was a moment of silence as I digested all this. "What was the name of the tavern?"

"The Salty Dog." Stilton wrung his hands. "I hope we did right, Miss Theo. We talked about following the mummy in, but by the sound of their laughter there were quite a lot of them, and rough, too. You hadn't said anything about confronting dockworkers, only to follow the mummy. Although what a bunch of dockworkers want with a mummy is beyond me."

"No. You did exactly right, Stilton. Thank you. And the others—thank them for me. I'll take it from here."

A look of concern crossed Stilton's face. "But not without

our help, right, Miss Theo? You wouldn't wander down there by yourself, now, would you?"

"I'll be sure to let you know when I need your services again." That seemed to appease him.

"Oh, one more thing," he said. "That young urchin that hangs around here, the one you're always slipping out to talk to?"

My cheeks burned. Had I been so very obvious? And if Stilton had noticed it, who else had? "Yes?"

"Well, he was down there, too. At the docks. He was hiding behind a barrel, watching the tavern." A look of reproach shone in Stilton's eyes. "I do hope you didn't send him to check up on us."

"No, no! Of course not," I reassured him. "It was just a coincidence, that's all. He and I didn't have a chance to co-ordinate our activities yesterday."

Looking greatly relieved, Stilton nodded. "Also," he said, "the grand master wanted to know if he could collect his magic favor today."

Already? "Oh, Stilton! I'm so busy today, with all the police and Miss Sharpe—I don't see how I can get away."

"Very well, Miss Theo. I'm sure the grand master can wait." Then Stilton stepped out into the hall. I heard a muffled *oomph*, followed by a sharp "Watch where you're going!" Then Miss Sharpe hurried into the room and slammed the door shut, practically catching Stilton's nose as he tried to catch a glimpse of her.

I gasped. Her entire face was covered in festering boils. More were popping up, even as I watched. "Miss Sharpe," I breathed. Oh dear. I had known handling that rope hadn't been a good idea.

Miss Sharpe rushed over to get her things. Keeping her face averted, she shrugged into her coat. As she reached for her purse, I saw that the backs of her hands were covered with boils, too.

"I must leave. Immediately. Explain to your parents that I've taken ill." She opened the door and nearly ran into Stilton again. "Don't look at me!" she screeched, and then, ducking her face, she ran down the hall toward the side entrance.

I am sorry to say, I couldn't quite muster up all the sympathy I should have for Miss Sharpe. Perhaps I'd feel more charitable toward her once the bruises from her pinching faded.

Before I had time to react to this latest development, a bellow came from somewhere in the museum. *What now?* Stilton and I exchanged a glance, then dashed toward the sound of the shout.

Apparently everyone else in the museum had the same idea. Like migrating geese we all made our way to the Egyptian exhibit, where the noise had come from. Three constables and Inspector Turnbull were deep in conversation. There was an empty spot on the wall of mummies. How odd.

Turnbull stopped talking to his men and turned to me. "Where is your father?"

I pulled my eyes away from the empty space. "He's somewhere around here. Did you check his workroom?"

Turnbull jerked his head at one of the constables, who took off toward the workroom. As we waited, I casually drifted to where the New Kingdom mummy Ikudidy had been.

"Careful, miss. Don't get too close to the crime scene."

"I won't," I said as Isis slithered between my ankles toward the row of mummies. She batted at something on the floor, and I peered closer. It was a small homemade Blood of Isis amulet. Undoubtedly the one I'd placed on Ikudidy only three nights before.

Had it fallen off? Or had someone removed it?

The constable returned, escorting Father with Mother trailing behind them looking worried. At the sight of Father, Turnbull swelled up like a self-important rooster. "You want to explain what happened to this mummy, Throckmorton?"

Father gaped at the empty spot. "I have no idea! The

mummy thieves must have broken in last night—" I could see him trying to work out how an intruder had gotten past him and his shotgun.

"And taken just the one mummy?" Turnbull scoffed. "When they've cleaned out every museum in London? I don't think so, Throckmorton."

"Well then, what *do* you think?" Father snapped back, annoyed.

"I think your greed exceeds your common sense. You were tempted to fence just one more, and now I've caught you red-handed."

"Red-handed at what? All you have is one more missing mummy!"

"Yes, but we caught a fence trying to sell off gold that is linked to one of the recent break-ins. We think you've taken the mummies in order to create a panic so people will take their gold from their vaults as protection. Once the gold is out of the bank, it is much easier to steal. And we think you're doing this in partnership with the Grim Nipper.

"Throckmorton, I place you under arrest!"

CHAPTER TWENTY-SIX

THE SALTY DOG

THE ENTIRE ROOM GASPED at Turnbull's announcement, and then everyone started to speak at once. "Surely you're mistaken," Mother said, her eyes shadowed with worry.

"I say, if I had any idea of the goings-on around here, I never would have taken this job," Weems muttered somewhere behind me.

Thinking fast, I stepped forward. "Excuse me, Inspector?"

"What now?" Turnbull crossed his arms in front of him and nodded, clearly humoring me.

"What about Nigel Bollingsworth?"

"Bollingsworth, Bollingsworth," he muttered. He pulled

out a small notebook and thumbed through it. "The ex–First Assistant Curator?"

"That's the one. Have you managed to track him down? Find him for questioning? He did just disappear with no explanation four months ago. Right after the Heart of Egypt went missing."

Mother's hand flew to her throat. "She's right," she said. "Bollingsworth did disappear right after we discovered the theft of the Heart of Egypt."

"You allowed an artifact of that importance to slip through your fingers?" Weems said. "Does Lord Chudleigh know about this?"

Father threw him an annoyed glance.

"We'll check into it," Turnbull said grudgingly. "But perhaps your father's working with the two of them. Now, take him away, boys."

And with that, burly constables appeared on either side of Father. They grabbed his elbows and escorted him from the room. To Father's credit, he maintained his dignity and didn't struggle or protest.

When the police had gone, we were all left staring mutely at one another. A throat cleared and then Vicary Weems clapped his hands. "Very well, then. Back to work. Go on, now. Move along." With great reluctance the others filed out of the room. Stilton glanced back over his shoulder at me. Once they had left, Weems approached Mother. "I should like to have a word with you, Mrs. Throckmorton."

The minute he spoke, I knew what he was doing. He was going to ask to take over Father's duties as head of the museum.

"Not now, Weems," Mother said, brushing him off. "I have to get this all sorted out." She turned to me. "Theodosia, I'm going to see your grandmother. Perhaps she can get that admiral of hers to help us."

"Good idea, Mum!"

She hesitated. "I don't know what time I'll be back."

"Oh, don't worry about me! I'll be fine."

The smile she gave me was strained. "That's my girl."

Weems gaped like a fish at her retreating form, still not able to believe he'd been so firmly ignored. "Well?" I said. "Shouldn't you get back to work as well? We're short handed now with Father gone, and Mother, too."

It wasn't until he left that I began to shake. My knees turned to jelly, and I eased myself down onto the edge of the display platform right behind me. Father had been arrested. And all because of this wretched staff. A sharp, hot lump rose up in my throat, and my eyes burned. I would not cry. I would not!

A warm furry rubbing at my ankles distracted me as Isis entwined herself between my feet. I reached down and picked her up, hugging her close, trying to fill the aching hole inside me. She seemed to understand how distressed I was and let me cuddle her for a long moment before she twisted away in mild protest.

I would just have to fix things, that was all. Which meant I could no longer delay. I had to get the staff back immediately. That night. Especially now that I knew where Chaos could be found.

A plan formed in my mind. I got to my feet and began making my way to the side entrance to see if I could find Will.

He shrugged and wouldn't meet my eyes. "Wot d'you mean, where was I last night?"

I pulled my eyes away from his bootblack brigade disguise. "It's a simple question, Will."

"I was wif me family. Like always, miss. Now, d'you have a message for Wiggy or not?"

I folded my arms across my chest. "That all depends. Did you already tell him that the Serpents of Chaos were meeting at the Salty Dog last night?"

Will squeaked, his eyes nearly bugging out of his head. "'Ow'd you know about that?"

I sniffed. "You aren't the only contact I work with, you know. I do have other ways of acquiring information. So let's try this once more," I suggested. "This time with a healthy dose of honesty. Where were you last night?"

Will looked away from me over to where Snuffles was waiting in the bushes. There was a long silence, broken only by a thick, wet sniff from his younger brother. For a moment I was afraid he was still so angry with me for trying to help him with the Grim Nipper that he would refuse to talk. But finally, he spoke.

"I was down at the docks." He looked up at me, annoyance snapping in his eyes. "Although if you knew that, why didn't you just say so instead of trying to trap me like that?"

I put my nose right up against his. "Because I'm not sure I can trust you anymore! You won't tell me why the Grim Nipper is following you all around London. You disappear on me so I can't get messages to Wigmere. Then I discover you've been hanging out close to the meeting grounds of the Serpents of Chaos. What am I supposed to think, Will? This isn't all fun and games, or even small-time thievery. This is life and death and letting chaos loose on innocent people!"

His gaze faltered under the force of my anger, and he

looked down at where the toe of his too-large boot was savaging one of the hedge shrubs. "I was just tryin' to 'elp. Trying to do wot you would've done if you could get out at night. But I knew somefin was going down on account of all the mummy sightings people was talkin' about down by the docks. So when I saw that one bony fellow trailin' bandages 'eaded down there, I asked meself, *What would Miss Theo do?* And so I followed." He shrugged and looked dejectedly at the ground. "I didn't know you'd given up on me and 'ad someun else working for you."

I was so relieved, I could have hugged him. Well, except for how grubby he was. And the fact that he would have likely squealed like a pig in disgust. "Oh, Will! I don't have someone else working for me. I just couldn't get a hold of you on account of you being so angry with me." Since we were in charity with each other again, I leaned in and tried once more. "You can tell me what's going on with the Grim Nipper, you know. I might be able to help."

Solemnly, Will shook his head. "No one can 'elp with the Grim Nipper," he said, his voice stark with hopelessness.

"You have to tell me, Will. They've just hauled my father off to jail because they think he's working with the Grim Nipper to fence all these missing mummies!"

"Oy, miss! I'm sorry."

"I have no choice anymore. I have to visit that tavern myself. I need to get that staff back and find a way to have all the mummies returned to their rightful places."

"You're not thinking of going alone, are you?" Will asked, shocked.

"I'd rather not," I admitted. "Would you come with me?"

There was a tiny pause as Will weighed the risk, and then he nodded. "All right, then. I'll come. When do you want to leave?"

I glanced at the sky overhead. It was almost dusk. If we left right then, we'd be there about sunset. "Now should do nicely, don't you think? Let me just grab a coat, and I'll be ready."

I dashed back to the cloakroom, my mind spinning furiously. I had to get some cab fare for the trip to the docks. It was simply too far to walk and I was out of time. Stilton. That was it.

I found him in his office, twitching madly as he tried to sort through paperwork. "Stilton?"

He jumped at the sound of my voice. "Yes, Miss Theo?"

"Er, may I borrow a pound or two?" At his surprised look, I rushed to explain. "I'm starving and who knows when Mum will be back. I thought I'd go get something to eat."

"I'll be happy to go for you, miss—"

"No!" I quickly interrupted. I thought briefly about telling him of my plan—he was a bit odd and a Black Sunner, and maybe he'd think nothing of it—but he was still an adult and might very well try to stop me. "I really need the walk. To clear my head and sort out what to do about Father."

"Well, I could accompany you."

"No, I'm too upset for company."

Looking slightly crestfallen, Stilton said, "Well, I don't know how Trawley would feel about that . . ."

Frustration spurted through me, and before I knew it, I stamped my foot. "Stilton! Can I just have the money?"

He blinked, and then, looking injured, he pulled a couple of pound notes from his pocket. "Here you go, miss."

"Thank you, Tefen." I hoped using his scorpion name would pacify him.

It seemed to work.

"You're welcome, Miss Theo. Do be careful!"

Careful? Why, Careful was my middle name!

The cab dropped us off at the oldest, seediest dock in the whole of London. At first the driver had refused to leave us there, but then Snuffles had held his stomach and pretended he was going to throw up, so the cabby booted us out of the hansom right quick. Heaven knew how we'd get back, but I'd worry about that when the time came.

There were a few men about, finishing up with their duties and whatnot. They all looked as though they'd slit one's throat as soon as look at one.

"Quit staring at them!" Will hissed, jerking me behind a barrel. "They take it as a sign of 'ostility."

"Oh, sorry." I concentrated on locating the tavern as Will led us on a winding path around barges and crates and ropes. Finally, he came to a stop behind a row of stacked wooden barrels. "There it is."

The Salty Dog looked as if it had been there for two hundred years. Its rough, salt-weathered timbers were blackened with age. Cautiously, Will slipped out from behind a barrel and made his way to the tavern wall, just below a shuttered window. When he was sure no one had seen him, he motioned for me to follow. Snuffles was to stay parked behind the barrels and sneeze if he saw anyone coming.

I stood on tiptoes and craned my neck at an awkward angle so I could peek through the crack in the shutter. There were dozens of men, peering into mugs of ale, but there was no one I recognized from the Serpents of Chaos. "I can't imagine that they'd meet and hatch their evil plots right under everyone's noses," I whispered. "Do they have a backroom or something?"

Will nodded, then quickly put his finger to his lips and nudged me so that I'd turn around. When I did, I spied a tall man wearing a greatcoat approaching the tavern. There was something familiar about his gait, and when he opened the tavern door, the warm light illuminated his scarred face. Nigel Bollingsworth.

I quickly returned to my post at the window to see where he'd go. He spoke to the man behind the bar, who gestured with his head toward the back. I turned to Will. "Is there a back entrance?"

He shrugged, then stepped away from the window and began making his way through more empty barrels and coils of thick salt-encrusted rope to the rear of the tavern. Picking my way carefully, I followed.

There *was* a back door! And even better, it was standing open, letting fresh air inside. Perfect. I headed straight for it, only to feel a hand clamp down on my arm and jerk me back.

"Wot d'you think you're doin', miss?"

"I have to hear what they're up to. I need to know their plans if I want a chance to get the staff back. And getting the staff back is the only way I can think of to clear Father's name. Do you have a better idea?"

"Aye. I'll go." He made to push past me, but I planted my feet and refused to budge.

"No, Will. I have to go. I know more about what's going

on than you do, and they might say something that would make no sense to you but would be perfectly clear to me."

Of course, being a boy, he immediately got all huffy, but I ignored it and stayed firm until he finally relented.

Once we'd gotten that sorted out, I worked my way inside the door, keeping a careful eye out for any signs of someone coming in the back.

The room reeked of stale ale and sour wine. I pulled the collar of my dress up to cover my mouth and nose. Hearing a murmur of voices, I dove for the far corner of the room and knelt down behind a barrel of hard cider. I hadn't realized they'd be meeting back here!

"You're late!" a voice with a German accent called out. Von Braggenschnott.

"No I'm not," Bollingsworth grumbled. "You're early."

"Either way, you're the last one here. Now we can begin."

There was the sound of a chair scraping against the floor as everyone took a seat.

"How did the experiment go?"

"It went just as Sahotep wrote it would. The moment we placed the head of the staff in water a yellow-green cloud rose up, thick and choking. Within seconds it enveloped our four prisoners. After that, it didn't take long. Four men dead in under an hour."

"Perfect. That will ensure we sail with the tide." He spoke

softly, a whisper really. And there was a huge barrel between us. Even so, I thought I'd heard his voice before.

"None of you suffered any ill effects?" von Braggenschnott asked.

Bollingsworth spoke. "No—the masks worked, although they were a bit hard to see out of."

"We won't need them for long if the fumes truly work that quickly. Plus, the breeze coming off the river will disperse them soon enough."

"Aren't you worried about the fumes harming others as the cloud moves away?" von Braggenschnott asked.

"No, their health is not my concern." The familiarity of the voice niggled at me.

"And the staff was able to raise them? They could function enough to follow orders and execute simple tasks?"

"Yes. They were a bit jerky in their movements, but they retained enough of their living thoughts to perform their duties."

"Excellent, gentlemen. We will make our move on the morrow." Where oh where had I heard this man before? With my heart thudding in my chest, I inched my head toward the side of the barrel. In the dim light, I recognized Bollingsworth and von Braggenschnott, but the third man was heavily cloaked and had his back to me.

"Are you certain there will be enough to take care of all seven hundred of them?" Bollingsworth asked.

"If not, we can always use our pistols."

Just then, a creak on the floor pulled my attention away from the conversation. An enormous round shape stood in the doorway, limned by the yellow light from the tavern room. I pulled back as far into the shadows as I could. "Cognac," he muttered. "They want cognac. Do I look like the kind o' place that has cognac? Why can't they just drink ale like normal folk? Brandy'll have to do or they can go find somewhere else."

And then I heard a sneeze. Then another. Someone was coming!

Moving as quietly as I could, I retraced my steps to the back door. I stepped out into the night, glancing around for Will, who was nowhere in sight. Someone grabbed my arm and yanked me behind the corner of the building.

"Someone's coming. Might be one o' them Chaos guys."

I looked to where Will pointed, then I squinted, trying to see through the darkness.

The good news was, it wasn't the Serpents of Chaos who'd followed us.

The bad news was, Edgar Stilton had. And he wasn't alone.

CHAPTER TWENTY-SEVEN

ALOYSIUS TRAWLEY CALLS IN HIS FAVOR

STILTON AND THE SIX OTHER SCORPIONS Trawley had assigned to me stood behind us. With one last glance at the Salty Dog, I gave my full attention to my guard, although I was quickly beginning to realize that was a misnomer. "What are you doing here?" I hissed at Stilton.

He stepped forward so he could keep his voice low and not risk attracting the attention of the agents of chaos or the local thugs. "You didn't tell me you were headed down here, Miss Theo! I would never have let you leave had I known that."

"And you didn't tell me you'd be following me."

"You had me followed last night without warning."

"I've already told you—that was purely coincidence."

"Oo are these men, miss?" Will's voice came from right behind me. "You want Snuffles and me to take care of 'em for ye?"

I looked from the seven Black Sunners, grown men all, back to Will and Snuffles and couldn't help but think that was rather optimistic on his part. "I think I can manage," I whispered. "But if you wouldn't mind watching my back for a few more minutes, that would be grand."

Stilton looked injured. "No one needs to watch your back, Miss Theo."

Drat. Heard that, had he?

"We mean you no harm. We're your guardians, you know. We're just here to keep you safe."

"And bring her to Trawley," one of the other scorpions— Basil Whiting, I thought—called out.

"Trawley?" I repeated.

Stilton shrugged and even in the dim light looked sheepish. "He really wants his magical favor, miss. Says the stars and moon are aligned just right for working magic and doesn't want the moment to pass."

"He also wants to be sure she's worth it," another voice called out. "If he's going to be going to so much trouble to guard her and do her favors, he needs to know she's the genuine article."

Looking pained, Stilton shrugged again. "You see how it is, miss."

"Do I have any choice?" I asked, my voice pitched low so only Stilton would hear.

"No," he answered, equally softly. "We've orders to bring you along, whether you cooperate or not."

Just as I feared. And Trawley couldn't have picked a worse time. "Very well. Let's go."

Stilton's whole face grew slack with relief.

"Just a moment, Stilton." I grabbed Will's arm and pulled him far enough away from the group of scorpions that they couldn't overhear us. Two of them made as if to follow, but Stilton waved them back.

"Ye want us to tail ye, miss?" Will's voice was barely more than a tickle against my ear.

"If you wouldn't mind," I answered, trying to move my lips as little as possible. It certainly wouldn't hurt to have someone know where I was. Or where their wretched temple was either, come to think of it.

"Our carriages are this way, miss." Stilton stood aside and indicated that I should precede him, which I did.

As I climbed into the scorpions' waiting carriage, I cast one last look back toward Will and Snuffles, but they had already disappeared from sight.

Once again I was blindfolded. Stilton tried to make small talk on the way there, but frankly, I was too peeved to appreciate it. It wasn't as if I didn't already have enough on my plate! I would have to tell Trawley I wanted nothing more to do with his beastly secret society. They were too much trouble and rather poor at taking orders, adoration or no.

The carriage lurched to a stop. Stilton gently helped me from the vehicle, then guided me to the door, where there was the same patterned knock before it opened.

"What took you so long?" a voice asked.

"We got here as soon as we could. Take us to Trawley."

"Aye, he's waiting for you. In here."

Stilton removed my blindfold, and I followed him down a familiar corridor that flickered with candlelight. I was herded into the same chamber as before, where Trawley waited with his band of acolytes draped in black cloaks. His wild eyes lit up when he saw me, and he rubbed his hands. "You came!"

"You didn't give me much choice," I said.

He ignored my sullenness. "I trust your scorpions have followed your every wish and done as you have bid them?"

"Except for the part about needing your permission and forcing me to come here, yes."

Trawley narrowed his eyes in annoyance. "Then let's quit wasting your precious time and get on with it, shall we? This way, please."

He stepped aside and motioned me toward an altar at the front of the room. I was so busy staring at the altar (and worrying about what he had planned) that I walked right into a bronze bowl that had been placed on the floor. With a resounding clang, I sent it skidding forward, the water inside splashing everywhere. "Oh. Sorry about that."

Trawley closed his eyes for a long moment. When he opened them again, he had a look of forced cheerfulness. "Someone get more water. Fell, you get the oil. Theodosia, would you please lie down over here." He indicated a row of four bricks on the floor spaced at even intervals. Four very hard and sharp-edged bricks, I might add.

"Face-up or face-down?" I asked.

"Face-down, if you please."

Gerton righted the bronze bowl in front of the first brick, and as Whiting filled it with fresh water, it became clear to me what Trawley expected. He wanted me to act as a medium so he could communicate with an Egyptian deity. What rot! This was late Egyptian magic and mostly showmanship. Surely he knew that much? But one look at his eager, shining face told me that he did not know that much.

Not at all. Resigned, I comforted myself that it was a very small, harmless bit of pseudomagic. His request could have been much, much worse.

Whiting picked up a smaller vessel and poured a thin film of oil on top of the water. With a sigh, I eased myself down onto the bricks. Luckily, they were rather large bricks. I rested my chin on the first one so I could see into the bowl, with the other three jabbing into my body at uncomfortable intervals. "Let's make this quick," I said, trying to get situated.

"As you wish. Silbert! Light the incense. Gerton, light the lamp."

Within seconds a thick, smoky-sweet, cloying scent filled the room, and I tried not to cough. In order to distract myself, I studied the bowl. The warm yellow light cast off by the oil lamp to my right illuminated the symbols of Anubis engraved upon its bronze surface.

Trawley began to chant. "Anubis, we call upon your power and strength. Open this child's eyes to your wisdom."

As Trawley repeated his chant, I let my eyes go out of focus. Egyptians weren't the only ones good at showmanship—I could play-act with the best of them. And the sooner this was over, the sooner I could get home and figure out what on earth Chaos intended to do with the wretched staff. The number seven hundred kept playing in my mind, seeming significant somehow. And they had mentioned sailing with the tide, which indicated a ship of some sort. Which made their new headquarters down by the docks make much more sense.

The light glowed off the film of oil, and the incense made me feel both dizzy and nauseated. I wondered what it would take to convince Trawley I'd had a vision. As my unfocused eyes stared at the bowl, the surface shimmered slightly. *Sail with the tide. Seven hundred. Sail with the tide. Seven hundred.* The words ran through my head and mixed with Trawley's chant.

My eyes grew dry, so I blinked. When I opened them again, a picture of the *Dreadnought* flashed in front of me and the penny dropped. "Of course!"

"She's seen!" Trawley called out, bringing my attention back to the chamber around me.

Quiet voices rose in murmured excitement. Bother! Now Trawley thought I'd had his idiotic vision. He knelt down next to me and tried to peer into the bowl. "What did you see?"

I had seen the *Dreadnought* and finally understood that Chaos was going to try and kidnap Her Majesty's Royal Navy's crown jewel. Which made perfect sense, as they loved to stir the pot between Germany and Britain, trying to provoke them into pandemonium and anarchy.

But that wasn't the answer Trawley was looking for. Instead, I made my voice toneless and flat and began speaking. "The Black Sun shall rise up in a red sky before falling to earth, where a great serpent will swallow it."

A quick glance at Trawley's face told me he didn't like that one bit. I rushed to add, "Then the serpent's stomach will burst open, and lots of tiny snakes will wriggle forth and disappear into the ground."

There. That was the best I could do. It's a lot harder to sound prophetic than one might think.

I snuck a look at Trawley's face. He was frowning but seemed lost in thought. I blinked my eyes rapidly, then began to stretch and wriggle a bit, trying to remind him I wanted up from these wretchedly uncomfortable bricks.

Trawley nodded at two of the scorpions, who leaped forward and helped me to my feet. As I brushed the dust off the front of my frock, I wondered what was to happen next.

Trawley seemed to finally realize that we were all waiting for him to respond or give orders or do something besides stare stupidly at the wall in front of him. He waved his hand in the air. "I must meditate on what this prophecy truly foretells. You are dismissed."

I climbed into the carriage and sat as far away from Stilton as I could, then folded my arms across my chest and stared pointedly out the window.

We rode in awkward silence for a while before he cleared his throat. "I'm sorry, Miss Theodosia. I didn't have any choice. Really."

I kept my eyes glued to the window.

"You don't understand. I'm not that high up in the organization. I don't have very much pull. What little I do have is due to you."

I turned away from the window and frowned at him.

"Because I discovered you, you see. And your powers. That's given me a bit of status with Trawley and the others, but even with that, they don't listen much to what I say. He . . . he seemed very taken with his vision."

"I trusted you!"

"But there was no harm done! You gave him his magical favor, and now he's quite happy and understands your power."

I shook my head. "Stilton—"

"Please don't be angry, Miss Theo! Please!"

It was quite disconcerting to have a grownup plead with me. Felt very wrong somehow. I supposed it wouldn't hurt to relent. At least a little. "Very well. By the way, what can you tell me about high tide? When is it, for example?"

He looked quite confused. "High tide? Is that something else you saw in your vision? Something you didn't tell Trawley?"

"No! I was just wondering, that's all."

"Well, normally spring tides are the highest, and this spring they're even higher with all the recent flooding and snowmelt."

"Yes, but what time of day do they occur?"

"I'm not sure I know that."

I scooted forward on my seat. "Stilton. It's absolutely essential that I know when high tide will be tomorrow. Can you find the information and bring it with you when you come to work in the morning?"

He blinked at me, looking shy. "Does that mean you're no longer angry at me?"

"Yes, yes. Of course. Now, can you do it?"

"For you, Miss Theo, yes."

When Stilton dropped me off at the museum, I pretended to go inside, but in truth, I hid just behind the door, hoping Will and Snuffles would be along shortly.

Sure enough, before very long I heard the soft slap of

running feet accompanied by a loud, wet sniffle. I stepped out of my hiding place so they could see me, then waited for them to catch their breath.

"Wot did them blokes want wi' you?" Will asked as he took in huge gulps of air.

"Oh, just a bit of idiocy, really. But I don't have time to explain. I've finally discovered what Chaos is planning!"

"Oy! Wot is it, then?"

"Chaos is planning to use the staff to kill the crew of the *Dreadnought*. Then once they're dead, Chaos will use the staff to bring them back to life. Since the staff has power over reanimated dead, Chaos can use them to kidnap the ship."

"Blimey!"

"Exactly. I need you to get word to Wigmere right away."

Will looked at me oddly. "I'm not sure 'e's still at Somerset 'ouse this late, miss. 'E don't sleep there, you know."

Oh. Of course he didn't. "Maybe he's working late, or perhaps you can find out where he lives, then? And as soon as you've found him, tell him exactly what I've told you, got it?

"Will do, miss. Anyfink else?"

"No, I think that's quite enough for one night's work, don't you?"

It was so late by this time that I didn't dare go check on Mother. I was counting on her being far too distracted by Father's arrest to have noticed I had been gone.

It was horrid, though, as I was rather desperate to hear an update on poor Father. The thought of him sitting in a cold, dark jail cell with all sorts of despicable criminals and brutes felt as if I'd swallowed a knife. Sideways.

I needed to come up with a plan. One that would stop Chaos from stealing the *Dreadnought*, keep Will safe from the Grim Nipper, and rescue Father from jail.

It needed to be a corker.

As I padded down the corridor to my closet, Isis trailed behind me like a wisp of smoke. Surely Wigmere would know what to do.

Except that the last time we were faced with something of this magnitude, I had ended up having to deal with it alone. In a foreign country.

But if this involved the lives and safety of seven hundred British sailors, Wigmere would have to step in and use his power and influence to the utmost.

The good news was that Miss Sharpe's festering boils would likely keep her away for at least one more day, which would leave me free to do all I needed to get done.

Just then, Isis stopped following me and looked back the

way we'd come, her back arched and all her hair standing on end.

"What?" I peered back into the darkness. There! I heard a . . . sniffing sound. And the faint click of nails on the marble floor. A dark black shape detached itself from the rest of the shadows and stood in the mouth of the hallway.

"Anubis," I whispered. It had taken me a moment to recognize the living statue that had burst out of our front window only the day before. But now he was back. The question was, why?

"Don't make any sudden moves," I warned Isis, keeping my voice low so as not to startle the jackal. Isis flattened herself against the wall. I hoped Anubis wouldn't see her and take up chase. There was nowhere for any of us to go.

The jackal lowered his head and advanced slowly down the hallway toward us.

Keeping my eyes locked on Anubis, I began to back down the hall. I'd nearly made it to the main corridor when Isis slinked out from behind my ankles and disappeared into the shadows. I braced myself, expecting Anubis to have seen her, but he kept prowling toward me, a low growl in his throat.

I glanced to the right and then to the left, but there was no safe place. No office I could take refuge in, no closet I could slip into. Just the open foyer on one side and the long corridor on the other. Both would allow the jackal to over-take me in a matter of seconds.

My hand crept up to the neck of my gown and fumbled for the amulets there. I gripped them hard and faced Anubis. "There's a good dog—er, jackal," I said. "Nothing to be angry about. You chased the silly cat away. You showed her what's what."

"*Grrrrr,*" was his only response. A bit of saliva dripped from his teeth. He was within launching distance now—one good leap and he'd be at my throat. Except he didn't leap. He tilted his head to the side and stared at me. The growl disappeared.

Heartened by this, I stood up a little straighter. "That's right. You and I should be friends, actually. I—eek!"

Anubis rose up on his hind legs, planted his paws on my shoulders, then began licking my neck. Well, no. Not my neck. My amulets! I glanced down around his muzzle, past his tongue, and saw that he was licking the Blood of Isis amulet. Of course! Anubis and Isis were great friends!

Remembering how fond my cat was of being scratched be-hind the ears, I reached out and tried it on the jackal. He stopped licking and angled his head under my hand for bet-ter coverage. Being a statue for decades, he no doubt ac-quired a number of itches that needed a good scratching.

As I worked my fingertips through the coarse, straight

hair that reminded me of brush bristles, a low, contented growl escaped from his throat. I ended up giving him quite a long scratch because I didn't know what he'd do once I stopped.

Finally, when my hand got tired, he opened his eyes, shook himself, then turned away from me. He put his muzzle to the ground and continued sniffing along the floor of the museum, as he'd been doing before he had spotted me.

Puzzled, I decided to follow him for a bit to see what he was up to.

Sounding a bit like the new Hoover that our maid used to sweep the carpet, the jackal moved along the corridor. After a few moments of this, his ears perked up and he became more animated. He sniffed twice more, then made a mad dash for the door that led to the catacombs. He practically shoved his nose under it, sniffing like a crazed thing and scrabbling with his claws.

"You want to go into the catacombs, do you?" I said, coming up behind him. He sat down and peered intensely at the knob, as if expecting me to open it.

"Well, I suppose you don't have anything to fear down there, do you?" I opened the door and he exploded down the steps like a shot, clattering the whole way.

What *was* he exactly, anyway? I wondered as I followed

more slowly. He couldn't actually be the god Anubis, could he? Perhaps he was a *bau,* a spirit manifestation, sent by Anubis to do his bidding on earth.

Whatever he was, by the time I reached the bottom step, he was pawing frantically at the wall where the mummies were leaning. Oh dear. It was where I had placed the staff. Where the jackal had last seen it before it had been stolen.

Which meant he must have been a guardian figure sent to protect it. Excellent! I could use a little help. Although how to best utilize his jackal skills was a bit of a puzzle.

After having sniffed every square inch of the floor in front of the wall, he returned to me, sat on his haunches, and whined in a mournful tone. I should have been more frightened of him, but he had a bit of cobweb stuck to his muzzle and it made him much more like a dog and less like a jackal.

I went to a shelf and grabbed the Canopic jar that had held the Orb of Ra. "Here," I said, shoving the jar toward his nose. "Is this what you're looking for?"

The jackal took a few quick, loud sniffs, then sat back down with his tail wagging back and forth.

"It's gone missing," I said. "Someone stole the staff, if that's what you're looking for." His ears perked up. "I bet you could track it, couldn't you? After all, that's what the hounds do on the hunt, and I know you're more clever and cunning than a mere hound." His long tail whipped back and forth, narrowly missing an Old Kingdom stele. But how does one explain the concept of docks to a jackal? How could I get him to understand where I wanted him to go?

And then it hit me! "I'll be right back," I said, then galloped up the stairs to the coat rack in the hall. It was still there! I grabbed my hat, the one the sailor had fished out of the water for me when we had toured the *Dreadnought*. I turned to go back down the stairs, but the jackal sat right behind me, waiting, and I nearly tripped over him. "Well, like I told you, the staff has been stolen. But I can give you a clue as to where you'll find it. It's down by the docks. Here." I thrust the ruined hat at him. "The docks smell like this."

His nostrils went into overdrive as they sniffed up every fiber of the hat. He was so thorough, I was half afraid he'd inhale the thing. When he was done, he looked up and met my gaze, keen intelligence shining in those dark eyes of his. "Good boy," I said. "Now, fetch."

He gave one quick, sharp bark, then exploded off his haunches and out into the night.

I was heartily sick of having to wait for everyone else to bring me information or take a message for me. Even that wretched jackal had more freedom than I did.

CHAPTER TWENTY-EIGHT

Snuffling Along

THE NEXT MORNING I WAS AWAKENED by a knock on my closet door. "Who is it?" I called. I stretched and rubbed my eyes.

"It's me, Theo."

"Oh, Mum!" Awake now, I hopped out of the sarcophagus as Mum came in. "Any word from Father?" I asked.

"No." She said it briskly, as if it didn't worry her one bit, but the dark circles under her eyes gave her away. "I have, however, heard from Miss Sharpe. She sent a note around saying she was unwell and unable to come today." Mother's gaze sharpened slightly. "You wouldn't know anything about that, would you?"

"No! Well, only that she left early yesterday because she was feeling ill. You can check with Stilton if you like. He was there at the time."

"No, no, that's fine. But I must warn you, Theo—I have much on my mind and am horribly busy this morning. I have a hundred things to do. You'll have to take care of yourself today without Miss Sharpe here."

A huge bubble of frustration rose up inside me. Didn't I do exactly that every single day? "Of course, Mother." Still hungry for information, I pressed on. "Who else have you heard from?"

Mother bent over, picked up my pinafore from the floor, and began smoothing it out. "The Royal Archaeological Society, for one. It seems I will not be joining their ranks at this time."

"Oh, Mother! I'm so sorry. Is it because of the mummies?"

"They say not." She hung my pinafore on a peg. "However, that's the least of our worries, I would think."

Which reminded me: "Were you able to talk to Admiral Sopcoate last night?"

"No, I'm afraid not. He was at dinner with a delegation from Abyssinia, but your grandmother said she'd send a personal note to him first thing this morning." She gave me a tired smile that I thought was supposed to give me fortitude, but instead left me feeling vague and uncertain.

Just then, there was an urgent rap on the front door. An unusually grim and determined look came over Mother's face. "If that is Inspector Turnbull again, I shall make him rue the day he ever set foot in our museum."

She sounded frighteningly like Father. I followed after her as a second knock reverberated down the hall. Mother jerked the door open and nearly missed being beaned with Grandmother Throckmorton's cane, which she was raising for a third knock. "About time," she sniffed, pulling her cane back to her side.

Before Mum could retort, Grandmother sailed in. "Where is that granddaughter of mine? There you are," she said. "What on earth have you done to Miss Sharpe?"

I swallowed nervously. "I-I don't know what you mean. Mum said she sent a note around that she was ill . . ."

"No. Not just ill. She sent me a letter resigning. She will not be returning, even when she regains her health. And after all the trouble I went to! You will tell me the meaning of this, young lady."

"Really, madam," Mother said. "With everything else going on right now, it seems to me that Miss Sharpe is not our most pressing concern."

Grandmother drew herself up to her full height, but instead of blasting Mother for her impertinence, she simply said, "Have you news of my son?" And then it hit me. Her outrage about Miss Sharpe was just an excuse! She'd really come over to see what was happening with Father. Honestly. Why couldn't she just say so?

Mum shook her head. "The inspector isn't exactly being forthcoming. Have you word from Admiral Sopcoate yet?"

"Yes. He sent a note around this morning. He'll be tied up escorting a delegation from Abyssinia on a tour of the *Dreadnought,* but once he's finished up there, he said he'll come right along and help us sort out this mess."

Admiral Sopcoate would be onboard the *Dreadnought,* and Chaos was planning to kidnap it! My stomach dipped at the full impact of this. I had grown quite attached to the jolly admiral. Besides, if something happened to Admiral Sopcoate, Grandmother would turn back into her horrid, grumpy self.

Taking a huge risk by speaking without being spoken to, I said, "Excuse me, Grandmother. But what time will that be? Did he say?"

She peered down her nose at me. "I suppose the strain of having your father arrested has chased away what few manners you had." But her words didn't have the normal sting to them.

"I'm sorry, ma'am. I *am* rather worried."

"As are we all, child," she said with a sigh, looking old and tired. It was shocking, really, seeing her this way.

"The time?" I gently reminded her.

"Their tour is scheduled for eleven o'clock. He said he'd be done by two this afternoon."

Maybe I was wrong. Maybe Admiral Sopcoate wouldn't be in danger after all. What I really needed to do was find out what time high tide was.

"Excuse me." I bobbed a quick curtsy, then left the room, anxious to find Stilton.

He was in his office, just sitting down to his desk. "Did you find out?" I asked as I burst in.

He glanced up at my interruption. "Oh, good morning, Theo. Yes, I did. High tide is at twelve forty-seven p.m. today."

Right in the middle of the admiral's tour! He *would* be in horrible danger! "Thank you," I said, then dashed toward the west entrance, hoping Will would be there early. Surely he'd realize we'd have much to discuss this morning, after our wild adventures of the night before.

However, Will was nowhere in sight at the west entrance. Instead, I found Snuffles hiding in the bushes. I would have missed him but for the loud sneeze that exploded from the shrubbery just as I was closing the door.

"Snuffles?" I whispered.

And up he popped. "Miss?" he said as he wiped his nose along his sleeve.

I winced, then spotted the clean linen handkerchief I'd

given to him sitting crisp and white in his coat pocket. "You're supposed to use your handkerchief for that," I said.

"Oh, no, miss! It's much too nice for that."

I blinked, then shook my head. "Where is Will this morning?"

Snuffles's face fell. "That's wot I was hopin' you could tell me. He didn't come home last night. He and Ratsy went out—"

"Ratsy?"

"Me next oldest brother, miss."

"Just how many of you are there, anyway?"

"Seven. There's Will, then Ratsy, next comes Sparky, then me, an' Pincher, Soggers, and the Gob."

"The Gob?" I repeated faintly.

"Aye. On account of 'im putting everything in his gob."

I hardly knew what to say to that. Luckily, Snuffles brought us back to the subject at hand.

"Anyway, 'e and Will went out last night after we got back but then never came 'ome this mornin'."

"Maybe he just went to give Wigmere the message?"

"Mebbe. But not Ratsy. Ratsy had a job this mornin', but we couldn't find a sign o' him anywhere."

My stomach dropped all the way to my knees. This was not good. Not good at all. Did they get too close to Chaos's plans? Or did this have something to do with the Grim Nipper?

And how was I going to get word to Wigmere now? "Don't worry, Snuffles. We'll find him."

Somehow.

"You wait here. I have to collect a few things, and then we'll go find your brothers."

Supplies. I needed supplies. The last time I'd faced the Serpents of Chaos, I'd been in a tomb with Egyptian artifacts loaded with ancient magic at hand. I would have no such help on the *Dreadnought*.

But what to bring, exactly? What would be the most effective weapons?

I dashed to my small carrel in the reading room and pulled my curse-removal kit from behind a bookshelf. I turned it upside down and dumped all the contents onto the floor. I sorted through them for a moment, wondering if there was anything there I could use. The problem was, Chaos was given to wielding modern weapons, such as guns, and I didn't have anything to counteract them.

I snagged the atropaic wand that I'd used to undemonize Isis, which I had been meaning to return to its display case for ages. It was shaped like a throw stick and might have some potential. That was all I found. Stuffing it into my bag,

I hurried into the reading room. One of Miss Sharpe's books lay open on one of the tables. Miss Sharpe! The rope! That could be an effective weapon.

Wishing I had a second pair of gloves to put over my first pair, I gingerly pulled the rope from the hiding place where I'd stashed it. I hesitated a moment, then quickly undid two of the knots, releasing even more of the malignant spirit's power, ensuring it would be a most formidable weapon, then I dropped it into my bag.

Hmmm. I wondered where Father kept his shotgun. That would be a comfort, no doubt. But that was silly. Where on earth would I hide it?

My next destination was the Egyptian exhibit. Chaos had the staff, and although I had a Blood of Isis amulet to protect me, no one else did. I wanted to collect the amulets from the mummies so at least a few others would have some protection. Grateful that the bodies had the power to move only at night, I plucked off the amulets and stuffed them into my bag. I paused again, searching the room for anything else that might prove useful. I spied a small collection of execration figures. Those had come in most handy back in the Valley of the Kings. I stuffed one into my carpetbag. And then I was out of time.

Except, once again, I had no money for cab fare. Bother! I was going to have to get a job if I was going to keep this up. Or ask Wigmere to cover some of my expenses, like the board of directors covered some of Father's. For now, there was really only one source to tap for the funds. I would rather have not brought him into this—I still hadn't forgiven him for the night before—but I felt that I had no choice.

I burst into Stilton's office. "Hullo again," he said.

"Hullo again, Stilt—I mean, Tefen."

He beamed at the use of his code name, which was exactly what I had been hoping for.

"What can I do for you now?"

"Actually, it's funny you should ask. I need a ride, and I'm afraid I haven't any money for a cab. May I"—the next word stuck in my throat—"borrow cab fare? I'll pay it back, I promise!" I rushed to add.

Just as I had feared, Stilton was immediately on alert. "But of course. Although if you're going somewhere, Mestafet and I should accompany you."

"I really don't think that will be necessary, Stil—Tefen. It's not like last night when I was out so late. It's morning and I'll be out and about in broad daylight. I'll be perfectly safe, I'm sure."

He began shaking his head no before I had even finished speaking. "I don't think so, Miss Theo. Trouble does seem to follow you around, and that's why you have us. To look after you."

Oh, bother. I'd so hoped because Stilton was a Black Sunner that he wouldn't be hindered by the same sort of hang-ups about safety that other grownups had. Clearly, I'd been wrong. "Wouldn't that get you into trouble with Weems?"

Stilton's face clouded a moment. "Yes. Most likely. But I can handle him."

"Actually," I said, thinking fast, "I have something else, something even more important, I need you to do."

His eyes lit up. "Really?"

"Yes. I need you to get to Inspector Turnbull and tell him that he will be able to find Nigel Bollingsworth at the Royal Albert Docks later on this morning."

"Bollingsworth! Really? Is he involved in all this?"

"Yes. But I haven't got time to explain it all now. Can you do it?"

"Yes, miss." Stilton lifted his hand to his forehead, saluting me.

Was that a Black Sun thing? Or was he just overeager?

He stood up and began fishing cab fare out of his pocket.

"Then," I continued, "go directly to Somerset House to the Antiquarian Society on the third floor. Ask to see Lord Wigmere. A wretched little beast of a secretary named Boythorpe will try to stop you, but ignore him and speak only to Wigmere."

Stilton nodded, absorbing every detail.

"Then, when you see Wigmere, tell him . . . Chaos is rising. Have you got that?"

"Chaos is rising," he repeated.

"Excellent. Then tell him I've gone to the *Dreadnought* at the Royal Albert Docks, and he'll know what to do from there. Oh, and let him know about Bollingsworth, too."

"Is that all?"

"Yes. Now repeat it back to me."

When he had, I took the cab fare he held out to me. "I *will* pay it back," I promised, then hurried from the room.

I ran smack into Clive Fagenbush.

"You were eavesdropping!" I hissed at him.

"No, I wasn't. I do work with the man. As I told you before, he owes me a report."

I had meant to ask Stilton about Fagenbush's prowling, but all the tumult of the past two mornings had chased it out of my head. However, I didn't have time to deal with that now—I had to get down to the docks.

Fagenbush eyed my carpetbag. "And where are you going in such a hurry?"

"None of your business," I shot back at him. "Now, excuse me." And off I went to the west entrance to meet Snuffles.

"Wot took you so long?" Snuffles asked, nearly hopping from foot to foot.

"Sorry. I had to collect some things. Now, let's go find a cab."

I hoisted my bag and marched across the street toward the corner. It was late enough in the morning that most everyone was at work, so it didn't take too long to get a cab to stop.

The driver squinted at me suspiciously and made me pay him up-front. With a sigh I did, then got into the cab and settled myself onto the seat.

Snuffles climbed in after me, but instead of getting on the seat opposite, he sat right up next to me so that our arms were nearly touching.

I remembered him wiping his nose on his sleeve earlier and scooted over a bit.

He scooted closer again, but before I could reposition my-self, there was a slap of the reins. As the cab lurched for-ward, the door opened and a tall, thin man stepped from the running board into the cab.

He lifted the tattered top hat from his head and we came face to face with the Grim Nipper.

CHAPTER TWENTY-NINE
A GRIM TASK

"YOU AND YOUR BROTHERS are hard men to find," the Grim Nipper told Snuffles, who shrank next to me.

"What have you done with Will?" I demanded, as if I had been the one who had accosted him.

"Nothing. I was hoping you might be able to tell me where he's gone."

"I don't know." I tried to keep my face from showing the panic I was feeling.

The Grim Nipper turned his watery blue eyes to Snuffles. "And you?"

Snuffles shook his head.

"Ah, now, that is too bad. You see, if I can't find your brother and convince 'im to come back to work for me, I'm afraid I'll 'ave to take you as compensation. I'm owed something for all me training of your brother, aren't I?" He reached into his coat pocket and began jiggling some coins he had in there.

Something tight inside my chest relaxed at the Nipper's words. He was still trying to convince Will to come back to work for him, which meant that Will *hadn't* returned to his old life. It also meant that he wasn't missing due to any shenanigans on the Grim Nipper's part, which left . . . Chaos. My chest tightened again.

The Nipper grinned, displaying a mouth full of brown and rotting teeth. "Besides, I got so much work now, what wi' all the gold people are saving to ward off mummies, that I could use two or three new apprentices."

Snuffles shook like a leaf in a stiff breeze, his eyes huge in his pale face. "Snuffles is much too young to work for you," I said, coming to his defense.

"Not really. Will was younger 'n that when I taught 'im everything I know. Besides, I've seen this young'un following Will around for a few weeks. I know Will's a-training 'im for 'is future career."

The Nipper pulled his hand out of his pocket. He was

wearing fingerless gloves, and on his palm sat a shiny gold sovereign. He held it out to Snuffles. "'Ere, now. Wouldn't you want one of these for your very own?"

As Snuffles watched, the Nipper began to walk the coin across his fingers in some kind of trick. Snuffles looked hypnotized, but whether from fear or the enticement of so much gold, I couldn't tell.

"Snuffles is not interested," I informed the Grim Nipper in my best Grandmother Throckmorton voice. "So you can take your leave of this carriage."

A look of annoyance flashed across the Nipper's face. "And just who exactly are you?"

"A family friend. Now please, take your leave, as we have an errand we must run."

"Take my leave? After I've just confessed to you me entire operation? I don't think so, me dear. Besides, while you're too old to train for nippery, you'd likely fetch a pretty penny if'n I sold you."

Sold me! I think not. As I watched the gold coin wind its way between his fingers, I got an idea. "Look," I said. "I have a very valuable artifact in my bag. If I give it to you, will you let us go? I'm sure you'll get more for it that you would me."

The Grim Nipper's eyes lit up as they fell onto the satchel I clasped on my lap. "In there, you say?"

Quick as a snake, he reached out and snagged the bag from my grasp.

Just as I'd hoped he would.

Keeping one eye on me to see if I would try to stop him, he pocketed his coin and opened the satchel. "You ain't near as clever as you look, thinking you can bargain with something I can just take." He lifted the knotted rope, studied it a moment, then laid it across his lap as he reached back into the carpetbag.

He groped around inside, then pulled out an execration figure. "What kind of toy is this?" He scowled, then tossed it onto the seat. Next he pulled out a handful of amulets. He stared at them for a long moment, appraising their value. With an exclamation of disgust, he finally tossed them onto the seat as well, his eyes flat and angry. "Thought you'd trick me, did you? Thought you could outsmart the Grim Nipper, did you? Well, I'll show you how they came to put the Grim in Nipper, you little cow."

He reached for the knotted rope on his lap, then raised his hands to strike me with it.

I gasped and stared in horror at the flesh of his fingers, which had begun to puff up and turn green, with the nails darkening to nearly black.

The Grim Nipper followed my gaze to his hands. "What—"

He flung the rope to the floor of the hansom and ripped

off his fingerless gloves as the effects worked toward his palms. He looked up at me with fury and horror in his eyes. "You've cursed me! You've gone and given me a mummy's curse!"

I didn't say a word, just shook my head. It wasn't true— not exactly, anyway.

"The gold!" he said, then shoved a hand into his pocket and pulled out a gold coin. He began rubbing it all over his cursed palms like a bar of soap. The boils and blisters continued to work their way up his wrists, disappearing into his coat sleeves.

"It's not working!" His voice was high and tinged with desperation.

The carriage lurched to a stop, and the cabby called out, "Royal Albert Docks! Out wi' ye!"

The Grim Nipper wrenched open the cab door and stumbled out onto the dock. I quickly grabbed the cursed rope from the floor—grateful for my gloves and four amulets— and stuffed it back into my bag.

"Wot did you do to 'im?" Snuffles asked, his eyes wide and full of awe.

"The rope was cursed."

"Blimey, miss. That was one neat trick!"

"Come on, we've got to hurry!"

No sooner had we gotten out of the cab than the driver

slapped the reins on the horse's back and took off like a shot. I heard him mumble something about a drunken sot. I looked up to find the Grim Nipper reeling on the dock, clutching various parts of his body as the curse worked its way through him.

Although there were scads of men working nearby, none of them spared the lurching Nipper a glance. Perhaps they also thought he was drunk. Whatever the reason, I was grateful for their indifference.

I didn't think the curse would kill him, but I didn't know for certain. If he died, I wouldn't have anyone to hand over to Turnbull in exchange for Father. I glanced around the docks, wondering what to do with the beastly man.

"Here, this way," I called out to him.

He lumbered toward me as I led him closer and closer to the edge of the dock. Quietly, I said to Snuffles, "When I say so, grab his coat and we'll push him into the water. Got it?"

Snuffles nodded.

The Grim Nipper nearly barreled into us and his shouts were growing louder and louder. If we didn't do something fast, he would attract far too much attention. "Now!"

I shoved the Grim Nipper backwards. Next to me, Snuffles pushed as well. There was a slight tug of resistance, and then the Nipper tumbled back into the water.

"Help!" he said, spluttering and floundering about. "I can't swim."

"You don't have to swim. Just grab one of the posts and hang on. Someone should be along shortly. And the salt in the water might even remove the curse."

I turned back to Snuffles just as he was putting something into his coat pocket. He caught me watching and patted it possessively. "Wot? I couldn't risk letting all that gold fall into the river, now, could I?"

"No, of course not. Now let's go!"

As we made our way to the dock where the *Dreadnought* lay at anchor, we did our best to keep hidden. I didn't want Chaos to find me before I found them.

Plus, I had to decide what to do with Snuffles. I didn't want to take him with me to face the Serpents of Chaos— he would be defenseless against their brand of evildoing. But as I looked around, the docks didn't seem like the best place, either.

I found a hiding place behind a stack of cargo containers— we were out of sight, but I had a good view of the ship's loading plank. There were sailors guarding the entrance, as there had been the day Admiral Sopcoate had brought Grandmother and me for a tour.

The thought of Sopcoate made my heart skip a beat. I

couldn't let anything happen to him. Grandmother wouldn't be able to bear it.

I glanced down at the watch pinned to my gown. It was nearly eleven o'clock. Sopcoate had told Grandmother he was escorting the Abyssinians at the top of the hour, so they should be here any moment. Chaos had said they'd need to be ready for high tide, at 12:47. How much time did they think they'd need to get the ship ready to sail? I glanced up at the giant vessel with hundreds of men scurrying around on its decks, tending to their duties. Hundreds of men whom Chaos meant to kill, then bring back as reanimated dead and use to kidnap the crown jewel of the British Navy. I thought how every one of those men would be horrified to learn that he would be committing treason within the space of a couple of hours.

Unless I could stop it.

"Here," I said, taking a Blood of Isis amulet from my satchel and handing it to Snuffles. "You'll need to wear this."

He recoiled. "I ain't wearin' no girl's frippery!"

"It's not frippery, you little dolt! It's an amulet, to protect against curses like the one that just attacked the Grim Nipper."

"Oh." He eyed it with great suspicion. "You sure about that?"

"Never mind. If you don't care if your fingers rot off, it's no worry of mine." I went to put the amulet back into the satchel, but Snuffles reached out and stopped me.

"No, miss. I'll wear it. I'm right fond of me fingers."

"Very well," I said, then slipped it over his head before he changed his mind. "You can wear it under your collar if you like, so it doesn't show."

Behind us there was a loud, hollow clattering as a horse and carriage drew up onto the wooden docks. My breath caught in my throat as I watched the footman hop down and open the door. Admiral Sopcoate alighted, followed by seven others. Except for Sopcoate, they all wore long flowing robes and brightly colored sashes. They had dark skin and full beards and wore turbans on their heads. The poor Abyssinians! They had no idea what they'd just wandered into.

The group laughed, and I heard raised voices speaking a strange language. Still using the cover of the cargo crates, I inched closer.

The tallest man had a strange forked beard. And blue eyes. Odd for such a dark complexion. The man next to him sneezed, knocking his whiskers askew.

One of the Abyssinians gave him a nudge and motioned to the man's face. The fellow who'd sneezed quickly reached up and adjusted his whiskers.

Except he didn't use a hand to fix his whiskers, but a hook. A horrid realization struck me.

I searched the rest of the faces. It was difficult to tell because they weren't all facing me, but it appeared as if the thick eyebrows on one man shadowed a heavily scarred left eye, although his skin was much darker than when I had last seen it.

With a sinking feeling, the brilliance of their plan hit me. Chaos was posing as the Abyssinian ambassadors! In mere moments, Admiral Sopcoate would be escorting them onto his pride and joy! I had to stop them, but how?

At the sound of quick, efficient steps on the dock behind me, I pulled back into my hiding place. A uniformed sailor was heading my way. I turned to Snuffles. "Whatever happens, stay here! Do you understand me? Stay here so you can show the police where I went. Oh, and may I borrow one of those guineas you lifted from the Grim Nipper?"

Snuffles tried to look shocked. "Wot guineas, miss?"

"Don't worry. I'd much rather you have them than they end up at the bottom of the river. I just need one."

At his continued reluctance, I sighed. "I promise I'll pay you back."

"Well, all right, then . . ."

I pocketed the coin, and then, without allowing myself to

think about it too much, I stepped out from behind a crate directly into the path of the sailor.

He stopped, surprise marking his face. "Out of my way, there, miss."

"Good morning, sir." I did my best to look a little lost and worried. (It wasn't hard, believe me.) "I am in a bit of a bind and was wondering if you could help me? I need to speak to Admiral Sopcoate before he goes onboard, but I don't want his visitors to see that it's only me who's called him away. Being foreign dignitaries, they might not understand."

The sailor scowled. "What's a slip of a girl like you want to bother the admiral for?"

I wanted to scream with frustration. "It is of the utmost importance that I speak to the admiral at once," I said, using my best Grandmother Throckmorton voice.

"Now, look here. We've all got more important things to do than play nursemaid to a hoity-toity young miss."

By this time, the sailor had raised his voice and was beginning to create a bit of a scene. I saw the admiral look over at us, his eyes widening as he saw me. He murmured something to the man next to him, then detached himself from the small group.

I stepped behind the sailor, not wanting any of the Serpents of Chaos to recognize me.

"What's going on, sailor?" he asked.

The sailor whirled around, his face flaming at being caught arguing with me. "This girl wanted me to disturb you, sir. I didn't think—"

"You did exactly right, but I happen to know this child. I'll take it from here."

The sailor gave a relieved salute, then hightailed it out of there.

Admiral Sopcoate gave me his full attention. "What on earth are you doing here?" He stepped closer, his face full of concern. "Is your grandmother all right?"

"Oh, yes. She's fine. But . . . it's about that group you're with. What I'm about to tell you might seem hard to believe, but you must try." I took a deep breath. "They aren't Abyssinians at all! They're evil men who work for a secret organization called the Serpents of Chaos. And they're planning to kidnap the *Dreadnought* right out from under your nose!"

The relief at being able to put this enormous problem smack into the hands of a competent adult was nearly overwhelming.

Sopcoate rocked back on his heels, a frown crumpling his brow. "You're quite right, my dear. This is a serious problem. But don't worry. I'll fix everything."

The admiral's face suddenly changed, going from his

friendly, pleasant manner to a chilling, unreadable mask. He reached out and grabbed my arm with an iron grip. "You, my dear, have meddled for the last time." Then, with my mouth hanging open in shock, he began to drag me toward the Abyssinian delegation.

CHAPTER THIRTY

High Friends in Low Places

"YOU MIGHT WANT TO GET YOUR FEET under you and pretend you're walking," Sopcoate said under his breath. "Otherwise I'll have to carry you aboard and that won't be pleasant."

Scrambling, I managed to get my feet working. "But . . ."

"You know, I doubted the others when they told me how much trouble you'd been. That's why I befriended your grandmother, in fact—so I could keep an eye on you and see if one eleven-year-old girl could really cause such a fuss." He tightened his grip on my arm and shook me. "They were right. But I think we've underestimated you for the last time."

We? He'd said "we"! My mind reeled under the implications. "You mean you're with *them?*" My voice squeaked.

"If you mean the Serpents of Chaos, yes. I'm with them."

Admiral Sopcoate was one of the Serpents of Chaos?

"I tried to play nice, Theo. I arranged for three governesses in order to distract you and keep you out of our way. But no, you were too clever for them. Too clever by half."

So that was how Grandmother had been able to find so many governesses so quickly. "And you're the one who told Bollingsworth where to look for the staff! Because I told you I'd been working down in the basement," I gasped.

"Exactly . . . Look what I found skulking around, gents."

Sopcoate thrust me forward so that I faced Bollingsworth, von Braggenschnott, and five other agents of Chaos I'd never seen before, all disguised as Abyssinians.

Von Braggenschnott raised his hook and took a menacing step toward me.

"Stop!" Sopcoate commanded. "We'll not risk our plans for a moment of petty vengeance."

"We should see how petty it feels when it is your hand she loses," von Braggenschnott muttered.

Bollingsworth studied me with cold, angry eyes and a disturbing smile. "Decisions, decisions—to kill her now or to kill her later."

"I'm not sure she should be killed, seeing as how she managed to outsmart all of you." Sopcoate's voice was scathing. When he had everyone's attention, he continued. "Our first move will be against the officers. If we cut off the head of the snake, the rest of the body will be easier to overcome. Who's got my mask?"

One of the men I didn't know pulled an extra turban from the folds of his robe. That was when I realized they weren't just slightly misshapen turbans, but masks to keep the men safe from the staff's deadly fumes. They'd managed to roll them up so that they looked like turbans and would be immediately accessible. It was brilliant, really.

"The captain is gathering all the officers in the wardroom for an official reception," Sopcoate said as he secured his mask inside his jacket. "Once they're there, von Braggenschnott and Janos will join me at the front of the room and the rest of you will take up your assigned positions."

"What about her?" a man with a Russian accent asked.

"You'll help Bollingsworth keep an eye on her." He shot the former First Assistant Curator a withering look. "D'you think you can manage her this time?"

"Yes," he snarled.

"I should hope so." Sopcoate thrust me at Bollingsworth, who clamped his beefy hand onto my arm.

I looked back to see if there was any sign of Inspector Turnbull. I could have used a contingent of policemen right about then. But there was no one. Bollingsworth shoved me forward. "I still think I should be the one to wield the staff, as I've got two good hands," he muttered.

Von Braggenschnott looked over his shoulder at us, his blue eyes burning in his darkened face. "Ja, but my magic is stronger."

"Stop your bickering!" Sopcoate ordered, and we made the rest of the way to the ship in silence.

We were met by a number of sailors on the dock, who saluted and instructed us to proceed up the boarding plank. Onboard, a small band had gathered on deck and was playing a jaunty bit of music. When they finished, Captain Bacon and a group of officers stepped forward to greet the dignitaries.

If he was surprised to see me accompanying the Abyssinian delegation, the captain gave no sign. Well, he blinked twice, but carried on as if nothing were out of the ordinary. Well disciplined, as Grandmother would say, which was too bad because I would have loved for him to ask a question or two right then. I thought briefly about simply blurting out what had happened, but a glint of steel in Bollingsworth's left eye convinced me to keep quiet. At least for now.

"The men will be ready for full inspection shortly," the captain explained. "They've just finished cleaning up after coaling."

"Ah." Sopcoate rocked back on his heels. "You're full of coal, then?"

"Aye, aye, sir. We'll be leaving tomorrow with the tide, so we're completing the last-minute preparations. All the officers are gathered in the wardroom just as you requested, Admiral."

"Excellent," Sopcoate said. "We'll go on down, then, shall we?"

With one last salute, Captain Bacon stepped in front of our party and led us to the hatchway to the next deck down. Bollingsworth kept a tight grip on my shoulder—so tight, in fact, that it was numb, which I supposed was a blessing.

We filed into the wardroom, which was half full of officers engaging in small talk as they began to take their seats. Admiral Sopcoate gave a friendly nod, then led our group to the very back of the room. "Everyone remember their places?" he asked under his breath. "Piotr and Franz, you take the far doors. Bollingsworth, you're in the back. Yuri and Jacques, you'll be in front of the pantry. The rest are up front with me."

The turbaned heads nodded back at him.

"You." He speared Bollingsworth with his gaze. "Have a care with her arm there or you'll have every officer in the place down on our heads for manhandling the child." The admiral pointed to a small supply pantry. "Tie her up in there. Yuri, go with him."

"With what?" Bollingsworth asked, indicating his empty hands. Well, empty except for me, of course.

"I don't know. Do I have to do all your thinking for you?"

Snarling under his breath, Bollingsworth dragged me toward the supply pantry. "Sit there," he said, thrusting me against a small footstool in the corner. His eyes narrowed as they alighted on my satchel. "What've you got in there?"

He tore the bag from my hands. "If you have another one of those ruddy execration figures, I swear I'll use it on you this time."

He yanked the satchel open. Frowning, he reached in and began rummaging around in it. "Rather slim pickings for such a clever girl, eh, Theo? Losing your touch?" He pulled out the atropaic wand, then tossed it onto the floor. His face lit up when he spotted the rope. "Look at this! You've very conveniently brought me just what I need to tie you up." He wagged the rope in front of my nose in a gloating manner.

However, I was afraid it was I who started gloating.

He wasn't wearing any gloves.

He grabbed my shoulder and twirled me around on the stool, then tied my hands together. Or tried to. The rope was too short. "What do you have all these ruddy knots in it for?" he asked as he began untying them. I shuddered at the thought of the *mut* getting loose on the ship. When there was still one knot left, I couldn't keep quiet any longer. "Honestly, I think it's long enough now."

He eyed me curiously. "Now, why don't you want me to remove this last knot?" Keeping his gaze on me, he moved his hand toward it. Just then, Yuri stuck his head into the pantry.

"Hurry!" the Russian said. "They're about to start."

Distracted, Bollingsworth forgot about the last knot and tied me up. Luckily, my dress sleeves were tightly buttoned at the wrist so he simply tied the rope over them. "I'll be back to deal with you in a while. Oh, wait." He tapped his turban. "I won't have to!" Laughing, he followed Yuri into the wardroom.

I didn't know whether he had meant to or not, but he had managed to leave the door open a crack.

The minute they were out of sight, I began struggling against the rope, but carefully so my sleeves wouldn't creep up and expose my skin. I wasn't sure how long my amulets would hold against a curse this strong.

Light conversation floated to my ears as the last of the officers took their seats. When I heard Captain Bacon's voice, I stopped struggling in order to listen. "My fine men, we have a treat in store for us today. Our own Admiral Sopcoate is here to say a few words and introduce us to his guests. Won't you welcome me in joining him?"

As applause followed, I worked even harder against my bonds, but it was no use. The clapping died down and another sound reached my ears. A muted scraping of metal on metal. I cocked my head. It was coming from behind me.

I tried to twist my head to see, but it was near impossible. The sound grew louder, so using my feet, I wiggled my body around on the stool until I was facing the wall.

And I nearly fainted when I saw two small, dark figures who looked as though they'd sprung from the Underworld.

One of them reached out and put a hand on my arm, and my heart almost stopped beating. I opened my mouth to scream.

"Quiet, miss! It's just me!"

It took a full second for me to recognize Sticky Will's voice. I realized that there was a small hatch in the wall that they had slid open.

"What are you doing here?" I asked in a strained whisper. "And what happened to you? Snuffles has been terribly worried." So had I, but I wasn't about to bring that up. Not after last time.

"Me and Ratsy snuck aboard during coaling, before dawn this morning. We're a bit dusty is all."

"My fellow officers . . ." Admiral Sopcoate began speaking.

"We have to hurry!" I told Will. "Can you untie me?"

"In a jiffy."

"No! Wait! Before you touch that rope, reach into that bag there and take two of the amulets. Each of you put one on. The rope is cursed," I explained at Will's dubious look.

When Will pulled out two of the homemade amulets, he stared at them in disgust. "We aren't wearing no necklaces!"

"They're not necklaces. I told you, they hold protective charms that will keep you safe from the cursed spirit captured in this rope. Now, put them on!"

Grumbling, Will and Ratsy slipped on the amulets, and then Will began to untie the rope. "After we left you, Snuffles went home and Ratsy met up with me. We went back to the Salty Dog. The German bloke and the one wi' the chewed-up face were stayin' there, in a room at the tavern. We followed, thinking mebbe we could 'ear anyfink else they 'ad to say. Instead, they led us right to a room full o' mummies! All the missing mummies are piled in the cellar of the Salty Dog."

"Excellent work, Will. What did Wigmere say when you told him?"

Will looked sheepish. "Well, I didn't have time to give Wiggy the message. We came aboard 'ere instead and never made it back to Somerset 'ouse." He gave a final grunt and the rope came away.

My heart fell. I had been counting on Wigmere and the Brotherhood to show up at any moment to help us out. But we were on our own.

Once I was untied, I stuffed the rope in my pocket, snatched the wand from the floor, and we all inched toward the crack in the door, careful not to make any noise. I peeked out.

". . . pleased to present to you Ezana Sehul, crown prince of Abyssinia . . ."

I pulled my head back in. "There are two men right in front of this door. Two are at the front of the room, two are on the far side, and one more is in the back. I'm pretty sure they're all armed with pistols, but they'll try not to use them for fear of raising the officers' suspicion."

"Do you 'ave a plan, miss?"

"Er, not quite yet. Give me a moment."

". . . and his high priest, Yeshaq Lebna," Sopcoate continued. "They are here today to view the greatest navy in the world as they begin to build a navy of their own. Even when starting out, why not start from the best, eh?" He laughed, and the room joined him.

I was close to panicking now. We were almost out of time and I had no tools and no ideas. Behind me, the boys were whispering together, but before I could hear what they were saying, Sopcoate's words snagged my attention.

"As a token of Prince Sehul's thanks, he will have his high priest perform a sacred Abyssinian Blessing of the Water ceremony, guaranteed to bring good luck and prosperity to our vessel. Prince Sehul."

We had just run out of time. Once the staff came into contact with the water, the poisonous gases would be released into the room. Perhaps I should just run into the room screaming the truth? That would at least put a temporary stop to the proceedings. I opened my mouth to take a breath when Will poked me in the shoulder. "What?" I asked, annoyed at having my momentum interrupted.

"We figure we can take four of 'em out, see. I got my flick knife, and Ratsy's got 'is slingshot. 'E can take out two, mebbe three, with it before they even know what 'it 'em."

"He's that good a shot?"

"'E's a ratter, miss. That's 'ow he catches the rats."

"Oh, well, yes, but that still leaves the others."

"Mebbe not," Ratsy said from the door. It was the first time he'd spoken and his voice was unusually deep, almost like a foghorn.

"What do you mean?"

"Look."

I looked out the crack and gasped. The back of Bollingsworth's neck had erupted in black boils and his skin was now a grayish-greenish shade. The rope had worked! Even better, he was swaying on his feet, struggling to stay upright as the curse overtook him.

Just off to my right, there was a flash of movement at the door as a sailor appeared. The officer on guard lowered his head to hear what he had to say. "A dog?" he repeated, so softly that only those of us near the door could have heard it.

"Yes sir, a dog."

A dog? My hopes rose. Could it be . . . ?

"Well, catch it as quickly as you can. We don't want our guests' visit to be marred by a beastly animal on board!"

At that very moment, Sopcoate and a dignitary were balancing a huge vessel full of water. They set it down in front of von Braggenschnott. He raised the staff in his hand and began to chant in a strange language that I recognized as a perverted form of Egyptian.

Everyone in the room was riveted.

Except the sailor at the door. "I say, sir, but what's wrong with that gent there?" He pointed at Bollingsworth, whose entire face was now covered in hideous boils.

"Good gad!" the officer said, probably louder than he meant to.

Heads turned to see what the matter was. A ripple of disquiet ran through the room as the conversation was repeated from officer to officer. In the front, von Braggenschnott said something with great flourish, then rotated the staff so it was upside down.

"Now," I said to Will. I bolted out of the pantry with the wand in my grasp. If I hit von Braggenschnott's hand, it would cause him to drop the staff. The only problem was, he'd drop it straight into the water, which would have the exact effect he wanted.

Over the chanting I could now hear the barking, but it was quickly drowned out when the most recent officer to have noticed the cursed man stood up and pointed to the back of the room. "The ruddy foreigners have brought us some nasty disease! Look!"

Many things happened at once then.

Will stuck the Russian with his flick knife, causing him to drop to the ground.

Slightly hidden behind the pantry door, Ratsy fired his slingshot. A small piece of coal struck Franz in the forehead, downing him like a ninepin.

In the confusion that erupted, a lean black shape burst through the wardroom door. It *was* Anubis! And he was heading straight for von Braggenschnott.

CHAPTER THIRTY-ONE

JACKAL AT THE DOOR

IN A HEARTBEAT, the jackal was at the front of the room. His sharp, pointed teeth closed around the staff.

Seeing my chance, I launched the wand.

It whirled unevenly across the short distance (thank goodness most of the officers between me and von Braggenschnott were still sitting or they would have stopped it with their heads) and struck von Braggenschnott's hand with a muffled *crack*.

Unable to help himself, von Braggenschnott let go of the staff. The jackal stumbled backwards, almost going end over teakettle, the staff still clutched in his teeth. Realizing he was free of a struggle, he darted out of the room. *"Nein! Nicht der zauberstab!"* von Braggenschnott yelled.

Pandemonium exploded.

"Get that jackal!" Admiral Sopcoate bellowed.

"The high priest is speaking German!" Captain Bacon exclaimed.

Thwack! Another piece of coal took out the Frenchman kneeling next to Bollingsworth, who had collapsed to the ground.

"Get the girl!" von Braggenschnott yelled.

"Now he's speaking the Queen's English!" someone said.

My eyes sought out Will. "Go back out the way you came and make sure the jackal escapes."

Will threw me a puzzled look. "But 'e's got yer staff!"

"I know, but he'll take it back to the museum. Now go!"

Will gave a quick nod, and then he and Ratsy disappeared into the pantry.

Four Chaos agents were down. Unfortunately, that still left four more.

Hiding behind the officers' legs, I crawled over to where Bollingsworth had fallen and slipped Snuffles's guinea into his pocket. Then, using a group of officers as cover, I duck-walked over to the door and slipped into the passageway. I tried to remember which way we'd come. From the left, I thought.

As I headed for the hatchway, a number of sailors were hurrying to the upper deck, intent on obeying Admiral Sopcoate's order to stop the jackal. When I reached the ladder, I saw one sailor coming down. Unlike the others, he didn't look confused—he looked purposeful and had a rather ruthless air about him. When he caught sight of me, he quickened his pace.

Bother. I'd forgotten they had agents hidden onboard. I whirled around and began running in the opposite direction, looking for a ladder that led up so I wouldn't be cornered in the bowels of the ship.

Not giving my knickers a second thought this time, I scrambled up the first ladder I came to.

As I emerged on deck, I took great heaping gulps of air, grateful to be outside at last. To my left lay the bow. Nothing there but anchor chains and vents. Certainly no means of escape.

I charged right, toward where the sailors had been lining up for inspection. Safety in numbers, I hoped.

The deck between the forward gun turret and the edge of the ship was relatively narrow, so I crept carefully, hugging the base of the tower as I went.

Once clear, I raced toward the bridge. As I ran, I glanced up at the chart house. Was that a flicker of movement I saw? I blinked against the bright sky, bringing my vision into sharper focus, but no, it had just been wishful thinking. There was no help from that quarter. All the officers who normally served on the bridge were down in the wardroom.

There was a shout behind me as Admiral Sopcoate and von Braggenschnott emerged on the upper deck.

I scrambled down the ladder that led to the level below. In front of me, two burly sailors were headed my way. My first thought was of rescue, until I heard Admiral Sopcoate shout out, "Squidge! Farley! Seize her!"

There was no place left to go. The smooth steel wall of the ship loomed on my left, the railing and the river on my right.

I glanced back at von Braggenschnott and Sopcoate, who were now coming down the ladder. Squidge and Farley were seconds away.

I decided I'd take my chances overboard.

Holding on to the top railing, I put my feet onto the bottom rail. It was wobbly and precarious, and I'd be lucky if I didn't end up going into the river headfirst. But surely the dark, foul water of the Thames was better than capture? Especially since I'd foiled Chaos's plans twice now. As Bollingsworth had said, they had a debt to settle.

I lifted my right foot to the top rail. I would have to push off hard to avoid hitting the side of the boat on the way down. I took a deep breath.

There was a flutter of blackness off to my right—between Sopcoate and me—as a great black shape swooped out of the sky in my direction.

An arm came around my middle, knocking a gasp of surprise out of me. My feet left the railing, and my heart, which had been lodged up in my throat, took a nosedive down toward my toes as the deck swayed sickeningly beneath me.

We landed with a bone-jarring thud (of which the cloaked figure took the brunt, I might add). My rescuer released me and I stumbled, then bent over to catch my breath. "You've simply got to find a better way to—you!"

The sight of Clive Fagenbush had me gaping in shock. "What are you doing here?" Honestly! Is no one who they seem anymore?

"Run, you little fool." He whipped a pair of pistols out from under his cape.

Shouts and yells from the officers' mess let me know that Chaos would be following, so even though I loathed doing anything Fagenbush told me to, I hightailed it out of there. With Fagenbush watching my back, I made my way aft, where, by the shouts I heard, the jackal had been spotted.

When I arrived, all the sailors were standing on the dockside, shouting encouragement to a handful of men who were chasing the jackal down the boarding plank. I breathed a sigh of relief. The staff would be out of Chaos's reach, at least for now.

Fagenbush was right on my heels. "What happened to the others?" I asked.

"They changed their minds and returned to the front of the ship," he said.

"But that means they're escaping!" I said in dismay. I started to run back, but Fagenbush reached out and grabbed my arm.

"No! We've got to get off this ship before Chaos decides they'd rather have revenge than a clean getaway. Besides, I was ordered to rescue you, not chase them down."

"Ordered?" I asked, momentarily distracted by this revelation. "Who ordered you to rescue me?"

"Wigmere," he said. "Now move."

CHAPTER THIRTY-TWO

UNEXPECTED FRIENDS IN HIGH PLACES

CAPTAIN BACON APPEARED ON DECK just then and gave the order to locate the Abyssinians. While everyone was busy with that, Fagenbush herded me down the gangway to the dock. I must say, my shock at Fagenbush working for Wigmere had me at a bit of a loss.

As Fagenbush led me toward a waiting carriage, we saw a small crowd gathered near the water's edge of the docks. "Haul him up!" I recognized Turnbull's booming voice and altered my direction.

"Where are you going?" Fagenbush asked. "Come back!"

Just because Fagenbush claimed he was working for Wigmere didn't mean I was going to start listening to him.

I reached Turnbull and his crowd of men just in time to see them pull a wet, bedraggled, shivering Grim Nipper from the foul water. His black and green blisters had subsided, so now he just looked like a week-old bruise. Turnbull scowled. "What happened to you?"

"A mummy's curse! Gave me a mummy's curse!" The old pickpocket was babbling and hardly making any sense. He caught sight of us watching. "Her!" He pointed directly at me. "She gave me the curse!"

Everyone turned to look. The minute Turnbull's eyes landed on me, he strode in my direction. "Where's Bollingsworth? You better not have been pulling my leg, because then I'll have reason to put two Throckmortons in jail."

"He's down in the wardroom on the HMS *Dreadnought*."

"That doesn't mean he's the one behind all this."

"Oh, I think you'll find that he is, Inspector. I think he may even have some of the stolen goods on him."

Still watching me, Turnbull called over four of his constables. "Go see if what she says is true, and if so, bring him down with you."

They took off at a trot, but the inspector stayed focused on me. "What makes you so sure he's guilty?"

Remembering Will's story, I said, "For one, we've located all the missing mummies. They are over at the Salty Dog tavern, in the cellar, I believe. You'll find that Bollingsworth has been staying there, although I'm not sure he's been using his real name."

Turnbull looked grudgingly interested. He called two more constables over and gave them instructions to get themselves over to the Salty Dog and see if all that was true. Once he'd sent them on their way, he gave me his full attention. "And how exactly do you know all this, miss?"

Oh dear! How much to tell him? I needed to stick as close to the truth as possible but not mention Will's or Snuffles's or even Wigmere's involvement!

Behind Turnbull, I saw Wigmere's carriage pull up. I needed to hold out for only a few more moments. "Well, I was desperate to get help for my father, you see, and Admiral Sopcoate had told us he would help, but he was busy today with a delegation he was taking on a tour of the *Dreadnought.* As I was rather anxious, I came down here to wait, so I could find him as soon as he was done."

Behind the inspector, I saw Wigmere, Thornleigh, and Bramfield get out and begin to make their way over to the ship.

"I happened to see the Grim Nipper, whom I recognized from the picture you'd been showing around the museum—"

"But I don't remember showing it to you!"

"No. You didn't, but I was, er, saw anyway."

He raised an eyebrow but said nothing further, so I rushed on. "When I saw him, I tried to think of a way to keep him here until you arrived, so I pushed him into the water, hoping he would never have had the chance to learn how to swim. And he hadn't."

"How did you know Bollingsworth was going to be down here?"

Oh dear. How was I going to explain that?

"Excuse me, Inspector." Fagenbush gave a short, formal bow. "If you are looking for a witness, I would be glad to offer up my services."

"You? You're the Second Assistant Curator over at the museum, aren't you? What are you doing here?"

"I saw the child leave this morning. Knowing her father was absent and her mother busy with her work, I set out after the girl thinking to catch up to her and escort her back home."

That diverted Inspector Turnbull's attention. Once again, Clive Fagenbush had come to my rescue. I hoped he wouldn't begin making a habit of that. I wasn't sure I wanted to have to change my opinion of him.

By the time Fagenbush had corroborated my story, one of the constables was heading back down the gangway.

"I just spoke to the captain. She was right, sir! Bollings-worth was there. Even better," he said, drawing closer and lowering his voice, "the captain said he had a gold guinea in his pocket, bold as brass."

I sent a silent prayer of thanks up for dear Snuffles and vowed to buy him a crate of handkerchiefs.

"Well, men have been known to carry guineas on them without any link to criminal activity," Turnbull said dryly. He turned to me. "However, coupled with everything else you've said, it appears you may be right."

I could tell by his face he hated admitting that, so I thought it rather jolly of him to be such a good sport.

"As soon as we've verified all that you've told us, if it checks out, I'll send your father home. That's the best I can promise."

"Oh, thank you, sir!"

It was an awkward cab ride back to the museum. Finally unable to stand it any longer, I pulled my gaze from the window and studied Clive Fagenbush. "How long have you worked for the Brotherhood?"

Fagenbush cast me a sideways glance. "Ten years."

"Really? That long?" I scooted forward on the seat. "Do

you have a tattoo as well? Right here?" I tapped the base of my throat, where I knew other members of the Brotherhood carried a symbol of protection.

"No," he said. "Not yet."

Well, what kind of member was he if he didn't have a tattoo? He couldn't be very good, then.

Almost as if reading my thoughts, Fagenbush made an impatient gesture with his hand. "I've worked for them in this capacity for only three years. It takes five to become a full member, which is when you get your tattoo. And your ring," he said, a look of dark resentment flashing across his face as he glanced down to my own hand, which bore the ring Wigmere had given me after our Heart of Egypt adventures.

"Oh. Took you a while to work up to being an agent, then, did it?"

"It wasn't that," Fagenbush said through clenched teeth.

"No, no. Of course not."

There was a long silence as his distaste of speaking with me warred with his desire to clear his own record. "I'd wanted to be one of their agents ever since I first joined. But my brother joined their service first." I waited for him to say more, but he stopped abruptly.

"And . . ." I prompted.

"And," he said coldly, "he was killed in the line of duty.

Wigmere refused to let me become a full agent because he felt that no mother should have to sacrifice both her sons to the Brotherhood." He returned his gaze to the window. "It wasn't until my mother passed on, three years ago, that he finally agreed to let me begin training."

I squirmed in my seat. I didn't want to know all this. It made Fagenbush much too human.

It also explained why Wigmere was so adamant that Fagenbush could be trusted.

"Here we are," Fagenbush announced without looking at me. He opened the door and stepped out of the hansom, then offered me his arm.

As I stared at the hand he held out to me, I realized I couldn't leave it floating there like a dying fish. Reminding myself that he *had* saved me—twice—I took it.

Once my feet were on the ground, however, I let go and flew toward the museum.

"Mother! Mother!" I burst into the foyer, which was empty, then rushed to the sitting room. Mother sat at the table, her head in her hands. At the sound of my voice, she looked up and tried to paste a smile onto her face. "Yes, darling?"

My good news nearly oozing out my pores, I ran right up to Mum and threw my arms around her. "I've got wonderful news. Inspector Turnbull is going to release Father!"

"What?" Mum half rose in her chair and clasped my arms in her hands to get me to slow down. "What are you saying, Theodosia?"

"It turns out it *was* Nigel Bollingsworth behind the mummy thefts, and Turnbull caught him red-handed. He found some stolen gold and knows where the missing mummies are and everything. Father's name's been cleared! As soon as Turnbull has a man free, he's going to send Father home."

"Oh, darling!" Mother wrapped me up in a huge warm hug. When she pulled back, there was a gleam in her eye. "I see no reason for your father to cool his heels in that jail cell one moment longer, do you? What do you say I run down and fetch him straightaway?"

"I say that's an excellent plan. The sooner the better," I agreed.

Mother grabbed her hat and coat and disappeared out the door. I was still so full of good cheer that I flung my arms out and twirled around, reveling in the fact that Father was going to be free, free, *free!*

Once I stopped twirling and the room stopped spinning, I remembered I had a few things to do before my parents returned.

But first things first. I needed to check on the staff.

CHAPTER THIRTY-THREE

REUNIONS

RESIGNED TO DESCENDING into the catacombs alone once again, I turned on the lights, gripped my amulets in my hand, and proceeded down the stairs, nearly tripping over Isis, who sat at the foot. She was staring at the stone statue of Anubis, her tail twitching back and forth.

The jackal himself sat proudly on top of his shrine, the staff and orb settled carefully between his front paws.

"Thank you," I said. "I couldn't have done it without you." Then, even though I knew he couldn't really feel it, I reached out and scratched the top of his ears, hoping he would some-how be able to sense how pleased I was with him. There was a whisper of movement near his backside, but when I turned to get a better look, all was still. Even so, I would have sworn his tail had wagged, just for an instant.

I left the jackal and went to the shelving to look for an old Canopic jar. Unfortunately, I'd left the execration figure in the hansom cab, and the atropaic wand was undoubtedly on the floor of the *Dreadnought*'s wardroom. I was quite sorry about that, as I hated to misuse museum property.

I did have one item to return, however. Gingerly, I pulled the cursed rope from my pinafore pocket and plunked it into a jar. Then I carefully put the top back on. I'd have to come back down the next day with my curse-removal kit so I could seal the jar, but this would do till then.

As I placed the jar on the shelf, I heard a small cough at the top of the stairway. I hastened over to find Will staring down at me.

"Wigmere's come to see you," he said. "'E's waiting in the reading room."

"Oh, excellent! I have so many questions for him." I took the stairs two at a time and followed Will to the reading room. "How's Snuffles?" I asked.

Will's face brightened. "'E's sitting right pretty, 'e is. 'E proved 'imself today. Might be a future for 'im yet."

Before I had too much time to dwell on Snuffles's dubious future as a pickpocket, Will motioned me inside the room. I found Wigmere in my carrel, holding his hat in one hand and his cane in the other. He was studying something on my desk.

I must have made a sound of some sort, because Wigmere looked up just then. "Ah, good afternoon, my dear."

"Good afternoon, sir."

Wigmere gestured at my desk. "Someone is doing some very interesting work here on the Egyptian calendar."

"Oh, thank you, sir. It keeps me out of trouble. Or so Father says."

His large white mustache twitched. "Indeed. Well, it's very fine work, my girl. And speaking of fathers," he said, "yours should be home very soon."

"Yes, Mum's gone to fetch him home." It was hard to keep from dancing on my toes, but that seemed too undignified to do in front of Wigmere.

He looked me straight in the eye. "He's very lucky to have such a clever, brave daughter."

My chest felt full, as if my heart were too big to fit inside me any longer. "Thank you, sir."

"I won't keep you too long—we just have a couple of loose ends to tie up."

"Did you catch them? Sopcoate and the others?"

"No, I'm afraid they had too great a head start. We got the four that you and Will disabled. How'd you manage to give Bollingsworth such a nasty curse?"

I explained about the *mut* I'd trapped in the rope.

"Ah. Quick thinking, that. Once the curse has been removed, Bollingsworth will be imprisoned in a high-security facility along with Jacques LeBlanc, Franz Stankovich, and Yuri Popov."

I wrinkled my nose. "But sir, I thought the French and Russians were our allies?"

"And so they are. You have to remember that these men don't represent their governments any more than Nigel Bollingsworth represents ours."

I brightened. "Then that should help to take some of the pressure from the Germans, won't it?"

"Some, yes. But members of government often see only what they want to see."

"It's quite disappointing, you know. I was so hoping we'd get them this time."

"You and me both. But we'll have to settle for having thrown a wrench in their works once again." He was silent for a moment. "That was a close call." He shook his head. "A poisonous fog that can kill? We'd always thought the Fog of War to be metaphorical."

"I would have made the same assumption, sir."

"It's a perfect weapon, really. Quite hard to defend against. We'll have to hope it remains firmly in the past."

I put my hands on my hips. "Speaking of the past, sir, why didn't you tell me Fagenbush was working for you? Wouldn't that have been much simpler than letting me go on suspecting him?"

Wigmere shook his head. "We never identify our agents to outsiders, Theo. That's standard policy."

"But I'm practically working for you!"

He smiled. "True enough. But you've now had occasion to run into each other on assignment, so all is made clear. And speaking of assignment, is the staff secure?"

"Yes. Am I to keep it or should I give it to you now?"

"We've decided it would be safest for all concerned if the Orb of Ra and the staff itself were separated. That way no one will be able to access all that power."

"That sounds like an excellent idea."

"At some point, we would like to return one of the components to Egyptian soil. I'd feel safer with a continent or two between them, myself. But for now, we'll settle for separating them. We'll take one piece and hide it, then you take the second piece and hide it, and we'll not reveal the hiding places to each other. That way, no single living person will know how to find the two pieces."

"Very well, sir. Which piece would you like?"

"Whichever piece you don't. It makes no difference to me."

I left the room and returned to the catacombs, where I approached the jackal cautiously. He'd been friendly enough when we had both had the same goal of retrieving the staff from Chaos, but I wasn't certain how he'd feel about the idea of separating the orb and staff. When he made no move for my outstretched arm, I snatched the staff and stepped back out of his reach. "Thank you again for all your help," I said. "We're just going to take this for safekeeping now."

I tugged the orb from the jaws on the head of the staff, then looked around the catacombs for a good hiding place. My eyes landed on the jackal's shrine. Really, I might as well continue to use him as a guardian. I opened one of the doors on the side of the shrine and carefully placed the orb inside, then closed the door.

Wigmere was waiting for me at the top of the stairs. I handed him the staff.

He carefully examined it, taking in the crooked jointed sections and the jackal head. "So this is what caused all that trouble?" He grasped the top section and straightened it.

"How do you think something this powerful ended up here, of all places?"

"Ah. We found an answer to that. Remember how I told you about the small, dedicated group who had vowed to protect the pharaohs and their treasures until the end of time? How they managed to smuggle a cache of Egyptian treasures out of the Alexandrian library before it burned?"

I nodded, my heart beating faster as I saw where he was going with this.

"If you follow that trail, something went awry and the group lost possession of the treasures. Their worst fears were confirmed when rumors of the artifacts circulated among the French in Egypt during Napoleon's occupation. Napoleon was said to have had all his agents searching for these artifacts of power in order to help him with his wars.

"But in a very tricky bit of patriotism, Reginald Mayhew, a British explorer masquerading as a Frenchman, got a hold of the artifacts and sent them to England. Only, the man was killed under mysterious circumstances before he could return to his native shore, and his crates lingered unclaimed in warehouses by the docks until the whole lot of them was auctioned off. The crates were purchased by one Augustus Munk, the original owner and founder of the Museum of Legends and Antiquities, who apparently didn't recognize their value or their power."

A forceful knock resounded through the building. A moment later, Will poked his head around the corner and made a face. "It's that gran of yours."

"Oh, dear," I said, turning to Wigmere. "What should I tell her about Admiral Sopcoate?"

"I talked briefly with Captain Bacon and the prime minister before I came here. It would be too disastrous for the country's morale to know the truth—that one of our highest-placed officials has betrayed us."

"But why? Why do you think he betrayed his country?"

Wigmere's eyes were heavy with sorrow. "Why does any man turn bad? Greed, sorrow, bitterness. A combination of all three? We will likely never know. However, the official story is that a secret unidentified group of rebels managed to trick Admiral Sopcoate into taking them aboard the *Dreadnought,* where he quickly realized his mistake and tried to overpower them. In the struggle, they took flight from the ship to a boat they had waiting. He followed and is presumed dead or missing.

"That story isn't going out to the general public. Only to those who need to know. I trust you to use your best judgment." He'd straightened the staff out by now and, tucking his cane under his left arm, placed the end of the staff on the ground. "I think that should work nicely." He looked back at me, his face solemn again. "I only wish I could sort out what to do with you as easily. It is unacceptable to have you in so much danger, yet for some reason, you seem to find yourself in the thick of things." He sighed. "Well, with Chaos scattered to the four winds, things should calm down now."

Grandmother knocked again.

"I'd best let you go." Wigmere handed Will his cane, then motioned for him to lead. As Will darted back down the corridor, Wigmere followed at a more sedate pace, leaning heavily on the staff.

I headed for the front door. Hopefully Chaos really had been dealt a debilitating blow this time. One could always hope—

"Stilton! What are you doing here in the corner?"

"Hello, Miss Theo." His gaze slid from my face to where Wigmere had just disappeared down the hallway, then back again. "I wanted to make sure you were all right. Trouble does seem to follow you about."

What rot! He'd been eavesdropping. How much had he heard? "Yes, well, you can see that I'm fine. And thank you so much for fetching Inspector Turnbull! He came at just the right moment. But I must run. My grandmother's here."

"So I heard."

"Well, thank you again. You were a lovely help. And thank the other scorpions for me, would you?"

As I continued on my way, I couldn't help but think of Aloysius Trawley and wonder what the Arcane Order of the

Black Sun would do when they learned I no longer had the power to raise the dead.

I made it to the front door before Grandmother beat it down and opened it to let her in. "Hello, Grandmother."

She swept past me into the foyer. "Is Admiral Sopcoate here?"

"No, ma'am. He's not."

"What about your mother and father?" she asked as she looked around the room.

"I'm afraid Mother's left to go get Father out of jail."

She looked relieved. "Oh, good, then. Sopcoate's with them."

"Um, I'm afraid not. Mother left alone."

Grandmother's face paled. "But I haven't been able to get a hold of the admiral. I expected to hear back from him by two o'clock at the latest, and I still haven't heard a word. I even sent a footman round to the admiralty to see if he'd gotten tied up there, but no one has seen him all day." She thumped her cane. "He promised me he'd help Alistair."

I stared at poor Grandmother. She'd fallen in love with a traitor, someone who had sold his soul to Chaos and was the worst sort of enemy Britain could have. Talk about errors in judgment! But of course, I could never point that out. I took a step toward her. "Grandmother—"

"What?" Her face was pinched, but I could tell she wasn't scowling at me. She was just . . . scowling in general.

"I'm afraid there's been an incident."

"An incident? Where? And how do you know?"

This was the tricky part, wasn't it? "I overheard Inspector Turnbull talking."

I waited for her to say something about the wickedness of eavesdropping, but all she said was, "Well, get on with it! What did he say?"

"He said there was a dustup at the *Dreadnought* today. It turned out that who Admiral Sopcoate was escorting wasn't a delegation of Abyssinians, but a group of unidentified rebels who were posing as Abyssinians in order to spy on the Royal Navy's newest technological advances."

Grandmother gasped, and then her hand flew to her mouth, as if she was surprised such a noise could have escaped from *her*.

"Admiral Sopcoate discovered their disguise and tried to apprehend them. Single-handedly," I added for good measure. "But he was greatly outnumbered."

"Why didn't the others onboard try to help him?"

"Because none of them knew what was going on. Until it was too late."

"Too late?" she repeated.

I nodded. "They presume the admiral died or was taken prisoner while protecting his ship," I said as gently as I could.

Grandmother grew even more pale, and she suddenly looked very old and very frail, not like a curmudgeon at all. It was then that I remembered she'd already lost one man, my grandfather, and now she was losing a second.

Hating the look on Grandmother's face, I couldn't help but embellish a bit. "They say he was quite brave. And fearless." It wasn't exactly a lie. He had been all those things, but for the wrong cause.

The front door burst open just then, and Mother and Father waltzed in. Father was tired and rumpled, while Mother appeared jubilant and relieved.

"Look, Grandmother, Father's home! Isn't that lovely?" Surely this would cheer her up.

And it did. For a moment her face softened.

Father held his arms open for me. I longed to run and throw myself into them, but something held me back.

I glanced back at Grandmother, who seemed old, angry, and a little lost.

Not quite sure what I thought I was doing—or why—I reached out and grabbed her hand, half afraid she'd bean me with her cane for taking the liberty. Instead, she stared in puzzlement at my hand holding hers.

Honestly! Did I have to do everything around here? "Come on," I said gently. "Let's welcome Father home."

And then Father was upon us, capturing me in a vast, uncharacteristic hug, which I savored. Even Grandmother standing next to me couldn't ruin that hug.

After a long moment we pulled apart. Beside us, Grandmother took a handkerchief from her reticule. "Really, Alistair, you must speak with your employees. This place has far too much dust floating around. It's quite unhealthy."

We politely looked away as she dabbed at her eyes. "And you," she said, spearing me with her now dry gimlet eye. "What on earth were you thinking, eavesdropping on policemen? Hasn't this family had enough scandal?"

"Yes, Grandmother." I bowed my head meekly, but the truth was, I much preferred this Grandmother, the one made of iron and starch, to the frail old woman she'd been moments ago. In fact, I had an almost overwhelming desire to hug her, even though she would never have allowed such a messy display of emotion.

Even so, I *did* have the urge. Surely that counted for something!

ACKNOWLEDGMENTS

Like Theodosia, I am lucky enough to have an entire secret organization behind me. However, since the Fate of the Known World does not rest in their hands, I think it's safe for me to give them the great big public thank-you that they all deserve.

First, to Yoko Tanaka, Artist Extraordinaire, whose illustrations captured the essence of Theo so perfectly and brought her world and surroundings to life.

Thank you also to Scott Magoon and Sheila Smallwood, whose creative vision for this book far exceeded my wildest dreams.

A round of heartfelt gratitude goes to Betsy Groban and Margaret Raymo for putting the weight of their amazing publishing house behind Theodosia. Surely I am the luckiest author alive (and if I'm not, don't tell me—I don't want to know)!

A very special thank-you to Molly Haselhorst and Thalia Chaltas for reading an early version of this book and giving me amazingly helpful feedback that kept my many plot threads from dangling.

Thank you also to Susan T. Buckheit for making sure all my *i*'s were dotted, my *t*'s crossed, and who kept my many participles from dangling.

I also want to thank Ann-Marie Pucillo, Alison Kerr Miller, Jennifer Taber, Karen Walsh, Nadya Guerrero-Pezzano, Linda Magram, Lisa DiSarro, Jean Thrift, and Jennifer Williams for all their efforts on Theodosia's behalf. What an amazing team you all are!

Thanks also to Erin Murphy, Keeper of the Details and loyal champion.

And last (but never least!), to Kate O'Sullivan for her eagle eye and gentle touch, proving once again that she is the Best Editor Ever.

THEODOSIA TAKES ON EVIL CURSES TO SAVE THE BRITISH EMPIRE
—AND HERSELF!—
IN THEODOSIA AND THE SERPENTS OF CHAOS!

★ "A sure bet for Harry Potter fans."
—*Booklist*, starred review

★ "A perfect blend of mystery and humor."
—*Publishers Weekly*, starred review

"Page-turning action and a plucky,
determined heroine." —*SLJ*